LUZ

Burnt Copper Press

San Francisco 2015

LUZ

a novel by
Luís González

Library of Congress Control Number: 2015911609
Burnt Copper Press, San Francisco, California

This book is a work of fiction and, although allusions are made to certain historical events, the characters, names, places and incidents are either the product of the author's imagination or are used ficticiously.

Copyright © 2015 Luis Gonzalez
All Rights Reserved.
ISBN: 0966305825
ISBN 13: 978-0966305821

Published by Burnt Copper Press
San Francisco, California, United States

Printed by CreateSpace, an Amazon company.
North Charleston, SC

Visit Luis Gonzalez on his website at: **cubawriter.net**
Like him on **Facebook.com/luzthenovel**
Follow him on **Twitter: @luzthenovel**

acknowledgements

I would like to thank the culture and the people of Cuba, an eternal source of pride and inspiration.

acclaim for LUZ

FOREWORD REVIEWS (4 of 5 STARS)

A hefty, surprising, and absorbing exploration of faith, both in political and divine redemption. Written with verve and sensitivity, Gonzalez crafts a humorous Cuban tale full of unexpected twists and rich characterizations, and whose surprises reward the suspension of disbelief. While sections devoted to God's conversations with his son in Heaven provide both levity and space for theological considerations, readers who enjoy the strangeness of this humorous and theological first installment will certainly look forward to future adventures.

KIRKUS REVIEWS

Gonzalez is a strong, sometimes idiosyncratic prose-stylist particularly adept at capturing the clash of idealism and futility that marks this period of Cuba's history. Gonzalez's considerable storytelling prowess is most fully realized in a chapter devoted to the backstories of Rigo and Clara's father. Here, flashbacks allow the story to move along while capturing the heartbreak of intellectual yearning snuffed out by an oppressive bureaucratic regime.

MIDWEST BOOK REVIEW

Luz is a highly charged saga of change and spirituality. The result is a striking, captivating, and dense read that unfolds like a flower and blossoms with a predestined heroine whose mother's world collapses and rises again from the fires of destruction, like a phoenix. Readers who appreciate a fine blend of spiritual and social insight, all held together by the glue of a feisty young protagonist surviving a Third World country, will find *Luz* a gripping, evocative story.

PALMETTO REVIEW

Gonzalez tells his epic tale with notable depth and compassion, as well as an intimate and abiding knowledge of Castro's Cuba, allowing the reader to feel Clara's anguish at being forced to make a seemingly impossible sacrifice no matter which path she chooses. Gonzalez writes seamlessly, allowing the reader to get lost in the world he creates, paying off all his premises with satisfying results. *Luz* is a heart-wrenching but ultimately hopeful tale of sacrifice and discovery — one of those few moments when both story and storytelling are of equal grandeur.

SAN FRANCISCO BOOK REVIEW (4 of 5 STARS)

Gonzalez relies on a heavily stylized form of storytelling in order to blend the epic with the everyday. Gonzalez takes his time to let you into Clara's mind as her life changes and priorities shift in an attempt to remind us that at the heart of every epic story, there lies the human heart. It is very rare to come across an author who attempts a story of this scale, but keeps the humanity of his characters firmly in place. A truly worthwhile read.

PORTLAND BOOK REVIEW

The novel is so strongly written, so well written, that one can easily focus on a story told from the perspective of an intelligent headstrong young woman whose life, like so many of our lives, takes a turn quite opposite of what she had intended and does so with miraculous results.

PENN BOOK REVIEW

Masterfully written fiction that simply cannot be overlooked. This is a fresh writer with a great voice. The only disappointment for readers, perhaps, will be the cliffhanger, and surprisingly wonderful ending. Gonzalez is aptly skilled in the art of "teasing" readers from the beginning in order to capture attention, and move the story into unforeseen territories. Intelligently written and very exciting. One of the best novels in the Latin American and Hispanic genre to date.

for María

contents

miracles. 1

setbacks 23

visitations 47

messes 97

    CONCEPTIONS 131

assumptions .169

solace 217

LUZ

troubled times

book i
comings and goings

so will I trust in the Lord,
all the days of my life

1

miracles

august 14, 1994
dusk

A *miracle.*

That was the way most of us saw it. The only way *I* saw it. A miracle had struck unexpectedly, and we all had to move quickly, we all had to act fast. How this miracle materialized, nobody really understood. How it unfolded so swiftly, no one was really sure. But one thing was evident. One thing stood clear. God was finally answering our prayers. He was finally acknowledging our long years of suffering, along with our petitions to the Virgin.

To be honest, I had never been religious. Not even spiritual. My mother was and from her I had witnessed much, especially on the days of the saints. Every year, on September 8, Mamá set up a shrine of flowers and candles to commemorate the Feastday of the Virgin and transformed our living room into a blessed chapel. *La Virgen del Cobre,* our beloved patron saint. Even during the era when it was absolute suicide for anyone to step foot inside a church, Mamá had always attended Mass. My mother was the type to die for her faith, a martyr if you will, and naturally she had tried instilling her beliefs in me. But I never fell prey to them, I was no believer. Myths and fairy tales—that's how I regarded religion. I much more took after my father, where education and politics were my religion. Writing, my salvation.

But no more. We'd been living in a Special Period the last four years in Cuba—*el Periodo Especial*, as the government called it—and I no longer believed in anything. There was nothing special about this period, nothing charming or endearing. What a misuse of words. What a travesty of terminology. And this from a master of language himself, the virtuoso of vocabulary and verbiage. *Special Period* indeed! Just one more marvel from our master manipulator, one more euphemism for the hell we knew as daily life. No future. No freedom. And certainly no food. But worst of all, thanks to our daily blackouts, no electricity or light inside our homes for up to twelve hours at a time. We all abhorred that the most: the long and endless hours without any power or interior light. But now everything had changed and even I recognized the incident for what it was: a miracle. I thanked God for His mercy. I thanked God for the opportunity. A pair of beneficent hands had sliced open the gates to this inferno—no, flung them open—and along with everyone else, I wanted out.

Only one major risk involved, one daunting drawback: the risk to life. But no matter. They had already ripped away my dream and destroyed me from the inside out. Those who ruled the roost around here reveled in that. They stole your hopes and tied the soul down with despair. All my life I'd wanted to be a writer, but that was never going to be possible. Not on this island. To live in Cuba was to exist in defeat: daily defeats, nightly defeats, defeats large and small that perpetuated themselves endlessly. Defeats that corroded you from within, and gnawed away at you from without. We were not simply awash in defeat, but drowning in it: in a deluge of dread and disappointment. To continue living here *was* to thrive in this defeat, and even at my young age, I felt dead inside.

But now, all those battling that vicious cycle were hopeful again. All those fighting for a surge of life were fleeing. An exodus from this living hell had sprung forth and, as usual, a frenzied flight across the water, a forced and feverish escape. But this time, miraculously, those who controlled the gates were not stopping anybody, were not throwing anyone in jail. Not our leader in green fatigues. Not his ministers in their menacing fashion. Not even his anonymous sentinels or mangy mongrels in blue. That was how I referred to the police around here, "mongrels in blue".

What else could this moment be, but a miracle? Surely God had bound their hands. Surely God had blinded their eyes. He must even be placing words in their mouths. Why else had the man in green made the announcement of a few nights ago? Declaring to the world we were free to leave. Gladly threatening everyone to let us flee. He was imparting his blessing on us; that is, if anyone thought him capable of such a thing. We knew then it had to be a miracle. We understood then it must be the working of the Lord. More than anything I knew I must avail myself of this miracle, and I too must take my leave.

It all began on August 5, the day God's wrath fiercely became manifest. And not only before the eyes of our homeland, but before the eyes of the entire world. Our miracle of August 5 in the year of our Lord 1994. Right here in Centro Habana at the Hotel Deauville, just blocks from where I lived.

Surely, something had preordained the events of that unforgettable day. Something or Someone or some Unseen Force out there. No doubt existed in anyone's mind. We were at the height of this Special Period and tensions had been brewing on the island for weeks, ever since July 13, when thirty-two men, women, and children were killed at sea, murdered right off our coast. The man in green and his pack of mongrels called it an accident, an "unfortunate incident". His legion of liars insisted they were only trying to stop a hijacked vessel and rescue the innocent passengers aboard.

But why then did they ram their speedboat into the ferry over and over again, pummeling the vessel until it split wide open? Why then did they spray their hoses at those on board to hasten their drowning? And why, if they cared so much about the innocent, did they wait more than an hour before radioing for help, as entire families drowned before their eyes? As their brethren screamed in agony and adults held up children to keep them from drowning? *Murderers! Terrorists!* Every time I thought about those helpless souls struggling to stay afloat and suffocating with seawater, it filled me with such rage I wanted to scream.

Ever since July 13 you could feel the tension roiling on the streets. Havana had turned into a hotbed of hostility, and my brothers and sisters were growing bolder, openly criticizing the police, whereas, never had they dared to challenge them before—that was something purely unthinkable. So plans of fleeing continued unabated even if it meant another hijacking, even if the attempt at escape ended in tragedy. And what a year of escapes it had been. In 1994 alone my brothers and sisters had fled in record numbers. The desperation was that high, the misery that great. Never had the everyday, ordinary Cuban felt so starved, so cursed. A tempest had been gathering in strength, and ever since the murders of July 13, we all felt possessed by some unstoppable force. That tempest finally reached land when, in the final days of July, a rumor started.

Like many rumors, there were always some parts that *were* true and some parts that *weren't*. A story had circulated that America, or the mighty Eagle to the North as some regarded it, had dispatched a giant ferry to pick up as many Cubans as could fit. We all believed this fairy tale, fantastic as the claim sounded; although to many it didn't seem that outlandish. Not with the exodus of Mariel still alive in our memory.

Before long, a giant crowd coalesced along the Malecón waiting and praying for the ferry to come. By some accounts

miracles

as many as five thousand of my brothers and sisters had converged along the seawall waiting for its arrival. It never showed up. It was a tale born of heightened hope and desperation, *a ferry tale*. But days after that crushing disappointment, the multitudes along the Malecón had not fully dispersed. Remnants of the faithful kept lingering and loitering and lowly simmering until, finally, on August 5, all hell broke loose: *El Maleconazo,* as it would come to be known.

I heard it from my house, only blocks from the flashpoint. I wanted to run toward the ruckus and join in, but Rigo forbade it. He wouldn't let me leave the house. But according to those fortunate enough to witness the incident, privileged enough to take part in history, a boy of no more than sixteen had deliberately tried entering the Hotel Deauville—a grave transgression for any Cuban: any ordinary, everyday Cuban.

From birth on we learned the cardinal rule around here: the only ones blessed enough to enter the gates of any hotel were tourists and foreigners, or members of the elite. We understood it was meant for our own good, meant to shield our eyes from the riches contained within: shoes meant *not* for our feet, food intended for bellies *other* than ours. Apparently this boy of sixteen had never learned this cardinal rule or didn't care for its adherence. No one knew exactly *what* ran through his mind, but one thing was known. As he argued with the mongrel who blocked his path, those standing nearby joined in the boy's defense and argued right alongside him.

"Why can't he go in?" they demanded to know. "Why can't he?"

What happened next unraveled in a blur. A sharp scuffle. A spontaneous spark. Someone pushed someone else and instantaneously a fight erupted, a violent one. Those standing nearby intervened and attempted to keep the policeman from arresting the boy. But it all swelled too swiftly, this fast-moving tide. It all surged too fast, this rapidly moving wave, bringing with it a surge of sights and sounds unfamiliar in our city. The most glorious sound of all came in the form of shattering glass. Who-knows-what or who-knows-who had smashed the large front windows of the Deauville and the most splendid sight to behold came in a shower of splintering glass. Not anyone or anything could stop the hail of crystal that came crashing to the ground.

El Maleconazo. They called it an act of terror, those who called the shots around here. But it was no act of terror. That was just political prattle, petty propaganda. El Maleconazo was an act of valor, an act of courage. It was a hotel defaced—that most hated symbol of class distinction here—especially a landmark hotel along the Malecón. But out of defacement came determination and an uprising had sprung to life. All of these hijackings and escapes and acts of defiance had ignited a resistance and, for the first time in thirty-five years, rioting and protests surged through our streets. For the first time in their sedentary lives my brothers and sisters felt restive and ablaze, and I, as a young insurrectionist working to subvert this regime, could not have been more thrilled.

That was how I saw myself: not as a dissident, not as a pacifist, but an insurrectionist. Dissident was too nice a word. Pacifist, pathetic. The word insurrectionist cut to the heart of our plight with a raw and ruthless ring. As rocks and bottles were flung at the Deauville, an insurrection it was. As chants of freedom were hurled in the air, a real revolution this time, an actual revolt. No more apathy. None of the staleness or stagnation that threatened to smother us all. The myth of that giant ferry quickly faded, but a resolve to flee and live again had newly spawned.

But not everyone viewed the events of August 5 as a miracle. Some, like my husband Rigo, regarded it as lunacy. Others, like Mamá and my sisters, viewed it as sheer stupidity. I was one of three daughters in my family: the middle sister, the one right in the thick of things or always getting lost in the shuffle. I had an older sister, Pilar, and a younger sister, Angélica. My mother, Inez, was still very much around, but as for my father, Alejo, well, it was usually too painful for me to think about him.

Determined as I was to launch my dreams then, I expected a few hurdles along the way, namely from the women in my life. But I could handle them. Rigo was a different matter. If I had always thought I possessed an unfailing partner in my spouse, never did I expect the only man I had ever loved to prove my biggest obstacle. But that's exactly what he'd become these last three days: an obstacle, a stumbling block I could not overstep.

They were leaving tomorrow from Cojimar, the nearby fishing village made famous by Hemingway. It was from Cojimar that nearly all my brothers and sisters were catapulting to sea. And it was also from there that my best friend, Amalia, and her boyfriend, Henry, were likewise taking off. Not the day after tomorrow or the day after that, but tomorrow: on August 15.

A talented painter and sculptor, Henry had built the raft all by himself. He could do anything with his hands and had constructed our sturdy vessel in one short day, fashioning it solely from sugarcane stalks and *maloja*. While the vast majority of rafts were strung together from inner tubes and other floatable plastics, Henry refused to utilize such distasteful material. He despised plastic so much that he even hated admitting his degree was in *Artes Plásticas*. Henry assured us that the raft did not need anything so unnatural as plastic. According to him, maloja, literally, *the bad leaf*—and which happened to be the green outer sheath of the sugarcane stalk—possessed a natural buoyancy far superior and more durable than that of plastic.

"There's much the world has yet to learn about maloja," he noted rather abstractedly. "And one day it will."

I should have known. For some reason, maloja always seemed to pop up in my life—always. Personally, I loved its delicately exquisite flower that resembled a whitish wispy flame. And it may have been the nurturing and protective leaf of sugarcane, but most considered it a useless weed, which is why maloja was burned so savagely in the fields during harvest time, this "bad leaf" as it was known. But Henry christened our vessel *"La Maloja"* anyway. Not the most auspicious of names, but fitting under the circumstances. I hadn't seen the raft yet and didn't want to. Not beforehand.

I'll admit that I was scared. But I also trusted in his abilities. If La Maloja was good enough for Amalia, it was good enough for me. Henry wanted out of Cuba for two reasons: his art and his ideas, which he considered one and the same. Art and Communism were two natural enemies, two siblings who not merely rivaled each other, but reviled each other. As for Amalia, she didn't care about anything *but* Henry. If her boyfriend was leaving, so was she.

It was dusk on this August 14. Some viewed dusk as that magical time of day when afternoon and night blended into each other with the softness of a lover's embrace. But dusk was my least favorite part of day. I had never liked it, that period of partial darkness when neither daylight nor nighttime could compromise on which should prevail. Dusk was not to be trusted. I found it dissolute, indecisive. Was it light getting lost in the shuffle, or light secretly scheming and right in the thick of things? Was it a thief on the run or a thief waiting to strike? There was only one thing I liked about dusk. Not the softness of its colors, but the swiftness of its descent: those fatal moments when afternoon fused into darkness with the quickness of a receding tide, when it drained all the errors out of day and devoured its disasters. Still, dusk was no delight, just simply the deterioration and death of everything.

Night was a salvation from dusk and how I wanted night to arrive. How I wanted morning here already. By morning I'd be gone. But Rigo and I continued fighting, and there was no dissolving Dusk's dogged determination. This dusk of August 14 clutched and clung onto daylight for dear life. If darkness usually flushed it out with the ease of a passing rainstorm, this dusk would not be doused or dampened any. It kept floating atop the vestiges of daylight, refusing to blend in with the night.

In much the same way, Rigo and I had wrangled for hours. For once we had the house to ourselves and could fight like a normal couple. But surely not for long. Mamá and my sisters were *I-don't-know-where,* and might return any minute, and I was truly at the end of my rope. No more reasoning. No more imploring. No more screaming, and no more time to waste. I just wanted to know one thing from my husband and would ask him one final time.

"I'm leaving tomorrow, Rigo. Are you with me or not?"

How I waited and waited for an answer. Dusk sat thickly in its particles of indecision, but so did my husband's thoughts. Then, suddenly, as Rigo put his books down and turned to face me, I gazed at him and braced myself. Here it came, the all-too-expected answer, the same response of the last three days. Slowly he walked over to me, and still I can picture exactly what he looked like that dusk of August 14. I can tell you what he was wearing, exactly what I was wearing. But the only thing worth mentioning about our attire back then was its drabness.

All clothes in Cuba were either drab or dreary or just plain dingy. Whether the pairs of pants were blue or brown or khaki, they exuded a drabness. Whether the shirts were olive or beige or tan, they lamented their own dinginess. And whether the skirts or blouses were the color of honey or lavender or the green of the sea, they languished in a dreary despair. Everything hung on our weary bodies flatly and lifelessly, while only our eyes contained the slightest hint of life. Rigo peered into mine deeply now before giving his response: those restless brown eyes of mine searching for a clue; my thin but forceful face squaring off with his resolve. He took his sweet time as he raised his hands to my face, smiling at me strangely as he slid his fingers down the sides of my hair, so long and silky brown then and hanging just below my shoulders.

"Yes," he uttered softly, barely audible in the din of this stubborn dusk. "Yes, *amor de mi vida,* I'm going with you."

I didn't hear him. I could hear only the voice in my head wanting to drown him out. I pushed him away from me and stepped back toward the dresser in our room.

"But chico!" I reacted excitedly. "I've told you a million times the way it works. Don't you get it? We don't have to make the full journey across the straits. We just have to reach international waters twelve miles out. That's where the rescue boats will be, where the Americans will be waiting for us. Don't you realize what this means? In just one short day or two, we can be in the United States—*the United States, Rigo!*"

"Amor," he tried to interject. "Listen to me—"

But, alas, I couldn't listen. I couldn't hear. As of late I had fallen prey to several bad habits that I attributed to growing up in a Communist State: always disregarding my opposition and, even worse, always repeating myself needlessly. I had not always been this way, quite the opposite. But I noticed the vice had come fully into bloom with the advent of our Special Period, during which I found myself constantly repeating my thoughts and ideas. I hated it too, this indelible stamp of Communist rule, where repetition was the basis of all communication and indoctrination. And I seemed to have developed a bad case of it. I asked myself repeatedly if there was some way I could have avoided this disease. If it was anything I might have done or failed to do. But, no—that was not it. How could any of us have shielded ourselves from this curse? How could any of us eschew the tendency to repeat or restate familiar refrains when it was all our leaders ever did? When, quite simply, it was all that we knew.

"No, Rigo! Don't interrupt!" I shot back. "I already know what you're going to say. You listen to me. You just want to blame Amalia. You think this is her fault, but don't blame her. This was not her doing. She hasn't brainwashed me. She hasn't filled my head with any grandiose schemes. I've made up my own mind, Rigo. Amalia is leaving because Henry is leaving, and she wants to be with the love of her life. If you loved me as much as she loves Henry, you'd go too—so don't blame her!"

"I do love you amor, just listen to me."

But I only shook my head furiously and gestured at him. "No, Rigo. *You* listen to me! I've heard all your reasons. I know you don't want to leave your family. I know you think you're abandoning them. But we're doing this because of family. The day will come when they want out of Cuba, and we'll be the ones to pull them out, the ones to save them. Sure, we won't know anybody, but we'll have each other. We'll make new friends and form a new family. That's what friends do, Rigo. Friends become family when they have nobody else."

"I agree, amor. Didn't you hear me? I said I was going."

I still didn't hear him, not fully anyway. Not with the restlessness that held me in its grip. Not with the ferocity of my thoughts all riled up and revved up and ready for a showdown. I waited for him to fight back, to refute my reasons point by point. My husband was a great debater, great at reasoning and skilled at arguing, and I loved to wage mental battle with him. It was one of our favorite pastimes as a married couple: debating to the death. But something was not clicking. Something was clearly the matter. He just stood there insensate and inert, sullen and almost sinking right in my presence. His eyes were those of a wounded little boy, and the hurt in their expression was now a spear that sank into me, much as the echo of his words finally began to do—seeping and sinking deep into my skull.

"You agree with what?" I continued, foaming in all my fury. "Agree with what Rigo?"

"With going, amor. I said 'yes'. You've convinced me, and I'm going."

I caught the words unmistakably this time, all of them. But I knew I must have heard wrong. This had to be a mistake, and I couldn't speak. I couldn't scream in my head because it made no sense. Not unless this was another miracle. And it had to be. It was happening too quickly, materializing out of nowhere, as all miracles do.

"You're what?" I asked again.

"I said *yes*, amor—*yes!*"

It was I who wanted to respond, but my words were being hijacked. I wanted to utter some appropriate reply, but my tongue felt tightly trapped even as the speedboat of Rigo's words kept ramming into the ferry of my thoughts over and over again, pummeling the vessel of my obstinacy until it split wide open. What a fool I was. Even as he sprayed me with hope and tried to hasten the drowning of my doubt, I couldn't escape. I couldn't flee. Not when this was all a setup. I was sure of it. Rigo knew what he was doing. He was no innocent. He was feeding me false expectation just to shut me up. If he was serious about going and this was no accident, why had it taken him more than an hour before coming to his senses? Before radioing reason and watching my life's goals nearly drown before his eyes? While my spirit screamed out in agony and foolish hope held up desperate dream to keep it from drowning. *Murderer! ¡Asesino!* That was all he'd become. As the helplessness of my soul struggled to stay afloat and fought to keep from saturating with stagnation, it filled me with such rage I wanted to scream. But I was too drained to scream. After all this silent wrangling, I formed my words softly and rather feebly.

"You're going? Is that what you really said?"

"That's what I said, amor. I'm going."

"But how, chico? For three days you've been saying that...you've been telling me that...why, you've even insisted that—"

I struggled to complete my thoughts, but Rigo approached me and prevented me, raising a hand and placing it gently on my lips.

"Listen, amor. You know me. I don't believe in miracles or much less, but you're right. Things are never going to change around here, and I have to accept it. I'm never going to make my dreams come true unless we leave. I'm going, amor. I'm going with you!"

"You mean it, chico? You really mean it?"

"I mean it," he said. "I'm going. *We're going.*"

But despite the tenderness in his eyes, doubt consumed me, and I couldn't accept it, not even if this was the response I had long awaited.

"But what's changed?" I insisted. "For three days you've been fighting me and battling me and swearing up and down you wouldn't do it. You've called it madness. Why have you now—"

Rigo placed his hand on my lips again, before my tongue could finish hijacking the rest of my thoughts.

"Amor," he replied. "Why can't you leave well enough alone? Why do you always have to push and push and push? I'm going, and that's all that matters."

That was when it happened, when I saw the light gloriously start draining from the interior of our room, when I noticed the pallor of its walls, a smooth and pale rust, deepen and darken into a crimson corrosion. Finally! Dusk finally in descent. Dusk finally dissolving into the tide pools of afternoon's death. An unmistakable darkness was now on the rise, but oh, I could see more clearly than ever.

"You're right, Rigo. I do push too much, don't I? I'll try to change, amor. Once I get to the United States, I promise I'll change."

A boyish and playful smile lit up his face, a surge of excitement infused his eyes. "Listen amor. Just so you know, I'm only going on one condition. I'm not settling in Tampa or St. Petersburg. I'm not living in Miami or any of the Keys. I don't want any part of Florida or all the *cubaneo* there. If you can agree to that, tomorrow morning I'll be on that ridiculous contraption of Henry's, which will be a miracle if it floats."

The sudden dose of levity caught me off guard, but his dig at Henry did not. Rigo didn't like Henry, not even when they should have gotten along fine. One was an architect, the other an artist. Their professions were not identical, but certainly fraternal. The two should have shared much in common, but instead of mutual respect, they shared a mutual distaste.

"Where, then?" I asked. "Where do you want to go?"

"To California. I want to live in California."

"Los Angeles?"

"No, not Los Angeles!" he said with scorn. "Remember

amor, above all I'm an architect, and a city like Los Angeles has nothing to offer an architect. San Francisco—that's where we're going."

"San Francisco?"

"Yes, San Francisco, an architect's paradise. I don't know if I ever told you, amor, but one entire semester of our studies was devoted to the architecture of San Francisco, and ever since then, I've been dying to go there. I've wanted to see and experience the city's architecture with my own eyes, especially a building there called the TransAmerica Pyramid..."

"The TransAmerica Pyramid? What is it?" I asked.

"Oh, you should see it, amor. It's the most ingenious building of the twentieth century. It was built in the shape of a pyramid, and it's the city's tallest building. It's a shining example of man's potential for achievement and something you'd never see here in Cuba."

"A pyramid, ey? How interesting."

"Oh, it's more than interesting, amor. It's magnificent, a true marvel of architecture and engineering. But that's only one of the many marvels and gems of San Francisco. There's another structure called the Ferry Building that's also impressive."

"The Ferry Building?" I repeated in my Spanish accent, with an awkward roll of the *r*'s.

"Yes, amor, the Ferry Building at Marketplace. You should see the clock tower there. It sits like a crown on top of the building. It was modeled after the Giralda bell tower in Sevilla."

"And?" I asked the beaming architect. "What about it?"

"What about it!" Rigo said in a huff. "Why, it's one of the most beautiful landmarks in the whole city. It was built so well that it survived the 1906 earthquake. It's where the Pacific Ocean ends and Market Street begins. Think of it as their Malecón."

I was stunned to hear so a bold comparison. Could this Ferry Building or this Marketplace really be as special as the Malecón? Our city's splendid and extraordinary esplanade? That golden necklace that curved around the bay and from which our hopes and dreams hung like invisible yet incandescent charms? I doubted it.

"You've never told me any of this, Rigo. You've never mentioned San Francisco or the TransAmerica Pyramid or this Ferry Building at Market Street."

"I've never told you about the stadium called Candlestick Park either, how it's located right on the water and how, for years, I've dreamed about seeing a baseball game there. I mean, why talk of things that have no chance of ever coming true?" he said. "Why even mention them?"

"Candlestick Park, huh? What an unusual name."

"It's a beautiful name, amor, and San Francisco is a beautiful city."

I kept ruminating, contemplating. "Market Street, eh? San Francisco? I just assumed we'd always end up in Miami."

"Never!" Rigo shot back. "Out of the question! San Francisco it has to be. I'll find work in a firm that designs clock towers and bridges and schools and libraries and come up with the best designs the Americans have ever seen."

"What about hotels?" I asked. "What about the luxury hotels you've always wanted to design?"

"Forget it!" he said flat-out. "I'm not interested in hotels of any kind anymore, luxury or otherwise."

"Yes," I said. "I understand."

"And I have a confession to make too," he added.

"Confession, Rigo?"

"Well," he hesitated. "If something had to be the catalyst of all this madness, this Maleconazo, I'm glad it was a rock through the Deauville, that's for sure!"

"Why is that?" I asked in surprise.

"That hotel is a complete eyesore!" he said "Not only Art Deco dull, but it's always looked as if somebody sheared it in half!"

I didn't respond. Personally, I liked the Deauville. But after what Rigo had been through the last couple of years, I certainly understood why he was averse to hotels and wanted nothing to do with them anymore. Maybe that would change in time, once we settled in the United States.

"Well?" he asked. "Are we in agreement?"

I hesitated. I didn't know much about San Francisco, beyond the Golden Gate Bridge and all the gays. But the more I thought about it, the more I liked the sound of it. It seemed that San Francisco was just as much a writer's city as an architect's.

"Fine," I said. "Agreed! San Francisco it will be. I don't know how we'll get there, and we definitely won't know anyone there, but if you want to live in San Francisco, San Francisco it is."

Rigo threw his arms around my waist and lifted me up before kissing me. He held me in place for the longest time and peered at me with his infectious smile. I hadn't seen him this happy in over a year and hadn't felt happier myself. He put me back down.

"Just one question, amor. Why tomorrow? Why so soon?"

"Why not tomorrow? Why wait and leave things to chance?"

"It's so soon, amor. How can we possibly get ready by tomorrow?"

"What's to get ready, Rigo? We're going by raft, remember? There's only room for four bodies, and that's it."

Rigo shook his head at me. He smiled and cupped my face with his hands. "You always have an answer for everything, don't you, amor?"

I pulled him close to me and draped my arms around his neck. "Well, remember that miracles don't last forever, Rigo.

We have to act quickly, move fast. What if tomorrow is the last day of it? What if today was and we don't know it yet?"

The expression on Rigo's face changed ever so slightly. His thoughts turned inward even though he looked straight at me. I wanted to know what worries had just invaded his thoughts, but I wouldn't push.

"You really think this is a miracle, amor? You really think so?"

"I know so, Rigo, and so do you."

"And you're sure it has to be tomorrow morning?"

"Tomorrow morning, amor, August 15, 1994. The day we'll leave this all behind and never look back."

He kept peering into my eyes, but his thoughts turned ever inward and silent. Something was bothering him and the look that hung on his face said it all. Whether it was a look of acceptance, resignation, or reality setting in, I couldn't tell. But I felt sorry for Rigo. At times he was a wounded and innocent little boy, and I must learn to go easy on him, listen compassionately. I kissed him on the mouth with all the feeling I could summon.

"Let's celebrate," I said. "Let's do it right now as long as we've got the house to ourselves. Let's make love for the last time in this homeland of ours."

"Right now?" he asked, his eyes darkening with ruggedness and lust.

"Right now," I replied.

He didn't decline my offer, of course. We made glorious and wondrous love, the last vestiges of dusk giving way to a nascent night, and light fusing into darkness with the feel and finesse of a fluctuating flame. I never felt closer to Rigo or more passionate about him than during our union that particular dusk. Partial darkness glowed with the frenzy of desire and distant points of light were all that I saw. When we finished I wanted him to love me over and over again. I wanted this dusk of desire to last forever and for Rigo to hold me and never let go. We lay in bed and I wanted desperately to stayed glued to him, but he had more pressing matters on his mind.

"I need to tell my parents," he said. "I need to break the news to Mamá."

"Right now? You have to do that right now?"

"*Coño mija*, I have to tell them sometime, don't I? We're leaving tomorrow."

He was right, and I knew it. As much as I wanted to hold on and never let go, Rigo was a practical man. He had to notify his parents and get it over with. I didn't want to think about my mother-in-law or how she would pin this on me.

"All right," I said. "I understand, amor. Go ahead."

Rigo slipped out of my arms and out of bed, and while I contentedly stayed put, he quickly threw his clothes on in all their splendid drabness. But I couldn't move. I continued on my side even though he was right: we had a lot to do, a lot to finalize. A restless and nervous energy stirred, but I sealed it off, closing my eyes and managing to drift off when his voice rudely awakened me. I found him sitting on the edge of the bed gently stroking my hair.

"I just want to tell you one more thing, amor, and remember this while I'm gone."

"What?"

"You know me, amor. You know that when I make up my mind about something, it's do or die, that I don't go back on things."

"I know, Rigo. Why are you saying this?"

"Because, amor, as of this moment I'm committed—we're committed. We go through with this no matter what. No backing out."

"Me back out? I won't back out, amor. I'm the one who just convinced you. The one who's been hounding you for three days."

That peevish and playful smile returned to his face. "All

miracles

right, amor, all right. I just want you to respect how I feel."

"I do, Rigo. You be the one to remember that when your mother is throwing a fit."

He'd had enough of me. Rigo bent over and kissed me goodbye, but I wouldn't let go of him. He had to peel me off of him. After some wrangling he finally freed himself and wasted no time in grabbing his wallet and watch and departing from the pale rust walls of our room.

"Be strong!" I called out after him. "Remember your own words when your mother tries talking you out of this. You know she's going to put up a fight, and a fierce one."

He responded not, but it didn't matter. I knew what the response would have been. Rigo's mother could never do any wrong. He stayed his course in silence and made his way down the narrow hall, reaching the front door and opening it softly. Rigo's family lived close by, and I hoped this wouldn't take long. I had longed for night's arrival, but our hated *apagón*—our nightly blackout—would soon go into effect, and I dreaded being alone in the house during the hours of blackness.

He was gone. From my bed I heard the front door close, but inside I felt another door open. We were leaving Cuba. We were leaving behind this *Periodo Especial*, and I couldn't believe it! Rigo and I had just made the most important decision ever as man and wife, and I knew it would lead to the richness and promise I had so envisioned. Finally could we emerge from the travesty of this tyranny. Finally could we depart from this twilight of terror. Finally could we spit upon this Special Period as it deserved to be spat upon.

I should have felt ecstatic, triumphant. But rather than triumph, I only felt deflated, lost in the midst of some barren emptiness. I sat up in bed, but didn't know what to do with myself. It seemed there were a million things to attend to, but nothing at all.

True, we were leaving on a trip tomorrow, but there was nothing to pack up, nothing to take with us. Maybe our identification papers, our birth certificates surely. I was sure

Rigo wanted to take some of his schematics, but I would let him worry about that. We were off to start a new life. Maybe some photographs of our old life, faded pictures of those we loved and were leaving behind. Alone in the house and with the silence of night encroaching, all I could do was wait, just sit and wait, or pace and wait, but definitely wait until everyone returned.

Amalia! I must tell her we had the green light, we were going! I must tell her not to give away our spots on the Maloja, for we were joining her and Henry first thing in the morning. I really didn't feel like getting dressed and venturing out, exhausted as I was from all the lovemaking, but I would pay my friend a visit and tell her I had triumphed, that a miracle of its own had just occurred.

I threw back the sheets. Despite the fatigue, I slipped into my own drab clothing, all the while thinking of how, very soon, I too would be breaking the news to my mother and sisters and pondered what their reaction might be. I'd given them fair warning. Since August 11 I had told them I'd go through with this and insisted nothing would stop me. Still, I contemplated the actuality of it now, and it saddened me greatly. How much like my father I had turned out to be: driven by wanderlust and blind ambition at the cost of home and family. With so much to do and think and feel, I felt paralyzed and did nothing at all. So I would wait. I would simply sit and wait.

Clara—that's how I was known. I had never liked my name. So old-fashioned, so Christian, and all Mamá's doing by the way. It had always reminded me of a Saint's name, and I was no saint. But I was nineteen years old then, Rigo twenty-six. The following day I would head for a new land, a new life, bearing with me all the dreams and hopes, all the fears and apprehensions that such a departure entailed. Exhilaration filled me, but so did dread. Whatever lay in store for us, the decision had just been etched. Life had drawn its design and engraved it into our destiny. Night was swiftly approaching, but darkness would soon be a specter of the past. Tomorrow morning a light would carry me forward.

Tomorrow morning I would start to live and no longer feel dead inside. Not anyone or anything could stop us or set us back. Tomorrow morning I would leave this homeland of mine forever, or so I thought.

2

setbacks

august 14
mid evening

"I did it, chica! It's all set! I convinced Rigo and we'll be joining you and Henry first thing in the morning! What do you think about that?"

I had gone to Amalia's to deliver the good news. After more pacing and restlessness I desperately wanted to visit my friend and firm up tomorrow's plans. Good thing I did, as Amalia had an announcement of her own. She too lived a few blocks away and grown up here in *Centro Habana*, right in the middle of the city where anything worth happening happened. I was thrilled when I showed up at her house. So excited that I barely took note of something curious and odd.

At first I thought my friend was merely resting, that she too must be drained and exhausted. When I found her lying in bed, face up and perfectly still, I thought she had turned in for the night, which meant we'd be getting an early start in the morning. But soon I didn't know what to think. Not as she lay wide awake, her eyes distant and glazed and fixed on the ceiling as if she were under some bizarre spell. And I knew not what to make of her large family coursing through the house and going about its business, while my friend remained alone in her room.

"That's wonderful, chica, that's just great," she replied, never turning to face me yet managing to produce a smile.

Only after she spoke did I realize something was clearly the matter. She sounded oddly disconnected, her voice frail and hollow. And she looked pale too, her complexion translucent but ghastly. Between a case of last minute nerves or coming down with something, I guessed it to be the latter. Amalia was not at all the nervous type. She was brash and fearless, always lively. So I didn't know what to think, not as she lay lifelessly on her bed unable to muster the energy to share in the good news.

"Amalia, chica? What's wrong? What's the matter?"

"Nothing, Clara. I'm fine. I'm just thinking about things."

"Are you sure? Are you having second thoughts?"

"Second thoughts? Are you joking?" she replied, her eyes fixed firmly on the ceiling still, her body perfectly supine.

She managed to inject some feeling into that last statement, but I remained unconvinced. I knew something must be the matter. "Everything is still on, right? You're sure we're still on?"

"Of course everything is still on, Clara! Did you ever think we'd get out of here? Did you ever think it possible?"

I felt tears well up in my eyes. Not only from the sweetness in her voice, but the sight of her so clearly troubled. But I didn't want to cry right now, not during this moment of happiness. I managed to contain the tears until they receded fully back.

"No," I confessed. "I honestly didn't think so. But it's happening, and nothing is going to stop us—nothing!"

I bent over and embraced her tightly, remaining at her side and unable to let go. She felt cold and mildly stiff, and I wanted to lend her some warmth. I felt I must infuse her with the raw exhilaration coursing through my veins. But despite her odd state, how beautiful my friend looked on that evening of August 14. I would always recall the peacefulness on her face as she lay still and motionless: the tranquility of her deep brown eyes, the silkiness of her wavy black hair resting atop the bedspread. Mostly her tender brown skin, pale and translucent, as if the glow of a white sun rose within her. My friend remained a natural Cuban beauty even in this peculiar state.

She didn't really resemble her parents to me, especially her father. But I did see the mother in her eyes: in their shape and size, in their color of chestnut-brown. The two women had long, thick lashes and identically arched eyebrows. And while Amalia's parents were short, light complected, and wide in frame, Amalia was tall, slim, and mulata. Truth be told, she was much prettier than I.

"You're right," Amalia said. "Nothing is going to stop us, chica, absolutely nothing."

I finally let go of her, sitting up bedside as my hand began stroking her forehead and my fingers wove themselves through her silky but lifeless hair. She never moved the entire time. She remained straight on her back in this fever of coldness, her vacant eyes never once deviating from the ceiling.

"What time are we meeting in the morning?" I asked. "The earlier the better, I hope."

I continued stroking her hair and smiling down at her, becoming acutely aware of another rawness brewing through the household. But this was hardly raw exhilaration. It was a combination of nerves and tension, a hailstorm of mirth as well as mourning. Amalia had a large family, and they'd assembled for the night's impending doom. Depending on who it was, the various family members had either come to talk her out of leaving the island or to say good-bye. But rather than address her directly, the relatives spoke of her as if she had already departed, had already gone, especially the two youngest brothers set to inherit her room who kept popping in and out. They were fraternal twins, eleven years old, and nothing at all alike.

"My bed goes by the window," declared the taller, leaner twin.

"Go ahead," spat out the shorter and wider brother. "I want my bed in the corner, where it's dark and cold and I won't have to look at you."

It was the strangest of gatherings, and I'd recall one thing the most about that night: all the *raspadura*, plates and plates of it everywhere I turned and looked. A large number of Amalia's relatives had poured in from the countryside—from the interior province of Cienfuegos—and brought with them that quintessential Cuban delicacy part candy, part elixir. Raspadura was pure raw juice pressed from sugarcane stalks and left to solidify. Cubans not only ingested it as a treat, but for its medicinal purposes. It could be molded into any shape whatsoever, but we loved making long bricks out of them or fashioning them into pyramids. That was why Havana's tallest structure—part tower, part pyramid—was affectionately known as Raspadura: a solemn memorial and monument built to honor our national apostle, José Martí.

I didn't know what to make of this. Why the entire evening everyone feasted on nothing but raspadura. Why despite the draining emotions weighing everyone down, a parade of frightened faces seemed fully alert and awake as if on watch for something. But feast away they did. Whether the faces were red from crying, red from drinking, or hardened with anger, they consumed raspadura. Or whether the faces were white with dread, white with resignation or white with fear, nibble away they did. The relatives from Cienfuegos had set a plate down by Amalia's bedside, but she wouldn't look at the raspadura, much less touch it.

"This will bring her back!" her aunts from the countryside insisted. "You'll see, if anything brings her back, raspadura will!"

All movement inside the house unfolded in a strangely supernatural state, including the sounds that enveloped us. Everyone gathered to see Amalia one last time cried wrenchingly or laughed heartily. While grandparents wept inconsolably and beat their chests, her three younger brothers chuckled and spoke of her fondly. While an array of aunts and uncles sobbed woefully and wailed in unison, Amalia's cousins laughed raucously from an endless supply of jokes. I hardly believed it when I saw Amalia's father, the last person ever to shed a tear, actually choke up.

Only one face seemed not the least bit affected by all the histrionics, displaying no emotion or producing so much as a single tear: Amalia's mother. She remained surprisingly calm throughout the gathering when, normally, *she* was the hysterical one in any charged situation. I didn't know what to make of it. Not unless the woman had taken medication or was simply holding it all back. The relatives from the countryside kept offering her servings of raspadura to put her in the right spirit, but she wouldn't be swayed. "Get that away from me!" she said disdainfully. "I don't want any part of it."

Through it all, the door to Amalia's bedroom remained wide open, but nobody ever stepped foot inside. No one came in to talk to her; no one came in to touch her. The family walked up and down the hallway and looked in momentarily, but after seeing her body resting peacefully and checking to see if she'd touched her raspadura, they'd disappear down the hallway again toward unknown regions of the house. Only her parents lingered outside the room, and we could make out all their conversations. They spoke as if nobody could hear them, as if neither of us was there.

"Don't worry," the mother told the father as they stood in the doorway and peered in. "She's not going anywhere. I'm telling you she's not. Tomorrow is the Feast of the Assumption, and I've pleaded with the Virgin to keep my baby from leaving. I know the Virgin will answer my prayers. I know she'll perform a miracle and keep Amalia from going—you'll see!"

This was unexpected, this effusive expression of piety. Amalia's mother was a small and slim woman, but feisty and excitable. She always wore her black hair short and walked around in high heels. I had never known her to be religious—nowhere near as religious as Mamá anyway—but tonight she wore a veil over her head. She had also transformed the Centro Habana home into a house of worship.

In the living room, on a makeshift altar backed against a corner, a statue of the Virgin Mary figured prominently, surrounded by flowers and votives and offerings of raspadura that the relatives from Cienfuegos had reverently placed at her feet. The family circulated back and forth in homage to the Virgin. They lit their candles, nibbled on their candy, and pleaded for their petitions to be carried out.

Only one person in that house remained unswayed by this all and certainly did not partake in any of the rituals, openly expressing his contempt for them all. Amalia's father was not the least bit religious. He made sure the house remained brightly lit and went from room to room insisting that all lights be kept on. He viewed religion as meaningless and ridiculous, as the contemptible thinking of backward people. He certainly did not view the events of this week as miraculous. He saw the attack against the Deauville as a criminal act and wished that those involved would be quickly arrested and executed by firing squad.

As for tonight, he made something perfectly clear to his wife: he couldn't stomach the sight of all the Catholic iconography, all the counterrevolutionary imagery: the statue of the Virgin Mary in his very living room (he allowed it, but only if she were firmly set back in the corner); the flowers and candles; the prayers and tears being shed in vain. The only thing he didn't mind was the raspadura. He hailed from Cienfuegos, and it was his relatives who had brought over the childhood treat. He didn't mind the jokes either and even chuckled a few times. Other than that, he viewed tonight's prayers and offerings as a colossal waste of energy and emotion. What his daughter needed was for someone—him most likely—to break through to her delusional thinking. Amalia's father did not believe in sobbing. He believed in sarcasm and cynicism and snide commentary.

"Isn't the Feast of the Assumption when Mary dies and her body rises up to Heaven?" he asked his wife.

"Yes, mijo. You didn't know that already? Or you just don't remember your catechism anymore?"

"¡Coño mija! Why then, of all the saints in Heaven, are you praying to her? Doesn't it make sense that tomorrow, on this Feast of the Assumption, the Virgin will only make it easier for our daughter to take off and leave? Doesn't that strike you like a ton of bricks?"

"First of all, the Virgin is not a saint. She's the mother of God. Secondly, she doesn't work that way—you'll see, you'll see, *cabrón!*"

"Well, that's what it seems like to me," he snidely pointed out. "That tomorrow will be the one day the Virgin helps everyone escape as if they're dying and going somewhere! Where, I don't know. But somewhere!"

"Don't be ridiculous, chico," she shot back. "As always, you never know what you're talking about—never!"

"Just make sure she takes a bite of the raspadura," one of the great aunts from Cienfuegos interjected. "That will make Amalia come to her senses, you'll see."

"Raspadura!" the mother spit out in disgust. "How is that going to help? That toxin! That crap that's nothing but pure poison!"

Amalia's father grew mortified. Not only had his wife just sworn in his presence, she had disrespected his family roots and their entire Cuban identity. He raised his hand high in the air and held it there as if to strike her down, but the gesture failed to faze his wife. It did not intimidate her in any way, especially under protection of her veil.

"Go ahead! I dare you!" she said to him, raising a hand too and hardening her face at him. "Go ahead, hit me! See then if this won't be the last night of your life!"

On and on it went, the entire time a series of one scrape after another. As Amalia lay there in her state of solemnness and tranquility, I didn't know if she was paying attention, ignoring it, or simply letting the snarling swirl all about her. But I caught it all: the sniping, the snippets, the sneering. It floated into the back room and back out again, wafting up and down the hallway and back toward uncharted regions of the house. Several times I wanted to get up and close the door, but I stopped myself. This was not my house; I had no right. Besides, each time I motioned toward the door, one of the Cienfuegos relatives popped a face in to have a look.

"No," they'd dutifully report before turning around and going along their way. "She still hasn't touched it."

Only her father made direct eye contact with either of us that night, especially me, waiting for everyone to disperse from the doorway before entering the room and kneeling at Amalia's bedside, before addressing her reverently and speaking in hushed and remorseful tones. All to no avail. Each time he did so, his daughter refused to acknowledge him. Each time the man knelt down and dug his fingers into the bedspread as emotion got the better of him, she remained motionless, staring up at the ceiling with both hands folded over chest. I was the only person in the entire house she communicated with that evening of August 14. Somehow we managed to shield ourselves from the ensuing antics by staying focused on our plans for the following day.

"Well, chica, it's a good thing you've brought that up," she said, her voice slow and hollow, her eyes fixed on the ceiling still. "You see, there's been a slight change in plans."

"Oh?" I said. "What type of change in plans?"

"Nothing to worry about. Everything is still on. It's just that Henry and I can't go to Cojimar with you in the morning. He's already there."

Just then I noticed her fingernails painted in a bright red polish and wondered where she'd gotten it. Cienfuegos, maybe? I hadn't seen polish that red in ages. And her complexion had just turned a shade lighter. Either the ceiling light kept blanching her skin into some vanilla veneer, or the rays of that inner white sun kept radiating across the expanse of her body.

"What happened?" I asked.

"Nothing too catastrophic, chica. Nothing that can't be fixed by morning."

"Catastrophic!" I said.

"Well, nothing too serious, just a little setback."

"What type of setback?"

"Well, it seems that for just one moment today, Henry left the raft unattended, and when he went back to it, one whole side was missing."

I wanted to bend over my friend again. Not to embrace her. Just to feel for her breath, just to feel for a pulse. I needed to see if she was merely playing dead or really not alive.

"What!" I exclaimed. "Are you joking?"

"No, chica, I'm not. But don't worry. He's fixing it as we speak."

"But how could such a thing happen?" I asked. "How did they have enough time to do that?"

"Are you surprised, Clara? Don't you know what it's like out there right now? What a mess it is."

Speaking of messes, something else caught my attention besides all the raspadura, besides the parade of faces from the countryside and the statue of the Virgin Mary surrounded by flowers and candles. As much as I loved my friend, Amalia was an inveterate slob, pathologically messy. Her room was always a walking disaster. But not tonight. Tonight everything was inexplicably neat and orderly. Not one item thrown about or strewn on the ground or mildly out of place. Not a fleck of dust anywhere in sight. Even her bed was neatly made, a pale pink bedspread hugging the mattress tightly.

"What does this mean?" I asked. "What are we going to

do?"

"Well, good thing is the thieves left all the maloja in tact, the outer lining. The bad news is they made off with most of the sugarcane stalks."

"The sugarcane stalks! Isn't that the crux of the vessel?"

"Yes, chica, but you know how smart that boyfriend of mine is, the way he always thinks ahead. He prepared for such an emergency and has plenty of stalks on hand."

I thought a dose of relief might be in order, but I remained anxiously silent. My heart pulsated and paced with worry and my eyes glazed over in misgiving. I stared down at the raspadura by the bedside and wished I could bite into it, but I focused on the bright red nail polish and wished I had that instead. I was relieved by one thing: that Rigo was not present to hear this. Not with his dislike of Henry or how he had mocked construction of the raft. If Rigo were to learn what I just had, he'd change his mind and immediately back out.

"So we're not leaving tomorrow then? Is that what you're saying?"

"Oh no, chica, we're definitely leaving tomorrow. But that's why we can't join you in the morning. You see, I'm leaving for Cojimar tonight. I need to help Henry weave the stalks back together."

"At this hour!" I protested. "You can't go to Cojimar at this hour. How will you get there? Not only that, you're in no shape to work, Amalia. Just look at you!"

What was happening? I couldn't decipher it—whether all this seeming casualness was merely a form of denial or there really was no cause for concern. My friend's revelation did not bode well with me, but maybe I needed to detach myself. Maybe I too needed to lie down and think about things. Or maybe I just needed a good bite of raspadura and feel the pureness of that sugarcane coursing through my body. I must admit, I hated the color of raspadura: a drab mix of olive green with a dreary hint of cardboard brown. But each time I looked at that brick of raw sugar at her bedside, how the blood rushed to my stomach and my mouth instantly watered: how badly I wanted to ingest that coarse sweetness; how badly I longed for that exhilarating elixir.

"Don't worry, chica," Amalia said. "I'll get up just fine, and Henry's brother is picking me up shortly. It's you I'm worried about. I feel horrible about stranding you and Rigo at the last minute like this. How will you get to Cojimar now?"

I would do it! I'd bite into the raspadura even though no one had offered me any, even though the piece lying within reach was intended solely for her. My hand hovered over the plate and finally reached down until I touched it. How cool and smooth and creamy it felt. I nearly broke into a cold sweat.

"I'm sure we'll figure something out," I said distractedly, wrapping my hand around the raspadura. "What I'm worried about is whether this raft will float tomorrow. That's what concerns me."

"Clara!" Amalia shot back, her voice hardening and her eyes stiffening. "Don't worry, chica! It's nothing to fret about. Some people are building rafts at the last moment, right on the beach before they leave."

"They are?" I asked.

"Yes, they are. Besides, you know Henry. You know he can fix anything. If he says the raft will hold, it will hold. Now, eight o'clock sharp tomorrow morning, Clara! But please excuse me for now, chica. I need to rest more and to think a while longer before I get up."

I dropped the raspadura back on the plate and retracted my hand. At least I had touched it, felt it momentarily. But I wouldn't be savoring any of its sweetness after all. I decided that I no longer wanted it, no longer needed it. I would much rather carry with me the lasting memory of its touch.

"Eight o'clock," I said absent-mindedly. *"Si Dios quiere."*

God willing indeed! I embraced my friend again, but only by rote. This time I felt no need to infuse her with any warmth or found it not the least bit difficult to release her. I kissed her good-bye and took a last look, wanting to remember her like this and remember this moment. I had not yet turned to leave when, once again, I heard a scuffle brewing outside the doorway, some new sniping. A flurry of voices coalesced into an indistinguishable blur of sound, except for one voice: that of Amalia's father, which rose above the rest. There was no subduing the man or the force behind his voice. I remained motionless at the bedside, unable to move as I took in this latest round of fighting.

"Let me in!" he insisted. "I'm going in there right now!"

"No!" Amalia's mother shouted, trying desperately to hold him back. "No! You need to calm down and stay out of this. You need to let the Virgin do her work. It's the Feast of the Assumption tomorrow, and my prayers will be answered. The Virgin will not allow our daughter to leave, you'll see!"

I remained fixed in my own motionless state, afraid to turn around and look. Her parents' beleaguered voices swirled behind me, and it even sounded as if one of the aunts from Cienfuegos had intervened, jumping in to keep the two from strangling each other. I'd had enough. I wanted to get out of there. Maybe they wouldn't notice me slip by. But just as I turned to go, a parade of hard and angry faces came barreling into the room with Amalia's father leading the way.

"Tell me one thing, Clara, just one thing! That you've come to talk my daughter out of this. That's all I want to know!"

Amalia's father may have been a short man, but he was physically intimidating: bulky and sturdy, with a deep and booming voice. He had thick black brows and dark prickly stubble. His eyes took on a possessed quality when pushed to the edge. Even as I stood face to face with him I towered over the man, but I couldn't answer him. I was too terrified. I could only marvel at Amalia's room and how I had never seen it so immaculate, so neat and tidy. I thought of the raspadura too, but only how it now disgusted me. How it represented everything I wanted to rid myself of. As my pulse raced and my breath quickened, my thoughts were being hijacked. The speedboat of this man's insistence kept pummeling the ferry of my silence, but he knew my answer only too well. He could divine it in my eyes.

"No, Clara! No, chica!" he intoned. "Don't tell me you're going through with this foolishness too! Don't tell me that!"

I wanted to counter with an appropriate response, but needed the raspadura to aid me, to infuse me with the power to stand up to him. One bite of that magical morsel and I knew I could fight back fiercely. I could pummel the vessel of his obstinacy until it split wide open. But my tongue felt tightly trapped and refused to budge.

"What about Rigo!" he persisted. "Surely Rigo won't be a party to this, not with how sensible and smart he is. Surely Rigo knows nothing about this!"

I needed to flee. I needed to escape this man's presence. As he sprayed me with the hose of his invective and tried to hasten the drowning of my hope, I needed to take immediate leave of him. And I refused to answer him but my silence said enough. All at once, as if in prayer, he clasped his hands and rocked them back and forth. But this was no gesture that presaged prayer; rather, a prelude to the diatribe he was about to unleash.

"That worthless *artist*!" he assailed Henry, uttering the word "artist" with particular derision. "How I wish I had him in front of me! I swear to God I would choke the life out of him with my bare hands. I would beat him raw with *caña*, that's what I'd do! Always chasing some half-assed dream, always taking advantage!"

A bull. Amalia's father was a human bull. Inside that immaculate room, with his thick neck and bulging eyes and nostrils that flared, he looked exactly like a beast. He resembled a mad bull as he snorted through his nose and his mouth began to froth. He pointed his head down as if to kick and charge and gorge his horns straight into some invisible target.

Amalia's mother did her best to calm him down. She even tried forcing raspadura down his throat. It was well known that bulls loved the taste of sweetness. But as he scraped his hooves against the floor and kicked and swung his head wildly about, the plate of raspadura by the bedside went crashing to the ground. The array of frightened faces all gasped in horror, mortified at the sight of their sacred elixir being desecrated in so undignified a way. But Amalia's father kept charging at some unseen enemy, some invisible red flag that kept taunting him, fighting some inner demon that had taken complete possesson of him. His wife did her best to hold him back, but there was no restraining this beast. He was in a savage rage and could not be subdued. Not as he charged toward his daughter's bed. Not as he knelt at her side and tears formed in his eyes. And not as he sobbed openly and uncontrollably and tried to waken her up. These were the moments he least resembled Amalia physically, when his complexion burned red and white and hers stayed a cool and sultry cinnamon. Despite all this fire and frenzy, Amalia remained fixed on her back unfazed, eyes to the ceiling and hands folded over her breast.

"No, *hija*!" he sobbed. "Don't you see what he's doing? This is all a setup! That boyfriend of yours is no innocent. He's feeding you false expectation. He's setting you up."

"She loves him," an aunt interjected. "And he loves her."

"Love!" the father sneered. "Artists don't know the first thing about love. Artists don't love anybody but themselves. Why couldn't she have fallen in love with a numbers man? Why couldn't she love someone good at math?"

I needed to leave, and quickly. As Amalia's family unraveled, this was no time for outsiders. This was a family crisis and I must bring my intrusive visit to an end. Just wait till she broke the news about leaving for Cojimar *tonight*. He'd really think it all a setup then. Or maybe she wouldn't break the news at all. Maybe she'd just up and float away. Amalia lay inert in her dispassionate gaze, and just before taking my leave, the bull tried one last time knocking some sense into me.

"Don't go, Clara! Don't go, chica!" her father begged me.

"What about your mother? What about your sisters? You can't do this to them. You can't do this to Pilar. She's innocent in all this, and she needs you! Who's going to watch over her if you're gone? Who's going to take care of her, Clara? Don't let that artist force you into this, too! What type of artist is he anyway? What has he ever created?"

Innocent! This man had the nerve to mention the word innocent when he knew exactly what he was doing! When it was no accident he had assembled the whole family here tonight and for over an hour now they had tried forcing Amalia to come to her senses. How dare he pump his daughter with so much guilt! How dare he force guilt down my own throat! This man was a dangerous fool, and I'd had enough.

I wanted out. I had to leave before reason radioed panic and my life's goals drowned before my eyes. I wanted out before my spirit screamed out in agony and my hopes plunged into desperation and despair. Murderer! ¡Asesino! That was all he was. Wasn't it time this man came to *his* senses? Wasn't it? As my soul struggled to stay afloat and it fought to keep from filling with frustration, the sight of this man filled me with such rage I wanted to scream. But I was too drained to scream. After so much silent wrangling I could only form a few words, all of them softly and rather feeble.

"I'm sorry," I said, giving him a hug and a kiss good-bye before I left. "I'm so sorry."

But he continued pleading and wouldn't let go of me. And the flushed and feverish faces that invaded the room rushed the doorway to block my path. If I didn't know how I would ever get out, I couldn't have asked for better timing when the house suddenly went dark and a chorus of wails erupted through the room, all the frightened faces scrambling in search of candles and oil lamps as Amalia lay in the middle of her bed oblivious to the confusion and whether it was dark or light.

"It's a sign!" her mother called out. "It's a sign she won't be leaving us."

"No!" her grandmother yelled out. "It's a sign she's as good as dead already. My *preciosa mijita* is dead and gone."

"No!" an aunt chimed in. "It's a sign she can still come back to us. Quick, get her some raspadura! And make sure it's not the one that fell on the floor."

"Don't be ridiculous!" Amalia's father finally boomed in, his voice rising about the litany of speculation. "It's no sign of anything! It's just our fucking *apagón* for the night, that's all it is!"

I hated to admit it, but the bull was right. As religious as I now regarded myself, this sudden power outage was no mystical incident, just our nightly blackout. It was eight o'clock, and the apagón would remain in effect for the next twelve hours. The time for escape had come. It wouldn't be easy, but darkness had snuck in as my accomplice.

A gauntlet. As I left Amalia's house for the last time ever, it felt I was passing through some medieval gauntlet. Arms to one side, arms to the other. Faces on both sides of me, voices all around. I tried focusing on the front door, but the arms along that gauntlet reached out and tugged at me, tried pulling me back. I tried shielding my eyes from the panoply of faces, but the ghastly glare in all those eyes terrified me and caused me to tremble. I tried covering my ears from the weeping and wailing, but the deafening walls of laughter still seeped through. It had all fused into a blur of sight and sound that didn't cease until I jumped into the street and shut the door firmly behind me! Finally, did it end—finally! Only one thing did I want to see before exiting the house: the statue of the Virgin Mary, just to ask for her blessing, but the darkness and the gauntlet completely blocked my view.

What in the world had I just witnessed? What on earth had I just lived through? I couldn't make any sense of it all, but one good thing did come of it: the emotional blackmail had not derailed me any; in fact, I felt more grounded than ever. How I pitied this family and any like it. So caught up in trite desperation they couldn't think sensibly. So intent on parental selfishness that they preferred to hold their daughter back and sacrifice her future just for the comfort of having her nearby. Thank goodness I had no interest in being a parent. Thank goodness I did not ever want to bear any children.

I just didn't get it. Couldn't the naysayers understand that nobody was forcing anyone to do anything? Didn't they realize this miracle had visited us for a reason? I loved Amalia's parents, but they were wrong. Even this minor setback involving the raft would not deter me any. Still, I must be more compassionate. It wasn't their fault. Some of us would always live in darkness, others would discover a hidden light. So I would not let Amalia's news discourage me. Henry could fix anything, and La Maloja would be fine come morning.

I coursed my way through the streets of Centro Habana, and for a few harrowing moments, a new chorus of wails rang out. As our nightly blackout doused everything in a suffocating black, residents clanged on pots from their balconies, pounded on windows from their living rooms, or banged on pans from their stairwells. Whether it was a chorus of resentment or a choir of rejoicing, I couldn't tell. I just wanted to get home. I wondered whether Rigo had yet returned and whether Mamá and my sisters might still be out. Would I be entering a dark and empty house or stepping into my own family crisis? My family was much smaller than Amalia's. We were not at all the size of a typical Cuban clan.

The streets were filled with people this evening, pulsing with a raw exhilaration of their own. It felt like New Year's Eve, like Carnival time even. That explained all the police out, all the mongrels in blue and in their black boots and belts. I hated men in uniform. I despised any kind of uniformity. But there were droves of those uniforms everywhere, which meant only one thing: they were expecting problems tonight. They were sniffing for any hint of trouble or looking out for any sign of resistance. I felt like an easy target, but despite the police presence I pushed on, coursing my way defiantly through the narrow streets and pulsing anonymously in my resolve.

Dusk had gone. No more partial darkness. No more sign of

its opaqueness as Night gave rise to a cool and thin air. A warm and inward light stirred within my breast and illuminated my path home, shining on a parade of faces so that with each one I encountered, I wondered what that face might mean. Was it the face of someone partaking of the miracle or of someone ignoring it? Was it the face of someone choosing freedom and life or submitting to death? In short, was it the face of a wise man or a fool?

If I had felt drained and exhausted earlier, I no longer did. Not as these silent contemplations swirled within. Not as they injected me with jolts of pure and raw energy. And certainly not as everything surrounding me surged and pulsed with life through all the twists and turns of our city.

Nine days since the miracle at the Deauville. Nine days since those who ruled every aspect of our lives here—the ones who kept constant watch over us—called it an "act of terror." Still, that didn't deter anyone from wanting to bear witness to the infamous act: ¡*El Maleconazo!* Many continued gravitating toward the flashpoint for any sign of last week's rebellion. Rumor had it that visitors from all over the island, as if in pilgrimage, kept pouring into the capital just to see the hotel for themselves, personally wanting to see where the incident had unfolded and hoping to view any remnants of the revolt with their own eyes.

The answer was no. The government wasted no time in fixing the broken windows of the Deauville and replacing them on that same August 5, all in a futile attempt to erase any sign of the insurgence. Did that explain all the people out tonight? Was that what all these faces meant? Were all these visitors merely attending a wake and paying their respects to the Deauville one last time before this historic act of rebellion was finally laid to rest?

I lived close by, on Calle Perseverancia, and reached my street in no time. I was just about to turn the corner onto my block of decaying and crumbling houses when I felt something tugging at me, something faint yet forceful: the unexpected pull of the Malecón. Our famous seawall beckoned me back in the other direction.

setbacks

I stopped and wavered, and in those fleeting moments of indecision, one of the mongrels in blue took note of me. I could sense his suspicious eyes all over my body. I could feel them on my back. What exactly were they keeping watch over? What exactly were they expecting? This had to be the only nation on earth where standing stationary was a threat to the country's security.

I was sure Rigo must be home by now. I was anxious to get back to him. But I couldn't break the pull of the Malecón. It urged me toward it. It called me back in the other direction. It was the taste of something sweet in my mind that wouldn't wash clean. I hadn't visited the seafront for weeks now. Not since the end of July when I'd waited with the multitudes for the ferry that never came. Since then I'd had no desire to return. But now, in a trance of sorts, I gravitated toward it, approaching that beloved part of our city where water met land and dreams delicately unfolded or folded back up.

I could no longer resist and caved in to its call. I would visit the Malecón one last time, even if just to say good-bye to my city and bid it a melancholy farewell. It was asking for trouble and I knew it. The majority of the mongrels were stationed there, keeping empty watch over our restive populace and expecting imaginary trouble. I knew who I was. I knew I had trouble written all over my face. No doubt they would stop and harass me, but I no longer cared. I was leaving tomorrow. So let the mongrels just try.

"Yes," I would snarl at them. "How can I help you? What do you want? You see, while you continue to rot in this cesspool of Socialism, I'm getting the hell out of here tomorrow. While you continue to corrode inside this trashcan of Communism, my body will float toward freedom and democracy. My body will take to the sea and there's nothing you can do to stop me—nothing!"

It may have been mid-August, but it felt cool out. I picked up the pace to keep warm. I managed to arrive at the seawall completely unnoticed, no contact with anyone or anything. Sure enough, the mongrels were all there: dozens and dozens fanned out across the Malecón, scores of them in full force.

They too seemed involved in some kind of wake. Not over those already deceased. Not over those who embraced the living death here and settled back into an afterlife of atrophy. Only over those with a hidden light. Those with a spark of energy and in a fury to flee.

Clearly, the mongrels knew which one I was. Clearly they sensed the firestorm of exhilaration burning within and thus they eyed me. Indeed, it didn't take long before a pack of them encased me on both sides, but I ignored it. As long as I stayed focused on the water, their presence had no effect on me. As long as I looked out to sea, I could shield myself from their gauntlet.

The Malecón. Like any native of Havana how I loved that delicate necklace that wound its way along the bay. Just as the Eiffel Tower was the face of Paris and the Empire State Building that of New York, the Malecón was the face of our city. For some time now it had signified nothing to me. I had come to view it as an old and crumbling seawall, a corral to rein in and further confine the heart of our city. Not tonight. Not the night before our departure. Now I saw it as an elegant and aged gate waiting to open up and eagerly show us the way out.

And what a beautiful night. As I stood at the wall by the sea, never had I seen the night sky so richly textured, so much in motion. It was layered in distinct shades of color: above the horizon lay a band of charcoal, raw and gritty. Above this a delicate layer of ashen gray spun in wisps of cotton. And above them both a thick blanket of black softly pressed down. What an unusual sight: these three bands that lay atop each other as if sharing a bed in the night sky. And what a dazzling array of light scattered throughout—not just along the skyline, but in a sprinkling of white and silver and even vanilla that hung high overhead. I couldn't be sure if all these lights resembled stars or granules of finely powdered sugar swirling and crystalizing deep in the tropical night.

What a magical spot where I stood, from where our stately skyline sparkled so brightly. If it were it up to me, we would leave from here rather than Cojimar. No better place existed to stage an exit. The Malecón, the launching spot of every Cuban's hopes and dreams. But for now I put such notions aside. I wanted to enjoy the exhilaration of the night sky and its glimmering pulse of lights, to intoxicate myself with the whispering sounds of the ocean and the seductiveness of its scent.

How I loved the water. I had all my life. Just not at night. How different the sea was at nighttime than during the day. In the light of day it was always a warm and friendly face, a familiar and smiling friend. But at night it was an unknown stranger with all its inherent dangers and something to be avoided. As much as I trusted in the events of this past week and knew them to be miraculous, thank God we were leaving in the morning. I could never take to the water at night. I could never let that unknown stranger blindly guide me. To think of all the brothers and sisters who had taken their journey under cover of night only to perish, who had trustingly accepted the hand of that stranger only to be betrayed by it. *That* was valor. That was raw courage and I shivered thinking about it.

But what did it matter? Regardless of where we left from, I loved the Malecón and always would. So much of my life revolved around this sturdy seawall and its sweeping vistas. It was here I came to realize I had fallen in love with Rigo and wanted to spend the rest of my life with him. It happened one night in late November. There were no lights sprinkled across the sky that night, just a thin canvas of clouds. I looked up and saw his face flashing before me, burning through the harbor sky. From that moment on his face wouldn't stop flashing across the expanse of my mind, racing back and forth between my heart and head and leaving no room for doubt as to how I felt: I loved him.

These were the lifelong memories I would always treasure of the Malecón, the way its essence was ingrained into mine. Those who visited our island admired the majesty of its views; those who grew up here appreciated its mystery and magic. Whether we leaned forward against the wall, sat on it restfully, or laid back and gazed up, the Malecón of Havana was intrinsically Cuban. How many dreams had come to life at this seawall as I stared at the sky that blended into the sea? How many plans were hatched here as I heard the whispering sounds of the water? And how many things, both good and bad, had developed or drowned here—desire as well as doubt?

I felt restless again, in the throes of that anxiousness that had gripped me earlier. Dusk was gone, but determination clung on. The evening air turned ever cooler and I longed for warmth. But as I stood and clasped my arms and even shivered in place, something other than a tingly breeze pricked away at me: gusts of hesitation, breaths of uncertainty, the slightest jabs of doubt started poking away. And these entanglements of emotion were bad enough, but now I felt the pangs of a nascent and nagging doubt.

It had to be the news my friend had given me. I must be fretting about our vessel, the Maloja, and whether it would be finished in time, whether it would float all right, whether Amalia would be feeling well enough by tomorrow, and whether Rigo might not just put a halt to everything. It had to be all these pulsings of preoccupation. How I longed to believe this even if something more powerful kept pulling at me, something more terrifying tugged at my heart. It was not the sight of Rigo that came to me at the moment, but of Amalia's parents gnawing and gnashing away at each other; the sight of those fretful family faces flittering all about. Mostly, it was the sight of Amalia's father as he knelt at his daughter's bedside and wept.

Was he right? Had we really thought this through? Had we considered all the consequences of leaving home and family never to return? I looked up for an answer, gazing at the sky as it slumbered impassively atop the water. Those bands of color had fully dispersed. No longer did they share a cozy bed in the night sky: the charcoal had clearly won out and churned the other two out. And that sprinkling of light had faded as well, receding behind a curtain of newly formed clouds to become the captive rays of a hidden white sun. The harbor sky fascinated me as it always did, but it was not Rigo

I saw or a feeling of love dawning on me. Instead, it was the image of my older sister Pilar and a growing sense of guilt. It was her face flashing before me and an ever-encroaching dread about abandoning her. But why was this striking me now of all times? Why was raw exhilaration being doused by some insidious dusk of doubt? For some reason a flimsy veil of incertitude was trying to cloak me in a partial darkness.

I didn't know what to make of it, but I wouldn't give in. I'd be strong and remember Rigo's words to me earlier: we were committed now, no turning back! Not even a sense of duty toward Pilar could make me retreat. How could I? How could I entertain a scintilla of doubt after what Rigo and I had gone through the last couple of years? Not just us, but my father, my sister—everyone in the family. Yet, as much as we all had suffered during this Special Period, Pilar was all I cared about. The mere thought of leaving her certainly left me feeling wretched and raw, but first thing in the morning Rigo and I were out of there. No turning back!

For the second time that night, tears filled my eyes. This time they did not stage a quick retreat. This time they marched straight down my face. No moving backwards. Not as the last few years in Cuba flashed before my eyes against the backdrop of a bad dream. Not as they unfolded like a giant flashback above a graveyard lit dimly in charcoal and ash. And not as I decided to bring an end to this never-ending wake and discard all the deaths in my life: the hardships, the frustrations, all the tragedies that had visited us.

I pushed back now. I resisted these newly festering qualms and told myself it was all very normal. This dusk of indecision was only natural and would soon begin to disintegrate until it fully dispersed. Miracle or not, whenever anyone arrived at a monumental decision such as this, it was only typical to be plagued by all sorts of second thoughts. By seeds, by shadows, by visitations of doubt. That was all this signified. Under such difficult and trying circumstances, it was perfectly natural to be hampered by and fall prey to and be visited by doubt.

3

visitations

august 14
flashback in the night

Three days prior, on August 11 when I first mentioned leaving, there had certainly been no doubt.

I thought Rigo would be thrilled by the prospect of fleeing Cuba, even on a homemade raft called the Maloja. He too hated life here and felt dead inside, he just never acknowledged that death openly. He buried it deep within and fed his foolish hope.

But if anyone had legitimate cause for abandoning his homeland, my husband did. All his life he had wanted to be an architect, dreaming of erecting skyscrapers and other towering structures. Even when I was twelve and Rigo was nineteen, when most guys that age spent their free time playing baseball or hanging out with friends, I, the neighborhood pest, could find him sketching and illustrating or making schematics of all the fantastic ideas firing off in his head. Science fiction, he used to call the drawings. Rigo intrigued me so, which made it easy to fall in love with him.

He realized his dream of becoming an architect, studying at Cuba's premiere Instituto de Arquitectura. Rigo possessed such talent that he was the first to be selected for a spot in Havana's internationally renowned institute and even graduated at the top of his class. My husband showed such promise throughout his studies, and his professors held him in such high esteem, that right before completion of his degree and becoming fully licensed by the state, Rigo was informed of an exciting new project. The Ministry of Economic Development not only wanted him to help design this project, but possibly lead it: a series of new luxury hotels along the beaches of Santa Lucía, Cuba's pristine archipelago off the northeastern coast of Camagüey.

Rigo reacted in a manner less than thrilled. "Camagüey? But I just got married. Will my wife be able to join me?"

"No!" came the resounding reply. "There aren't the funds for that. You can come home one weekend a month if you want, but that's it. Are you interested or not, compañero?"

Rigo sensed it might put a strain on our new marriage, but he was interested, more than interested. He was so excited he couldn't sleep nights, and on many occasions, I'd find him awake at two or three in the morning sketching and drawing and drafting blueprints when he should have been resting by my side. This project along the beaches of Santa Lucía had received such staunch approval from the highest levels of government that the ministry decided to accelerate its launch. A couple months ahead of schedule, Rigo received word to start packing. The ministry was dispatching a planning committee to Camagüey's northeastern coast.

"We want to see some of your schematics," they told him. "And right away."

Rigo couldn't wait to break the wonderful news. Of

course, I was upset. We'd been married less than a year, and I didn't want him gone from me. I never felt more whole or complete than when I had him at my side. Not to mention that Camagüey seemed so far away: a tedious ten-hour train ride from Havana. But I figured this was our punishment, what we got for growing up in the same neighborhood and knowing each other all our lives. Even so, I remained passionate and loved him with all my heart. I was only twelve when I fell in love with Rigo, and he was nineteen. I knew I was much too young for him, but even then I wanted to marry Rigo some day and spend the rest of my life with him.

True, Rigo wasn't the most handsome of men, but he did have strong hands and a great body that I worshipped. More importantly, he possessed a humble heart and loved his family. He was loyal, affable in nature, and everybody liked him. He had glowing reports from his professors, all of whom had very strong ties to the ministry, and it was easy to see why they selected Rigo for this project. He had the talent, personality, and drive. Rigo was the full package. That was why it made no sense when, out of nowhere, the night before he was all set to go, after fully preparing his suitcases and packing some pre-preliminary sketches he wanted to take on the expedition, Rigo received the most upsetting call of his life.

"Start unpacking, chico," officials informed him matter-of-factly. "The trip is off."

Rigo refused to believe it, he *couldn't* believe it. He thought it must all be a practical joke and somebody would call back right away and confess. But nobody called or stopped by or sent any other form of communication. Maybe he'd done something wrong. Maybe he'd offended the wrong person or had inspired jealousy among a superior. Rigo was so intent on being a part of this project he called back and agreed to work for free if necessary.

"Consider it volunteer labor," he said, determined to get his foot in the door and wanting to know what he'd done.

"You haven't done anything," officials assured him. "You have a sterling record and a bright future in this country. All we can tell you is the project has been put on hold—indefinite hold."

If this was meant to make him feel better, Rigo felt himself drowning in devastation. He'd never experienced any form of disappointment in his life, and this crushed him. But he suspected something else at play here and meant to find out. He visited someone who would know and whom he trusted implicitly: a professor who taught North American form and design with an emphasis on the twentieth-century architecture of San Francisco. Of all his six years of intense study, this was Rigo's favorite class.

As expected, the professor knew precisely what was going on, and there was, indeed, something brewing behind that thin explanation they had doled out for his student.

"Well, chico," his former professor began. "The project is on hold all right; that part is true."

"There's another part?" Rigo asked. "What and for how long?"

"Forever," the professor bluntly informed him. "You didn't hear this from me, Rigo, but there's been a big change of plans around here, real big."

"What type of change of plans?"

"I know I can confide in you, Rigo, just as you can always confide in me. Still, I have to stress the confidential nature of this. Effective immediately, all projects on this massive a scale will be granted to companies of foreign governments."

"What!" Rigo asked in shock. "No!"

"Yes, chico. The ministry has conducted a resource planning study and concluded that Cuba lacks the means to execute so enormous a project, that it lacks the skill to put in effect so grand a scheme. They've decided to outsource."

"*Outsource?*" repeated Rigo, barely able to pronounce the word in his thick Cuban accent. "What in the hell is that?"

The professor explained the idea behind outsourcing and how, just now, the concept was barely taking form and still highly experimental. But soon it would set a trend for the future, whether a country was Capitalist, Communist, Democratic or a Dictatorship.

"Like it or not, it's the way of the future," he said sadly. "Only one good thing will come out of this outsourcing."

"What's that?" Rigo asked.

"Local jobs, albeit low-paying jobs."

Rigo apologized for his outburst and for his use of foul language, even though, in Cuba, foul language was not the exception but the norm. Still, he had meant no disrespect to his favorite instructor and felt ashamed. And had shame been the only emotion Rigo grappled with it might have been easier to pick up the pieces, but it was not. Again came defeat: a sweeping defeat; a dizzying, demoralizing defeat that descended on him and totally displaced him. For weeks my husband functioned in a daze, moping around the house and doing absolutely nothing. I'd never seen him so sedentary or morose. I knew not how to help. I couldn't reach him. It pained me to take so drastic a step, but I had no choice. I'd have to call the one person I hated resorting to in any time of trouble: my mother-in-law Mihrta. I knew she could help, but I also knew she'd find a way to make me feel useless in this crisis—and she did. I'd never seen her more animated or in higher spirits than the day she came over to see what ailed her baby.

"He'll have to move back home for a week," Mihrta announced. "Maybe two."

"But he is home," I protested. "We're married, remember?"

"Of course you are, mija. I mean his *home* home, not his adopted home. Now don't worry, one week won't kill you. Just think of how you'll have your husband back to normal and good as new."

Mihrta had never liked me and decided that even when I

was twelve, she should be brutally blunt with me. "I know what you're after," she said one day. "Just stop wasting your time, mijita. My son is too old for you, and he's not going to wait around."

But she was wrong. Rigo *did* wait, and she'd never forgiven me for it. Just as she'd never forgiven me that, upon our marrying, we decided to move in with my family rather than his. Like every newlywed couple in Cuba, we had to choose living with one set of in-laws or the other. No such thing as marrying and having your own place, much less owning your own home. Not with all the severe housing shortages, especially in Havana. After my father's death it made no sense to move in with Rigo's family, which included two younger brothers. Mihrta blamed me for that decision too.

After the wedding she fell into a depression so deep and mournful the doctors recommended electroshock therapy. Everybody tried talking her out of it, terrified of what so drastic a treatment might do, fearful it might leave her in a permanent vegetative state. But it worked. Mihrta came back stronger and livelier, more determined than ever. The voltage in her brain worked such wonders she swore by electroshock therapy as a miraculous cure-all. Rigo's younger brother was studying electrical engineering and Mihrta insisted he invent a home version of the therapy. He managed to come up with something all right, but almost burned the house down in doing so.

I didn't know what was going on over there, how Mihrta was putting her healing hands to use, whether she was feeding him chicken soup or hooking him up to a cord and lamp. One week turned into two, and two became three, and I feared I might never see my husband again. Then Providence intervened and brought Rigo back to life and back to me, or so I thought. It happened without notice again. He had decided to visit his favorite professor to discuss the prospect of switching to teaching when, unexpectedly, he got a call about another exciting project.

"Don't tell me," he began sarcastically, knowing all about

outsourcing and how, soon, it would set a course for the entire future. "More luxury hotels?"

"No," they replied, missing the sarcasm in his voice. "Nothing as glamorous as that, but infinitely more important."

They had piqued his curiosity with their cryptic teasing. Maybe the Ministry of Housing had approved a new construction project. "Well?" he asked. "What is it?"

"A school!" they announced excitedly. "A very special school!"

"What type of school?" he asked cynically.

"One the Revolution is in dire need of," they explained. "One the Revolution can no longer place on hold or put off indefinitely, and we want you in charge of it, chico. We want it to be a prototype for all future schools in Cuba."

Before they provided him with any specifics, Rigo's mind fired away. He wished he had pencil and paper right then and there because he could already see this school vividly in his mind. Not a single-story complex typical of the traditional Latin American school, but a tall and futuristic structure fashioned from steel and glass and metal and windows on all four sides, windows from floor to ceiling that allowed a panoramic light to stream in and from which faculty and student alike could gaze into infinity. Rigo had already calculated the height of the building and how many stories it should have, and just to teach everyone a lesson, he would design this new school like a hotel, a luxury hotel. It may have been years away from completion, and even years away from rising off the ground, but already Rigo couldn't wait for the christening of this landmark building that would punctuate Havana's skyline with a bold exclamation point.

"Just wait!" he told the officials. "I'm going to design a school like no other. It will be the most innovative and recognizable school Havana has ever seen."

"Havana?" they scoffed. "Who said anything about Havana?"

"Isn't that where it's going to be?" he asked. "Isn't the school for right here in the capital?"

"Absolutely not!" they declared. "The last thing Havana needs is another school. In fact, the ministry recently decided there are too many schools in the city and wants to shut some down."

"Oh," said Rigo. "Well, where then?"

"¡Camagüey!" they proudly announced. "In the little town of Rio Piedras in the historic and colonial province of Camagüey."

Rigo's heart deflated and sank. *¡Camagüey! Again!* No, he couldn't have heard correctly. "Did you say Camagüey?" he asked.

This time the officials caught the tinge of disappointment in his voice and homed in on it. "Is there a problem compañero?"

"No," he said. "No problem. It's just that, as you know, I'm married and all, and—"

"You were willing to go there before," they countered.

"I know, but you see, I feel bad about leaving my wife now, and, well—"

"You didn't feel bad about leaving her when it was luxury hotels you were going to build. You only feel bad now that the project involves a school and your prospects aren't quite as glamorous."

"Oh no," Rigo replied, trying to do some quick damage control. "It won't be a problem. I can assure you, no problem at all."

"Glad to hear it, compañero, glad to hear it. Don't worry," they said. "It's only nine hundred kilometers away. One weekend home a month will be more than enough for you."

Rigo took hold of his senses and further acquiesced. "Yes," he said. "That'll be fine."

"Good to hear," they assured him yet again. "Good to

hear. And listen. We know you're a newlywed, but just wait. In a few years you'll be begging us to send you to Camagüey. No, you'll be begging us to send you to Angola."

Rigo didn't know if they were joking or not, but regardless, the officials were totally off base. My husband loved me more than anything and didn't find their jaded humor the least bit amusing. Still, he knew they were due proper respect and acknowledgement.

"That's funny," he said with a very thin laugh. "Very funny."

"Listen," they further advised him. "You just concentrate on building this school and doing a good job, and the sooner you complete it, the sooner you'll come home to your wife seven days a week. How's that?"

Rigo couldn't ask for anything more, and he knew it. "Do you think I can work in Havana then?" he asked. "Do you think some projects might open up in the capital?"

"Oh, yes," they replied. "Projects are always opening up in the capital, compañero, you know that. And with someone of your exceptional talents, well, you'll get top choice of any project you want."

It seemed a done deal. He either went to the town of Rio Piedras in Camagüey to build this school, or he could kiss his fledgling career good-bye. With Mihrta's unwavering insistence, Rigo chose Camagüey, ashamed to admit that he really didn't know much about this silent province to the east. Only that it relied on cattle production and agriculture for its existence and was known the world over for its *tinajones*—giant clay pots used for collecting rainwater. Maybe it wouldn't be so bad. All by himself and without Havana's big city distractions, Rigo could bury himself in his work. He could complete the project ahead of schedule and return home all the sooner. His housing would be provided at a large cattle co-op, but this did not mean extra meat in his diet; in fact, when it came to working and living at cattle co-ops, the state required workers be strictly vegetarian.

Rigo was promised a team of ranch hands from this co-op

to help with construction, and he planned on cracking the whip. He would not permit any delays or allow anything to derail a tight timeline. He wasn't just doing it for selfish reasons either. He thought of the time, money, and resources he'd be saving the Revolution. It was a laudable goal, especially for someone so young.

But commendable and ambitious as his objectives were, almost immediately upon stepping foot on Camagüey soil, Rigo knew he had problems, big problems. It happened the moment he submitted his schematics to the local leaders who'd been appointed to oversee the project and report back to the ministry.

"What's this?" they asked. "This doesn't look like a school. It looks like a hotel, a luxury hotel."

Rigo calmly explained the way officials had presented the project to him: that it was supposed to be a school of the future, a prototype for all subsequent schools on the island, and more than anything, the ministry wanted some groundbreaking, revolutionary design. Rigo whipped out his portfolio and all who had gathered around savored his visionary sketches and designs. Not surprisingly, by the end of the presentation, Rigo had won over every official with his intellect and charm. They had never met anyone like him. They were more than impressed and recognized that, in Rigo, they had secured a talented and driven individual who could make things happen. Unfortunately, they had some bad news. They were sorry to inform him that clearly, some grave miscommunication had occurred.

"Look," they said. "We don't know what you were told in Havana, but all we need is a simple primary school house on our rolling plains. That's all, with two, maybe three rooms at most."

"That's it?" Rigo asked.

"Yes. You see, there's a community of cattle ranchers here, meat eaters, who not only refuse to read and write, they refuse to let their children learn to read and write. This is a crime against the state, as you know, and we've been instructed by party leaders that these hooligans and their offspring must come into compliance within a year and become fully literate—without fail!"

"I see," said Rigo.

"Yes, and they have finally agreed, but only as long as the school is located at the cattle co-op where the children can tend to their duties and learn."

"Oh," said Rigo.

"That's all we need, compañero—a little schoolhouse. Besides, how could you possibly build a school of your proportions here? Where would all the workers come from?"

"Right here," he said. "I was told they'd come from right here in the cattle co-op."

"Impossible!" local leaders countered. "Again, I don't know what they told you in Havana, but everyone here is busy helping with the new project in the province, even us."

"New project?" Rigo asked. "What new project?"

Every pair of eyes lit up magically, electrically. "Why, a series of luxury hotels along the coast," they replied. "And they're going to be beautiful."

Rigo felt himself in the grip of some inner trembling but managed to quell it. "Not in Santa Lucía?" he asked.

"Why, yes!" they exclaimed. "How did you know?"

Rigo's heart pounded savagely. Had he been lied to after all? Had they tricked him? Was the project back in the works with Cuban firms and Cuban workers? It had to be. Local leaders had no reason to lie to him. Had he offended someone after all? Had he stepped on the wrong toes? Rigo immediately wanted to call his favorite professor, but the phone lines in Camagüey did not reach Havana. Unable to take any action, he was beside himself. Rigo had planned on laboring and toiling through his first weekend in Camagüey, but now he issued a statement canceling all scheduled work.

"Both days?" they asked.

"Both days," he replied. "You see, I've got a couple aunts who live right here in Camagüey, and they insist I come over for dinner my first weekend or they'll never forgive me."

Residents from the co-op understood. Those from the countryside knew better than anyone about the politics of extended family. But Rigo had no aunts in Camagüey. Not any aunts, direct or through marriage. Not any close family or distant. He didn't know a soul in the province. Rigo lied because he needed to settle something critical before lifting so much as a finger at their request.

That Saturday morning he paid a driver to take him from the remote pueblo of Rio Piedras toward the beaches of Santa Lucía, knowing exactly where to go. He had, after all, been privy to the coordinates in the blueprints and knew precisely where groundbreaking for the project was slated. Rigo wasn't sure what he might discover there, but suspected he had been lied to. Well, he was partially in the right. On the one hand, they had lied to him, but on the other hand they hadn't.

Outsourcing was definitely thriving along the pristine coastline of Santa Lucía, and in full force. This was evident as he looked around and noticed the corporate placards of numerous foreign companies staked in the ground there: Canadian companies. Spanish companies. Japanese firms, and even Chinese ones. Yes, Chinese! Those who were supposed to be stauncher communists than the Cubans.

But that did not come as the big shock. If Rigo remembered that all this outsourcing would create local jobs, that could hardly be the case at the moment. Not with every worker in sight running around with an efficiency and intensity he had never witnessed in his life. The everyday Cuban did not work like this; clearly these were all foreigners. There were definitely some locals there, but only a few. He could tell from their appearance, from their manner of dress and their diction especially. Camagüeyans actually pronounced their words rather than ate them. Rigo recognized a few cattle hands from the co-op, some of the vegetarians, and approached them on their break.

"What's going on here?" he asked. "What is all this?"

"The new Varadero," they proudly informed him. "Cuba's new international hotspot."

"Was it hard getting hired?" Rigo asked. "Are they paying you well?"

"Well, we're not exactly hired," the cattle hand explained. "And we're not actually getting paid."

"I don't understand," Rigo said.

"Well, technically we can't get hired because that would be accepting foreign currency, and the state won't allow it. But we can put in hours of unpaid volunteer labor."

"And you don't mind?" Rigo asked. "You wouldn't rather be earning something?"

"Well, of course! But as long as we have to put in volunteer hours anyway, it might as well be for something exciting. Besides, sometimes we get tips on the side—but you didn't hear that. Hey, aren't you that new architect in town? That visitor everybody's talking about?"

Rigo felt so disgusted by all he had heard, he couldn't think straight. These were the local jobs created by outsourcing? Measly menial labor with no monetary compensation? How would he ever get his school built? How, when all the able-bodied townspeople preferred building hotels for free just to be part of the experience? How, when all the locals preferred the paltry handouts of foreigners to the stoicism of self-dignity? Even here, all the way in Camagüey, the residents preferred to lend themselves to visitors of foreign lands than give of themselves to their own posterity. On the ride back from Santa Lucía to Rio Piedras, Rigo did some long, hard thinking and decided that the moment he arrived at the cattle co-op, he would resign immediately and head back to Havana. My husband had had it with all the deception and chicanery and no longer wanted any part of it. But when Rigo made his announcement to local leaders, they wouldn't hear of it.

After only one week with their new visitor, everybody

from Rio Piedras had grown quite fond of Rigo and did not want to see him go. People from the countryside understood disappointment better than anyone else in Cuba and told him to forget about the schoolhouse along the rolling plains. It turned out that, while he had been visiting his non-existent aunts over the weekend, a strange cable came in from Havana about a new project slated to take precedence over all else and for which ministry officials were seeking an appropriate candidate. Local leaders from Rio Piedras hoped Rigo might be suited for the position even though it didn't seem related to architecture in the least.

"Do you know what calculus is?" they asked him. "Have you ever heard of the word *calculus*?"

"Yes," he said. "Of course I have."

"What is it?" they asked.

"Well, it's higher math," he explained. "It's one of the branches of mathematics that focuses on limits, functions, derivatives, integrals, and infinite series; in short, it's the study of change. That's all calculus is—change."

They all looked at Rigo with vacant expressions on their faces, as if he had just uttered a foreign language to them.

"Never mind," he said. "Why do you ask?"

"Well, are you any good at it?" they persisted.

"I'm excellent at it," Rigo replied. "As architecture students we not only study theory and design, but engineering, physics, drafting, and we go all the way through calculus, both differential and integral."

Perfect, they thought—*absolutely perfect!* Local leaders had no clue as to what Rigo had just said, but it appeared they could keep utilizing his talents. They revealed the contents of the mysterious cable and this new project that had received the blessings of officials from key ministries in the capital: a grassroots calculus program for students all across the country, including those in the most remote regions of the island. They wanted no child left behind and meant it. Strangely, it was not calculus for accelerated high schoolers or university students who had already gone through geometry, advanced algebra, and trigonometry, but calculus for fifth graders who barely understood decimals and fractions.

"It's called Early Exposure," they told Rigo.

Cuban researchers had recently concluded there was only one way to produce a truly competent society: by ensuring that everyone thoroughly understood calculus. But the calculus had to be instilled before the other branches of math that preceded it. Years of data showed that those exposed to calculus before geometry, algebra, and trigonometry grasped and retained the calculus all the more when they were finally ready for it later on. Data also showed that subjects were less interested in change as a result, now that change had been dissected and demystified for them. The Revolution planned on leading the way with math, science, and technology into the twenty-first century, and this, they determined, was the optimal way to do it. Personally, Rigo thought the whole thing absurd and slightly insane, but he'd grown tired of battling all the elements conspiring against him.

"Fine," he said. "I'll do it. I'll go ahead and teach the calculus."

They were thrilled! Ecstatic! Normally, those who hailed from the outer provinces had to petition Havana vigorously for any request, no matter how minor. But local leaders from Rio Piedras decided to sidestep all that. They were taking no chances on losing the likes of Rigo. Everything in the capital always got mired in red tape and miscommunication, but Rio Piedras leaders took their own initiative, wiring a cable back to ministry officials and respectfully notifying them that they had located the perfect candidate for teaching all this calculus stuff. Best of all, he could start right away. Residents from the cattle co-op expected a long and protracted battle, but much to their surprise, the response came back quietly approved.

It was settled. Rigo would start teaching these math classes immediately. But his new adopted family from Rio Piedras hoped Rigo could help with one more pending matter. It had nothing to do with architecture and nothing to do with calculus, but they sensed that, with his talents, Rigo might be just the man for the job. They also hoped that being so devout a workaholic, Rigo wouldn't mind devoting his free time to this pet project.

The province of Camagüey certainly did not possess the glamour or glitter of Havana, but it remained a vital province of the republic regardless. It even had a more impressive history when it came to academics, and Camagüey was the first province in all of Cuba to erect a library. It housed more libraries per square inch than the rest of the country. Just one problem: Camagüeyans had not devised an indexing or cataloging system in keeping with the complexities of computerized collections or the databases of the twentieth century. They hadn't even devised a system in keeping with the indexing of the nineteenth century. But they longed desperately to be brought up to date. Camagüeyans wanted their libraries to be ranked among the best in the world, especially the central one in their provincial capital. One day a minor delegation from Ciudad Camagüey showed up at the cattle co-op in Rio Piedras to pay Rigo a visit. Officials could barely contain themselves from excitement over the new project.

"What is it?" Rigo asked, knowing he would regret asking.

"Do you know anything about library science?" they asked him.

"No," Rigo said. "I don't know the first thing about it."

Members of the delegation looked at one another and came to a tacit agreement, having heard of his distinguished accomplishments in teaching calculus and forming a gut feeling that Rigo would be perfect for the job. "Well, as long as you're so good at numbers and designing and drafting, do you think you can help us create a system that will index and catalog our books?"

In dazed resignation, Rigo looked back and forth and from side to side at the vacant faces of his Camagüeyan hosts. How could he refuse them? They were so nice to him. And so in need. He wanted to accommodate them, but how had he ended up in this predicament? How had he gone from wanting to fulfill a lifelong dream of designing luxury hotels to being stuck in a cattle co-op in the Camagüey countryside teaching calculus to fifth graders who barely knew basic arithmetic? From wanting to alter Havana's skyline, to library cataloging! This was what all his years of studying and passing rigorous exams had amounted to? It made absolutely no sense, but the answer he provided made even less.

"Sure," he replied. "Why not? I'll try it."

If his new friends were ecstatic before, they were overjoyed now, exuberant. Soon, local leaders from Rio Piedras held a banquet in Rigo's honor and even invited neighboring towns. The feast included generous servings of beef and goat and pork, and even the vegetarians from the co-op found themselves partaking in the meal. Amid all the hoopla, Rigo had not the slightest clue as to what he would be doing or how to accomplish it. But if the people of Camagüey had selected him for this task, he was all theirs. They could do whatever they wanted with him, whatever their hearts desired. He was at their disposal as long as he never had to build so much as a four-by-four mud hut anywhere on this earth; as long as he never had to gaze upon another hotel anywhere in Cuba built and owned by foreigners, while the everyday, ordinary Cuban could not so much as step foot on such a property. For what seemed an eternity now, a whole year, my husband and I saw each other only once a month. Naturally, when he came home to Havana for those very brief weekends, I was only too eager to hear about Rio Piedras and Camagüey and how the school was coming along.

"Is everything going as you planned?" I would ask. "Is the project ahead of schedule?"

"Ahead of schedule!" Rigo shrugged. "We haven't so much as dug one bucket of earth from the ground yet. That's how ahead of schedule we are."

By now Rigo had been working in Rio Piedras for months, which made no sense to me. "But why?" I insisted on knowing. "What in the world is the hold up?"

| 63 |

How could he explain? How could he accurately describe all his misadventures? I found out much later that for months he had hidden the truth from me. He'd been too embarrassed, too ashamed to reveal the unexpected turn of events with his career. For the longest time I believed the delay was all due to lack of materials and lack of workers, lack of planning and communication, revolutionary red tape and bloated socialist bureaucracy—the US embargo even! I pressed Rigo for answers and information, but each time he brushed me off. He didn't want to go into it. To explain was to relive, and he didn't feel like reliving all his frustrations. He'd say that he was in Havana for only two weekends a month, and preferred to spend his thoughts on anything else but his second life in Camagüey.

Or had it become his primary life? Rigo didn't know anymore. There were times he felt and acted like a visitor in his own home. Even here, a ten-hour train ride away, Camagüey was all he thought about. And there were times he felt and acted like a visitor in his own home. Especially with some grains of truth to the government's Early Exposure Theory after all, for officials were already reporting positive results. Only one year after the program's initiation, Rigo's fifth-grade students barely knew how to multiply and divide decimals or add and subtract fractions, but they were scoring in the top tier of national calculus exams. As for the libraries of Camagüey, they now employed an efficient and sophisticated cataloging system that rivaled that of the Biblioteca Nacional in Havana.

More than ever the people of Camagüey did not want to see Rigo go. But should he feel honored or trapped? Should he feel that this experience had opened up new opportunities and directions in his life or turned into one giant holdup? Maybe he should accept his fate; after all, these undertakings in Camagüey represented a form of architecture, and he was indeed functioning as an architect of sorts. But since he couldn't formulate an adequate conclusion, Rigo pondered his predicament and continued feeling torn between his two lives.

When turmoil struck him the hardest, and when a swirl of confusion left him hanging in the balance, only one act freed him from insufferable abeyance, only one act provided the clarity he desperately craved. It pained him to do it, especially since he'd sworn off the urge for months, but on those rare occasions when he had nothing to do in Rio Piedras, Rigo could not resist, could not keep away. He'd hire a car to drive him to the white sandy beaches of Santa Lucía to satisfy the itch of mordant curiosity.

Each time he did so, Rigo regretted it deeply. After one year of breaking ground along the northern coastline of Camagüey, those luxury hotels being outsourced to foreign companies were weeks away from a grand opening, and it plunged him into deep despair. His heart felt like imploding. Most depressing was the ordinariness and nondescript appearance of these luxury hotels, the rush job being employed. They looked little better than the sardine can, Soviet-style apartment buildings of the last thirty years in Cuba—row upon row of them.

It nearly slayed him, knowing he could have done a much better job, a much more innovate job of designing a new generation of edifice. But the hell with it. It wasn't his problem. Every once in a while I would ask Rigo about the initial project he had been promised upon graduating, and if there were any updates on it. But Rigo brushed off my inquiries without any detail or explanation.

"No," he'd reply. "Nothing new. Just chalk it up to life in Cuba, where you can never count on anything being different or calculate how things will turn out. It's no coincidence that nothing ever gets done around here, especially when nothing ever seems to change."

But Rigo wasn't the only one stymied by disillusion. Our system had frustrated my passions too. Even from a young age I had fancied myself a writer, always receiving excellent marks in literature and composition, but for good reason: I loved language. Words were my passion. Syntax my spirituality. As far back as I recalled, I had made it clear to professor and advisor alike that I wanted to pursue a career in writing. Not as a creative writer or a novelist—the thought of what novelists did and the process they went through terrified me—but as a critic. I loved critique and analysis and the dissection of art form.

"Don't worry, chica," they told me. "With your grades and determination, you'll have no trouble getting accepted. You're a shoo-in."

Sure enough, during my senior year in high school, I was first to be notified by the Ministry of Education of full acceptance into an elite program at the University of Havana: an honors literature curriculum with emphasis on literary criticism. I couldn't have been more thrilled. Among other things, the university boasted a great hall known as the *Aula Magna*, and I couldn't wait to bask in the greatness of that sacred hall and absorb all its history. That summer I read rapturously, dissecting and deconstructing everything I got my hands on, analyzing and breaking everything down in an effort to foster the critic in me. Then, in August of '93, one week before I was set to start classes at the university, I received another notice from the ministry—a less than thrilling one. They were sorry to inform me that, due to very low interest, the elite literature program had been eliminated and replaced by a course in advanced mathematics. Furthermore, this would render my university admission null and void.

"Null and void! But why?" I asked officials, calling immediately to demand an explanation. "I'll just study something else. I'll study journalism, creative writing even."

"Sorry, compañera. It doesn't work that way, and you know it. Those spots have been filled and allocated for the next five years."

"Five years! But under the circumstances that rule shouldn't apply to me. Shouldn't I be able to try for something in one year?"

"Five years, compañera. You know everything in Cuba is on a five-year plan. *That's* when you can try again. If you'll excuse us now, we've got planning to do!"

Five years! What was I supposed to do for the next five years if not study? How was I supposed to cultivate and sharpen my mind during all that time? How would I ever make up half a decade lost? The period following high school was ripe for the mind's development, crucial years for the brain to hone its ability in tackling complex thought patterns and mastering abstract concepts, for developing intricate skills that could be refined into a specialty. To start five years from now would mean starting too late and losing too much ground.

Besides, by then the ministry would most likely deny me all over again, especially since I knew what this was really all about—my parents. My acceptance had not been revoked due to cancellation of the program. My acceptance had been revoked due to my mother being openly religious and my father having been fired from his job.

That was the only thing happening here. Nothing else made any sense—the way it happened so quickly, so unexpectedly. You had to grow up in Cuba to understand how things worked: the Revolution and its repercussions. My father Alejo—this was really all about him! Let me just say I had always respected and admired him tremendously. I had always regarded my father as an intellectual, and only because of his towering intellect did I aspire toward greatness with my own writing.

My father loved language too, but in a different way. I had a love *of* language, he had a love *for* language. He was not a writer, but an interpreter—a translator and researcher, a professor too. He was fascinated by the way languages spoke to one another and interrelated. He was not an interpreter of Spanish or English or Russian. He was fluent in several Middle Eastern languages including Arabic, Farsi, Hebrew, and even Armenian. There was only one Middle East language he never truly mastered: Aramaic. It had always given him great trouble, and nothing put him in a worse mood than speaking and writing or trying to read in Aramaic. My father didn't understand his impediment with it, especially since Aramaic was merely a derivative of Arabic.

But he had one. To us it sounded fine and he seemed to speak it perfectly, but in private, my father ranted and raved that his Aramaic was slow and clumsy and his accent sloppy and awkward.

My father always seemed wrapped up in his work, and even when I was little, I viewed him as emotionally detached and distant. I was forever devising ways to lure him from his detachment. One day, when I was ten, I thought I found the way: by showing a genuine interest in that which captivated him so.

"What is it about that culture that fascinates you?" I asked.

"The marketplaces," he replied wistfully. "Whenever I see pictures of marketplaces in the Middle East, or of the surrounding architecture of the squares, or of the men sipping coffee and smoking cigarettes while discussing politics and history in that sea of sound and smell and color, I long to be there. I *ache* to be there."

I didn't get it. To me it seemed like an incongruous pairing: Cuban and Arabic, especially since, as far as anyone knew, nobody in the family carried a drop of Middle Eastern blood in their veins. Thank goodness too. Even from a young age I felt no affinity with that culture, especially their treatment of women and how the men from that region of the world required females to cover up from head to toe just to appease their primitive insecurities. My father's side of the family hailed from a long line of teachers, so it made perfect sense that he always stressed education and higher learning. He went on to earn a doctorate from the Institute of Advanced Linguistic Studies in Havana, and the state certified him with a rating of native speaker in Arabic, Hebrew, Farsi, and Armenian. Only in Aramaic had he received a rank of mediocre, and this forever proved a thorn in his side.

My father taught classes, not only at the language institute where he earned his doctorate, but all over Cuba. He was that renowned. One day officials from the Ministry of the Exterior approached him about a thrilling new project for which he had been recommended and personally selected. Representatives came to him with a proposal shortly after the start of the Gulf War in '91, and if he accepted, it meant my father would be traveling to the Middle East posthaste. It didn't take him long to make up his mind. Nor did it pain him any to arrive at the decision on his own.

"I'm going to Iraq," he announced matter-of-factly, only three days before he was scheduled to go. "I leave on Friday."

"*Iraq!*" my mother protested. "What are you talking about, Alejo? With this war that just started? With the Iraqis and Americans killing each other? I know you love all this Middle Eastern stuff, chico, but why would you want to go there now of all times? Are you crazy or something?"

"It's not that I *want* to go," my father explained. "I've been personally selected because of my language expertise. I'll be forming part of a diplomatic mission that includes engineers, medical personnel, agricultural experts, and of course, other linguists."

"Diplomatic mission for what?" my mother balked. "What in the world does Cuba need from Iraq and Iraq need from Cuba?"

My father swore Mamá to secrecy, explaining that he was about to share highly confidential information with her, and she could not mention it to neighbors or friends—not even family. No worries there. Mamá hardly had any friends. She was devoutly religious and cared only about lighting votives and expanding her collection of prayer cards and relics.

"It seems," he began, "that in recent years Iraqis have acquired a penchant for Cuban sugar. Well, the government of Iraq is interested in cultivating and harvesting its own strain of sugarcane to meet the country's increasing demand. For obvious reasons—since Cuba produces the best sugar in the world—the Iraqis have selected us as their consulting partner in this venture. In exchange, Cuba will be allowed to purchase Iraqi oil at a greatly subsidized cost."

The Revolution couldn't have asked for a better way to bring an end to our crippling Special Period, especially since it was the end of Soviet oil subsidies that had brought the Special Period into being.

"Of course!" my mother said scornfully. "Now it all makes sense. Oil! Sugar! These matters always include the vices of the world. I'm surprised there's no mention of tobacco."

"There is!" my father continued. "Believe me, there is! But that's five years away. For now, if we can get the Iraqi sugar fields to thrive in the desert regions of the country and become self-sufficient, they've agreed to build refineries right here on the island and teach us how to refine our own oil."

The Cuban government reacted with such joy and hopefulness at the prospect of refining its own oil on a large scale that they even sweetened the deal, offering Cuban health-care professionals to provide educational training for Iraqi medical students. The Iraqis were genuinely touched, overjoyed by this proposal, knowing that Cuba ran a world-renowned medical program. They immediately accepted the offer and wanted the Cubans to start coming right away.

There was just one problem. Most Iraqis did not know a word of Spanish; they mainly studied English for their foreign language requirement. Thus the reason for my father being selected for this Middle Eastern mission: to head the language team now responsible for teaching Spanish to this first generation of Iraqi medical students, who, one day would study medicine right here in Cuba for a premium price.

"Just wait," my father said. "In a few years, we're not only going to be refining our own oil, we're going to have a thriving community of Iraqis who'll demand their own marketplace, and officials will have to accommodate them. I can't wait!" he said. "We'll have a Little Baghdad right here in Havana."

But my mother wasn't buying any of it, and neither was I. How was all this going to happen with a war going on? A war that involved the Americans? They would never allow this type of venture between the Cubans and Iraqis. They would claim it violated international law and scorch the sugarcane fields first chance they got. Besides, how could you possibly cultivate sugarcane in the desert? *Impossible!* we both thought. Mamá lit candles and offered up prayers for something to impede his voyage, while I seethed in silence. I was fifteen when he blindsided us with this announcement, and I could think of only one thing: there went the Quinceñera I had expected later that year.

"How long is the mission?" Mamá asked him.

"Same as everything else," he said "Five years. But don't worry, Inez. They told me if the demands of the project permit, I can come home every six months for a week at a time."

"You might as well not come home at all," Mamá said. "Why even bother?"

My father had clearly made up his mind, especially since ministry officials had given in to a personal request of his: my father wanted a guarantee that he could devote 30 percent of his time to research. For years he'd wanted to write a dissertation on the history and evolution of Aramaic, and there could be no better place to do this than in Iraq.

"As long as it doesn't interfere with your teaching or interpreting duties, it's fine," they said.

For the next two days Papi barely uttered a word as he moved throughout the house, wrapping himself up, as he always did, in his latest undertaking; this time packing and making sure he set aside everything he needed, especially key textbooks and journals and teaching materials. On the day he shipped off for Iraq, Mamá and my two sisters cried inconsolably, but I didn't. My blood merely churned. My heart seethed. I was the second sister, the middle of us three, and I could think only of how much I hated him, especially as I felt the raw exhilaration coursing through his veins, the spirit of adventure brewing in jubilant impatience and frothing in its eagerness to be in those Middle Eastern marketplaces already.

I did not expect to hear from him for the first year, but much to my surprise, we received letters almost immediately.

Never did my father say a word, however, about missing us or missing Cuba or counting down the days until his first visit home. All he wrote about in great length—ad nauseam I might add—were the different marketplaces he had visited and how each one had its own feel and personality and how each managed to surpass the other in vitality and charm beyond his wildest expectations.

"And the coffee," he added. "I've never tasted anything like it. I don't know which I like better. Turkish coffee, Arabian coffee, Syrian coffee, or Greek. I can drink coffee from anywhere in the world here—anywhere!"

I hated him all the more after reading this. I despised my father with every word he wrote about his blessed marketplaces and Middle Eastern coffees. I loathed his letters that were nothing but history lessons on that part of the world. And since he had a fascination with coffee now, my sisters and I learned all about how the first instance of brewed coffee dated back to fifteenth-century Yemen and how the word coffee itself, in most languages, came directly or indirectly from the Arabic word *qahwah*. But it wasn't just hearing about exotic coffees that tantalized and teased us. It was learning about an endless array of cheeses and oils, of spices and even breads.

"The breads!" he would write. "Middle Eastern bread has got to be the most delicious in the world, especially the flat kind. You should taste it when it's soft and warm, when it's dipped in oil and slightly salted. There are times I look at it and swear I want to cry."

I wanted to cry too—from the way his description of all these foods left my mouth watering. How could he be so thoughtless? So shameless when we were all starving from the effects of this Special Period? It was clear that he loved his new life there. He'd taken to it as a fish to water. One day my father wrote us about a new friend he'd made in Iraq, a native of Baghdad named Ehn al-Salahm, head of security at the language school. We all thought it strange that a linguistics professor should associate so closely with what was essentially a security guard, but my father explained that Ehn al-Salahm longed to learn Spanish so he could impress one of the Cuban girls at the embassy. Aside from that, Papi explained that he and his new friend shared a lot in common.

Soon my father wrote us about Ehn al-Salahm every chance he got, explaining how this new friend had even invited him over for dinner to meet his wife and family. My father said that he received the shock of his life when the front door opened and he was greeted respectfully by Ehn al-Salahm's three beautiful daughters. *Three daughters. Just like us.* But they were younger, as my father was in his midforties at the time and Ehn al-Salam only in his early thirties.

"Wait a minute!" Mamá said. "This Ehn al-Salahm is married with three daughters, but he's trying to impress one of the Cuban girls with his Spanish? Wonderful friend your father is making!"

It certainly didn't affect Papi's opinion of Ehn al-Salahm. Not as letter after letter regaled us with tales of intoxicating evenings spent at the man's home, during which Papi described extravagant gatherings rich in food and wine, full of conversation and music and dancing, along with the endless assortment of Middle Eastern coffees.

"I hate him!" I confessed to Pilar any time I read one of the Ehn al-Salahm letters. "I despise Papi."

"Why?" she asked me. "You shouldn't begrudge him, hermana. Papi is an ambitious man, and that's how ambitious men are."

"Yes, they're so ambitious that they love their passions and careers more than their own families. I hate him, hermana! I hope he stays in Iraq with this Ehn al-Salahm guy for good, and I hope he never comes back!"

"Don't talk that way, hermana," she reproached me. "Really. Take that back or you'll regret it one day—you'll see."

But I wouldn't take it back. I wouldn't apologize for my feelings, and this outburst swelled into a shameful secret we both shared. Fortunately, Pilar did not resent me for any asperity in my words. It only brought out the mother in her all the more, and she lectured me about feeling happy for Papi and being proud of him.

"Don't you see that this opportunity is precisely why he's slaved away all his life, hermana? Why he's made so many sacrifices and concessions. Don't you see that Papi has reached a level of success in Cuba that less than one percent of the entire population ever achieve!"

I didn't care. It got to the point where I wouldn't read his letters anymore. Pilar possessed far more a forgiving nature than I ever did, and I truly admired her for it. She had always been athletic and physically gifted, but never ambitious or career oriented at all; yet it was she who understood our father's burning desire to excel and attain distinction. It was she who sympathized with him while I continued to hate him and wished I would never see him again, especially since a whole year had gone by and my father had apparently forfeited both opportunities to come home to visit.

But if there were ever times in a person's life when one had to be careful with what one wished for, this played out as such. Not only would I certainly see Papi again, but much sooner than expected. After a year and a half of his five-year assignment in Iraq, my father sent word he was coming home. Not for a brief visit, but for good. He didn't elaborate. Not in the cable received and forwarded to us by the ministry.

But if we would have to wait to hear all about this unexpected shift of events in person, I wanted only one explanation the day my father came home from Iraq for good: Why hadn't he brought us even one can of café? Just one! I understood no breads and cheeses; they would have spoiled on the long journey back. But how had he failed to bring home even one *jodida* can of coffee after writing all those letters about all those Middle Eastern coffees? Just like him!

"What happened?" Mamá asked, knowing from the look on his face and the disengaged expression in his eyes it could not be good.

"What do you think happened?" he said. "The usual thing that happens anywhere and everywhere: envious colleagues, jealous coworkers, backbiting and gossip, the usual knives in the back."

"Alejo, can you be a little bit more specific?" Mamá urged. "Can you tell me who did what to you?"

But Papi would not reveal more. He refused to talk about whatever had happened, while subjecting us to an atmosphere of dark brooding and sullenness for days and weeks on end. We left him alone and afforded him his space.

"When do you return to work?" Mamá asked one day. "When do you go back to the language institute?"

"I don't," he said.

"You don't? Well, how are we going to live?" she asked. "What are we going to do for money, Alejo?"

"Does it matter?" he replied. "Is the Cuban peso worth anything anyway?"

He had a point there, but we still needed *some* money. So while Papi languished in his state of abject misery and solitary dejection, Mamá mobilized quickly and managed to find a job right away. Of all things, too: patching up the horde of defective wheels and inner tubes to all those Chinese bicycles flooding the streets of Cuba during this Special Period. It turned out that Chinese rubber was highly corrosive and flimsy. It either melted quite easily in the Cuban sun or exploded without notice. Wheels were either eroding right on the asphalt or popping like crazy. Mamá hated the work. The first thing she did the moment she came home each day to was detoxify herself from the handling of all those dirty wheels and from inhaling the fumes of rubber cement. True, it wasn't a glamorous job: repairing rubber and inflating inner tubes, sometimes by mouth even. And it was rather embarrassing too, considering she was married to a renowned linguist. But this was no time for conceit or pride. It was no time for self-indulgence or moping either. Whatever had taken place in Iraq, Mamá insisted on knowing the full story, but Papi would only offer her the same diluted and watered-down version.

"I've told you, Inez: personality conflicts."

"But you were the supervisor, Alejo. You were running the show. Personality conflicts with whom?"

"The underlings, Inez. The underlings banded together and turned on me."

Mamá wasn't buying it. She knew there had to be more to it than what his monosyllabic replies suggested. She knew he was keeping her in the dark about something, and she was right. One day my father finally opened up to the one person he had always felt a kinship with in our household: Pilar. He at last divulged to her the details of his fate in Iraq, but she swore me to secrecy. I was not to tell Mamá any of this. While Pilar and my father had always been particularly close, Mamá and I shared the same closeness, and Pilar knew this. I was not to utter one word to our mother or how it all revolved around this new friend of his, Ehn al-Salahm.

"I knew it!" I said. "I knew that guy had something to do with this. I never liked that individual just from what I read about him. What happened, hermana? Tell me!"

"Well," Pilar began. "It seems that this fast and furious friendship not only caused envy and hostility among his coworkers at the language school, but speculation as well."

"Speculation? What type of speculation?" I asked.

"Well, I didn't know this, hermana, but apparently the men in the Middle East not only greet each other and say good-bye with a kiss, but when they're really good friends, they hold hands and drape their arms around each other's shoulders—whether or not they're in public."

"Really?" I said. "They hold hands in public? Grown men?"

"Yes, and it seems that on more than one occasion, Papi and Ehn al-Salahm were spotted holding hands walking through the various marketplaces and word got back to the embassy."

"What happened?" I asked.

"Well, Papi told me that when he showed up for work that Monday morning, two diplomats from the embassy were waiting for him at the language school. They marched him straight into conference and demanded an explanation as to all these alleged physical displays of affection—the hand holding, the shoulder draping."

"What about it do you want to know?" he asked.

"Is it true?" they said.

"Of course it's true," he replied. "It's the custom here. It's what they do."

"It's what the Iraqis do!" they replied. "It's the custom between Iraqi and Iraqi, not between Cuban and Iraqi. You're a visitor here, do you understand?"

But nobody was going to correct or instruct Papi about a culture he had read about and studied all his life. "It's the custom here between good friends *regardless* of where you come from. And if you don't partake of the custom, you offend them. Is that what you want me to do? Offend our Iraqi hosts?"

"Precisely!" they fired back. "They are the host, and you are the guest. You are not supposed to be befriending anyone anyway. You'll recall that, before coming here, everybody was expressly warned *not* to fraternize with the locals. You know that Middle Easterners snap and go crazy."

"I'm not fraternizing," Papi shot back. "Fraternization is nothing but a superficial act, civil artifice. Ehn al-Salahm and I are friends—actual friends. You understand?"

"Friends!" they said. "No wonder! Now it makes sense why your colleagues have been complaining. They see that you're friends with one of the locals and they're jealous."

"Well," Papi continued in self-defense. "If they're so jealous, why don't they make their own friends? That way they don't have to waste their time worrying about me."

"Because they're busy actually working!" the officials shot

back. "You see, Alejo, if it were just a matter of you and this guy being friends, there would be no problem. But your colleagues are vigorously complaining that you're never around, that all you do is delegate and take off, that you don't teach any of the classes or correct any of the papers. That you give yourself the best shifts—oftentimes when your friend is around. They claim that when you're not at the marketplaces with him, you disappear for the weekend, and there's even speculation that the two of you have been taking unauthorized weekend trips. Do you know how we learned of this, Alejo?"

"How?" Papi asked.

"Because his wife has called and shown up at the language school several times looking for him and asking if anyone knew where he was."

"So?" Papi said. "What about it? I'm not a marriage counselor. I'm a linguistics professor. What do I have to do with that?"

"What have you two been doing?" officials demanded to know. "Where have you two gone?"

"Mosul," Papi said matter-of-factly.

"*Mosul!*" they reiterated, a look of horror on their faces signaling they must have heard wrong. "Mosul as in…all the way up in the northern part of the country? Mosul as in…hours and hours away by car?"

"Precisely," my father replied. "You'll recall that, before I signed up for this mission, I did so on one condition: thirty percent of my time could be devoted to research. Well, my research thesis happens to be on *Aramaic and its Dissolution in the Modern World—Causes and Effects*. The reason I've been taking these weekend trips to the north is because the University of Mosul happens to be one of the largest educational and research centers, not only in Iraq, but in the entire Middle East. And it just so happens that Mosul is where the Assyrians of Iraq still reside: ancient descendants of Mesopotamia and the last remaining group of the modern world to speak Aramaic still. That, compañeros, is why I've been taking these unauthorized trips as you call them. Because the northwestern part of Iraq is the only place on the entire planet where Aramaic is still spoken and heard."

Both diplomats felt their heads spin from so much download all at once. *Damned intellectuals! They thought they were so much better than everyone else.* "We understand," they began smugly. "We get it. Your friend goes to keep you company, and to help you if any problems arise."

"Precisely," Papi replied. "Plus, I'm teaching him Spanish, so he uses the travel time to practice his conversational speech."

"We absolutely understand," they reiterated. "And do you two hold hands all the way there? And hold hands all the way back?"

My father wasted no time in joining the steps to this trite tap dance or choreographing it himself with obscenity. Neither of my parents were ones to swear, but one must remember that being coarse and vulgar was an inalienable Cuban trait, and Papi, despite his professional standing, could be extremely vulgar.

"¡Oye, chico! If what you're doing is trying to accuse me of being a fucking queer, why don't you just come out and say it! That's what's going on here, isn't it? You think I must be a fucking queer and that Ehn al-Salahm and I suck each other off every chance we get."

Both officials regarded each other with a stunned artifice, their eyes opening wide before proceeding with their mockery. "We're not saying that, Alejo, of course not. We're just telling you how it looks to us *and* your compatriots. This isn't ancient Mesopotamia, Alejo. You know what our culture is like. It's not just mega-machista, but uber machista. Nobody else from this mission has made the type of friendship you have, and that's why they talk about it nonstop. Some of your colleagues even suggest you might be doing drugs, Alejo, indicating that you're constantly wired and pumped up, *alborotado* all the time."

"Drugs!" my father scoffed. *"Drugs!* Are you joking? If I

seem wired, it's only from the coffee. It's only because for the first time in my fucking life my body is drinking real coffee and it's not used to it. It's strong and makes me alert and enables me to put more hours into my research. I've noticed that after several cups of Moroccan coffee, my Aramaic is even better than ever."

"How insulting!" they shot back, appalled by such hubris; all long-time residents of Havana were endowed with hubris it seemed. "Are you telling us we don't have real coffee in Cuba? Are you? We're famous for our coffee, chico. Just like we're famous for our sugar and tobacco. Why else do you think we're here?"

"Not like this coffee," Papi said. "Not at all."

"Well, you listen up, chico. We're here to tell you something you need to know. Word of your antics has reached the wrong ears in Havana, and there are new stipulations for your continued involvement with this mission. This is a very sensitive project, Alejo, and we can't afford any scandals. According to this cable from the Ministry of Economic Development, which came in overnight, this research of yours in Aramaic or Mesopotamia or whatever it is, comes to an end right now! Understand, Alejo? As of this moment, you are here to teach and teach only. You are not to fraternize or make any more friends. You are not to take any weekend trips anywhere with anyone. And you are authorized to visit the local marketplace only once a week! Is that clear, Alejo? Don't forget this country is at war with the Americans right now, and by befriending the locals you not only endanger your life, but ours as well."

"Are you telling me I'm not allowed to make friends while I'm here? Is that what you're saying?"

"That's exactly what we're saying, Alejo! No more holding hands, no more putting your arms around another man's shoulder, and especially, no more kissing."

They both laughed uproariously at this.

"To hell with you!" my father burst out, rising up and stepping away from the table before storming off. "To hell with all this! Effective immediately, I quit! I didn't come halfway around the world to be treated like a prisoner! That's not why I came all the way to Iraq! I could have stayed in Cuba for that!"

That was it, the reason his assignment came to a premature end. I remained transfixed by the end of this account, eerily entranced. I shook my head slightly in disbelief and fought back tears I felt forming. Not just from learning the truth, but because this depiction of my father seemed so uncharacteristic of the man I knew. I had always regarded Papi as a quiet and bookish intellectual. But the man Pilar just finished divulging revealed a passionate adventurer and courageous individual, one who would not be defined or hampered by social conventions.

No wonder he returned to Cuba without even one can of coffee. Customs officials had either confiscated it, or he wanted no reminders of his year and a half in Iraq. No wonder my father refused to talk about this even with Mamá. What a fall from grace. How demoralizing and ignominious an ending. I felt horrible now. I hated myself for all the times I had said I despised him and really meant it. Pilar was right. My words came back to haunt me and filled me with sharp pangs of regret. Never haunting me more than now, forced to observe him around the house with nothing to do, for now he had no job either. Little did my father suspect that when he resigned from his mission in Iraq, he'd be resigning from his entire career.

"What are you doing here?" the chief administrator of the language institute asked him when Papi showed up for work his first Monday back. "You resigned, remember? And when you resigned from your post, you resigned from everything."

"Really?" he said. "And who will you find with my knowledge and skills? Nobody, that's who! Nobody!"

"You're quite mistaken, Alejo. Not only have we found your replacement, he starts tomorrow. Good thing too. We really needed a change around here. Fresh talent—an emerging intellect, if you will."

There it was. The final nail in my father's heart. By taking his teaching job away they might as well have deprived him of the air he breathed. From then on he languished and lacked all motivation. He wouldn't talk either, answering yes or no to the simple things, providing only the most minimal response whenever necessary. He would sit alone and stare pensively at the floor, his expression inscrutable but melancholy. All we could do was watch him withdraw into himself. What could anyone say? What could anyone do but let him swirl within a torment intent on smothering him? Nobody could reach him, not even Pilar. Needless to say, never again would we hear him speak a word of Arabic or Hebrew or Aramaic especially. Never again would he look at or touch his beloved texts in the towering bookcases inside his room. The books sat silent and ignored, gathering but a thick sediment of neglect.

Only once more would I witness my father come to life, coinciding with the unexpected arrival of a letter. Not just any ordinary letter, but one from overseas. The return address coded in that indecipherable Arabic script, the stamp containing the image of some elaborate mosque awash in tones of blue. It was a letter from Iraq, from his friend Ehn al-Salahm.

At the sight of the envelope, my father alternated between excitement and agitation, retreating to his room and hurriedly closing the door. He longed to read the contents, but in shielded privacy.

I had to know what was going on—*I just had to!* I crept toward his room and put my ear to the door, but would soon regret it. After a few minutes I heard him sobbing. He tried crying inaudibly, but no mistaking the muffled sobs. What the letter said, we had no clue; it was, after all, written in Arabic. And whether he had any intention of writing Ehn al-Salahm back or not, we couldn't surmise. He certainly didn't sit down to pen an immediate response. I don't think he ever revealed the contents of the letter even to Pilar. But I did note a marked change in his demeanor the day after its arrival.

From that moment on, my father couldn't seem to sit still.

He seemed constantly in motion. The only thing he now took interest in were neglected houseplants tucked away in our side patio: a sad and meager collection of greenery that he tended to religiously until they flourished anew and our side patio resembled an oasis in a Roman atrium. And he focused most lovingly on the leaves until they glistened in their verdancy. Plants, coffee, and smoking—that was all he cared about. He drank coffee morning, noon, and night. He smoked more than ever too. And when we ran out of coffee he had to have more, right away. He and Mamá fought constantly since he insisted that she locate additional sources for him. But when she couldn't or refused, Papi turned into a crazed fiend, going from house to house and neighbor to neighbor asking for what little of it they might be willing to spare and even bartering against our future rations. Some were willing to trade their precious café for a choice selection of his fine creations, famous throughout the neighborhood now, but my father's plants were strictly off limits, non-negotiable.

I must admit I found this hopeful. At least he'd regained a sense of living. It was better than sitting around and staring into inner space and collapsing within himself. One day I even caught a glimmer of the old light in his eyes. He'd gotten out paper and pencil and I thought this was it. He was getting back to his work and research.

"I'm writing my friend," he announced. "I'm replying to Ehn al-Salahm."

I felt a throbbing of old resentments as his pencil formed the incomprehensible Arabic script. He managed to jot down the date and a greeting, but before eking out even one word, my father stopped. He doubled over in excruciating pain and collapsed at the table, complaining about a pain in his stomach so sharp we had to rush him to the nearest clinic. On the way there little could we imagine he would be leaving us again, but this time for good, that our beloved but troubled father would actually die that same night.

Of all the vices to do him in, never did we suspect coffee to be the ultimate culprit. Doctors at the clinic said they had never seen anything like it: a caffeine-induced ulcer that had gnawed away at his intestines and bored a hole through his stomach the size of a baseball. Whether it was from the Middle Eastern coffees he had consumed in Iraq or the Cuban coffee he had consumed all his life, or a combination of both, nobody could say for sure. But coffee had taken its toll and they pronounced my father dead on November 11 of 1992.

"But what did the letter say, hermana? The letter from his Iraqi friend? I know that you've got to know something about it." The thought of using the term "friend" in conjunction with my father and this individual made my stomach churn and turn as if I had developed an ulcer of my own.

"I don't know Clara. Really, I don't."

But I found this hard to swallow, especially now that Pilar had divulged all that she had. Papi must have said something to her—*something!* My older sister was the only one he had ever confided in and, whatever that letter contained, it must have been too great for him to keep to himself. I knew my father. I knew he must have been bursting at the seams to share some part of its contents, however minimal, and so I pressed.

"But you must!" I insisted. "He must have said even the slightest of things to you. Just think, Pilar! Think back to anything he might have uttered."

Sure enough, my insistence was about to pay off.

"Well," Pilar finally acquiesced, not having to take me into the strictest of confidence because she had honestly not given it any importance. "He did say something, but I really didn't pay any mind to it. He was not acting himself. He was almost irrational, hermana. His thoughts were jumping from one thing to the next and he was almost incoherent. I mean, Papi of all people! *Papi, incoherent!*"

"About what?" I urged. "Incoherent about what?"

"Something that made no sense, chica. Something about the sugar and the Iraqis and even maloja."

"Maloja?" I asked confusedly.

"Yes, maloja," she repeated. "*Maloja* of all things! Don't

you remember how, ever since he started tending to all those plants in the patio, all he did was carry that big book of his around and refer to it constantly?"

I didn't respond. I was too spellbound. I could think only of how we all knew about our father's furtive fascination with leaves, his passion for them even, as if he had secretly wanted to be a botanist all his life. Why, one of his most guarded possessions was this big reference book called *Hojas*. It was a thick book with beautiful illustrations, all hand-made, of all the different leaves of the world. All three of us sisters knew that we had to treat that book with the utmost of care and respect or we could never touch it again. Many a time he had warned us so.

"Now do you see why I didn't pay any mind to it?" Pilar continued. "I thought he was just going on and on about leaves again. I'm telling you Clara, he was delirious at the time. I think he knew the end was near."

Her words haunted me. And if this was truly the case, his was not the only state of delirium. I too felt delirious, under siege after his death, under constant attack by my conscience. Guilt for having been so selfish in my thoughts and words overwhelmed me at times. How greatly it pained me that I had never told him how much he meant to me or how much I admired him. True, it was he who had always inspired my love of expression and an ardor for language, but it was he who now inspired me to proceed with life.

It was only upon his death that I came to understand this, that I came to recognize the rushing force behind all my aspirations. No doubt his fall from grace had sealed my fate with the university. No doubt at all. That was what happened in Cuba: the sins of the father always visited the son, or the daughter. But I would not blame my father entirely for the rescission of my acceptance. There was someone else who I held equally responsible and whom I despised for his part in my father's demise. His name was Ehn al-Salahm. He lived somewhere in Iraq. One day I would take his letter and have it translated. One day I would learn the truth of all that had transpired between my father and him in the marketplaces of

Iraq. And one day I would also learn what in the world maloja had to do with any of this.

Forget it then! I wouldn't apply to the university in five years or ten years or even fifteen. I'd never step foot inside the Aula Magna. I wouldn't study anything in Cuba. Not under this miserable system that slanted everything in a way officials saw fit. I would get married instead. Rigo wanted me to wed straight out of high school anyway, so now I had the perfect excuse. We would become man and wife. We would start a family. Damn all the ministries and the university and everything else! I never wanted to read or write another critique as long as I lived. I believed this at least. I made up my mind and refused to deviate from the decision until, one day, unexpectedly, a fellow student and good friend of mine named Nelson heard about my predicament with the university and approached me with a strange proposition.

Nelson was also a writer. He too was an intellectual and reminded me of my father somewhat. He was funny and had a mordant sense of humor, an acerbic wit. But Nelson was funnier for something else: his eyeglasses. While nobody in Cuba under the age of forty ever wore eyeglasses—they were considered unsightly and unfashionable—Nelson refused to dispense with his dark-rimmed pair. He considered eyeglasses an essential component to a writer's appearance.

"How would you like to be part of a group?" he asked. "A writer's group."

"A writer's group? Maybe," I said. "I guess so."

"Great!" he replied. "There's just one catch."

"What?" I asked.

"It isn't exactly a typical writer's group. We're not going to sit around in a circle and read each others stories or chapters or verses from poems and suggest ways to make them better."

"What are we going to do?" I asked.

"We're going to sit around in a circle all right, but we're going to be discussing all the things wrong in Cuba and how to make them better. We're going to shine a light on all the defects here in the hopes of exposing every single one of them. We're going to document and distribute, we're going to quietly inform the world about what's really happening in our homeland, highlighting the injustices and figuring out how to set them right, like the injustice done to you with the university. You do know that the elite literature program was not canceled, mija. You do realize, I hope, that it was just a lie they fed you. So are you in, Clara? Are you in?"

It didn't take long for me to formulate a response. Even before Nelson finished explaining the nature of the group, I felt the fire of his words fanning the air. I felt the sting of his ideas sizzling through my blood. How quickly things changed at times, how unexpectedly. Here I'd been denied the opportunity to study that which I loved most, literary criticism; here I was never going to write a critique again as long as I lived; but here I was being given the chance to become a critic anyway. Who would have thought?

"I'm in!" I said. "Count me in!"

Nelson leaned forward. He gave me a heartfelt hug and I hugged him back. We smiled at each other with brewing enthusiasm. I liked the look of his eyeglasses. Everybody gave him a hard time and urged Nelson to switch to contacts or get surgery, but I liked how intellectual they made him look. I hoped he never got rid of them.

"Just one thing," I said. "What's the name of the group?"

He wasted no time in responding. "Insurrection!" he replied. "Insurrection is the name of our group. How do you like it?"

Insurrection, I mused, instantly connecting with the word. I loved it too. I loved the meaning. I loved the connotation. I even loved the sound of the word, so raw and rumbling. Insurrection seemed the perfect name for an underground group, for rebels dedicated to exposing all the savagery and disillusion, all the unfairness woven into the fabric of daily life here.

"Does this mean we're dissidents?" I asked.

"No, mija. We don't waste our time with the word dissident. We're insurrectionists; that's what we call ourselves: *insureccionistas*."

Again the perfect word, the ideal concept and I loved it. Nelson was right. "Dissident" was too nice a word, too pacifist and pathetic. The title insurrectionist highlighted our plight with a focused ruthlessness, and now I had a new anchor in life.

But I also got married since my university career ended before it ever started. And now that Rigo was in Camagüey for long stretches of time, I occupied myself with writing and editing and confirming facts for our publication *¡Insurrección!* I had never felt more motivated or determined; the very danger excited me. I was getting a real education now, reading the works of José Martí from start to finish and coming to learn that no greater model for criticism, no better source of inspiration existed than the poetry and essays of our liberating father. To hell with the university! To hell with it! The only words and ideas I needed to thrive on and sharpen my mind with were those of our national apostle.

My involvement with the group eased some of my suffering then, but did not entirely erase the injustice I felt, especially after learning the elite literature program remained very much intact. It only reinforced what I knew deep down: I needed formal training. If ever I were to be taken seriously as a writer, I needed the proper scholarly credentials. Nelson did what he could to help. He brought over his study materials and urged me to follow the syllabi of his classes as if enrolled right alongside him. What a colleague. What a friend. I embraced his magnanimity, and for the first time since Papi's death, life coasted smoothly, a faint but hopeful light stirring within. If not for Nelson's efforts, my spirit would have broken. But thanks to this serendipitous union I enjoyed a respite from the turmoil.

Naturally, I mentioned nothing of the group to Rigo, especially the fact that, before long, I became Nelson's right-hand man. My husband would have adamantly disapproved. Rigo liked Nelson and respected him, but why create strife with unnecessary revelations? Hadn't I experienced enough setbacks and untimely tragedies? Enough of these crippling curses then: Rigo and I married, only to be forced apart. My admission to the university accepted, only to be denied. My father's life dedicated to his work, only for his reputation to be trashed. And worst of all: now he lay dead.

All of these misfortunes were more than what the everyday Cuban should have to endure. Rigo, me, everyone we knew—we were all the product of taunting disillusion, bitter disappointment. My family in particular had suffered its share of setbacks. But a new plague would strike to eclipse them all, even my father's death. This time it afflicted the one person who least deserved it: my older sister Pilar, whom I cherished and loved dearly. It happened on March 30 of '93, the culmination of a week I would never forget.

An everyday, ordinary headache—that was how it started. We were assured that nothing could have prevented the outcome. Pilar had just come home from afternoon training that day. A third-year college student, she was a long-distance runner at the university and one of their best. She would tell the doctors that it all began with a pain that had burrowed itself deep in her forehead. But even during two days of intense aching, she knew it was no ordinary headache. The pain had embedded itself deep in her eye, and any eye movement, no matter how minimal, only worsened it. This persistent pain lasted several days before it finally dissipated, but only to be replaced by a flashing and flickering of lights even when she closed her eyes.

"That's it, hermana! You're going to the doctor!" I insisted. "This isn't normal, and you need to be seen right away."

"I'll be fine," Pilar insisted. "I've been working really hard lately, that's all. I bet it's my blood sugar that's really low."

The next couple of days she undertook much lighter training and it helped. The splitting pain vanished. The flashing and flickering of lights all but dispersed. But little could anyone imagine that, right around the corner, the next phase of this ailment sat poised to strike.

"It's so strange," she announced one afternoon that week. "I don't know what's happening, but the color in everything seems all drained and washed out."

"Are you sure?" I asked.

"Yes," she replied. "Everything seems less vibrant, especially anything with red in it."

"How long has this been happening?" I asked.

"A couple of days," she replied.

I didn't know why, but I felt a sense of urgency upon hearing this, and no longer would I postpone the necessary.

"That's it," I said. "I'm taking you to the doctor's right now, whether you want to go or not."

We were standing in the kitchen when I demanded this. I was prepared to drag her from the house, by force if necessary, but within seconds, such efforts were rendered pointless. I knew circumstances had taken a dire turn when Pilar couldn't move, or lift either foot off the ground, and had to remain stationary as if to maintain balance. She jutted her arms and hands about too. She shifted her head slowly as if some wave of dizziness were about to topple her.

"What's happening, Pilar? What's the matter, hermana?"

"I can't see!" she cried. "I don't know what's happening, but I can't see!"

I would never forget the fear and panic in my sister's voice, nor the taxi ride to the hospital and how she clung to me as we both cried. In between sobs Pilar explained how, right there in our kitchen, a black vapor enshrouded her eyes and she nearly fell to the ground. Worse, this black fog did not retreat. The entire way to the hospital it only thickened, entrenching itself firmly in the mirror of her eyes. By the time we saw a physician, it was too late. Not only could she no longer see, the doctor informed us the vision loss was permanent. I couldn't stop shaking. I couldn't stop sobbing hysterically.

"It's my fault!" I wept. "It's all my fault!"

The doctors insisted that I stop with the hysterics. Pilar needed us more than ever now, but she needed clear and calm heads to prevail. They assured me there was nothing that anyone could have done to prevent this. Surely we'd been following the events of the last year and a half. Surely we knew Pilar wasn't the first person in Cuba to succumb to this affliction during this Special Period. We certainly knew what the doctors were talking about. Who hadn't followed the events of our recent health crisis? Still, I couldn't keep from crying or blaming myself or believing that, if only I had dragged her to the hospital on the first day of her headache, she wouldn't have lost her sight.

But I was wrong. As much a natural critic as I was, I couldn't argue with science: an epidemic was an epidemic. It's just that, deep down, even if the doctors were right, I needed something to blame myself over, a way to punish myself for all my self-centeredness and self-absorption, a symptom of being a middle sister. Pilar was not the only everyday Cuban who had mysteriously lost her sight in the last year and a half. The first cases surfaced in early '92, in Pinar del Río, our westernmost province. But those initial cases involved middle-aged men who smoked heavily and drank alcohol, those with hardened vices. Pilar hardly seemed a candidate for the ruthlessness of this epidemic and it made no sense.

When it first struck the island, nobody understood what was happening, where this plague had come from or how it was proliferating so swiftly. There were those who called it a curse, a just punishment for a government alienated from God. Why else had thousands of our brothers and sisters developed physical ailments that ranged from loss of vision and loss of use of both legs and arms to total paralysis and complete blindness? Why else? If many believed this, I never bought such explanations. If anyone deserved punishment around here, it should have been them: all the ministers and secretaries, all the diplomats and officials, our bearded uncle in his olive-green fatigues. But they weren't affected. Just the ordinary, everyday Cuban.

It didn't take long for a major visitation, for doctors and scientists from all over the world to descend on the island and figure it all out, the odd etiology of this epidemic. They soon had a name and face for it: *neuritis*, an inflammation of the central nervous system. The effects were sometimes temporary, sometimes permanent. But if neuritis turned into an international riddle, I found it all rather comical, ironic that it took the greatest minds of the global medical community to arrive at such an obvious conclusion: neuritis was the result of near starvation. Over the last two years the Cuban diet had deteriorated miserably. Our bodies were starved for vitamins and minerals, especially vitamin B. No wonder those from the government emerged unscathed, their eyes and limbs fully intact. They weren't starving in the least and everyone knew it.

The Ministry of Health responded swiftly, handing out vitamin supplements so that, in some cases, the ailments stopped or even reversed themselves. But a year and a half after the outbreak, thousands remained afflicted with one form of the disease or another. There were two versions of the ailment: those left paralyzed and those left blind. The two sides of neuritis were like the faces of two fraternal twins: somewhat the same, but very much different. By the time neuritis hit Pilar, over thirty thousand had succumbed.

This plague did not strike without notice, as some believed. It spread swiftly, as all plagues do, but its nucleus had been a long time forming, a long time nurturing, its incubation silent but steadfast, and all a result of this Special Period, this dreadful era of scarcity and self-denial. Even the term *Periodo Especial* mocked us: a term usually reserved for nations at war. We were in a war all right: at war with our own bodies. Three years into this Special Period and its hallmark was a diet intent on destroying us. Not to mention the blackouts we had to stomach. *Apagones* we called them, the twelve-hour blocks of time when officials cut power to the city and left us drowning in darkness. How I hated our nightly blackouts, those long and terrifying hours when we lit candles, a few lit kerosene lamps, just to assure ourselves someone was out there.

How unjust. How unfair that the tentacles of this affliction had tightened themselves around Pilar. My older sister, the kindest, most loving person in the world. Pilar, who hardly fit the profile of those at risk. She was twenty-two and an athlete, in great physical shape, without an ounce of fat on her bones. Little did anyone suspect during the early days of the epidemic that fitness only fed the vengefulness of the disease. A lack of body fat left muscle and nerve vulnerable to attack, while heat and exercise intensified its effects.

According to all the specialists then, an unfortunate pairing of events conspired against Pilar to minister her condition permanent. But no matter *what* anyone told me, I blamed myself, believing that if only I had taken her to a doctor on that first day, she would never have lost her sight. I needed to punish myself. I needed to pay the price for my neglect. And so, one day, not long after Pilar lost her sight, I was only too happy when I came down with horrible cramps that raged somewhere within my abdomen. I knew I should go to the hospital, but I refused. I suffered the pain as long as I could.

For three days I was on the brink of delirium, bedridden with chills and high fevers, convulsions pulsating deep within. How I reveled in the aching. How my body soaked up all the pain as it marinated itself with infection. I wished I would burn up and die, but the thought of Pilar blind and helpless pulled me back. And it was only from Mamá pulling me out of bed and dragging me to the hospital that I received antibiotics and the infection subsided. But the doctors had additional news for me. A week after being hospitalized, I received a call to return. My lab work had come in. Physicians wanted to meet with me personally and discuss the results. They advised I bring my husband along with me.

"Compañera, have you heard of calculus?" they sat me down and asked.

"Calculus," I said. "As in math? You mean *that* calculus?"

"No, not that calculus. Calculus as in plaque, as in buildup."

"Well, I certainly know the term," I replied. "What about it?"

"Well, it seems you're the victim of the Cuban diet too."

Doctors proceeded to inform me that, somehow, I had managed to contract an even rarer form of neurological apathy: an intrauterine calcification affecting the peripheral parts of my reproductive system.

"But how?" I asked. "How is that possible? It doesn't make any sense."

But the voices of the doctors droned on as they explained it all with statistical exactitude. "Well, compañera, it makes perfect sense. You see, in the prolonged absence of essential vitamins and minerals, especially among young women of child-bearing age, the right set of circumstances can combine, wherein, the pituitary gland produces an elevated concretion of mineral salts. Sometimes these salts turn toxic and concentrate around organic material in the hollow organs or ducts of the body. Well, it appears that a thick layer of calculus has formed inside your fallopian tubes and left them permanently scarred."

"What does that mean exactly?"

"What it means is that you're never going to bear children, compañera. Whenever there's this much calculus, the condition is irreversible. We're very sorry, really."

Rigo took the news stoically, telling me not to worry, insisting the doctors were either wrong or didn't know what they were talking about, or that we could simply wait until some treatment cleared this all up, even if it meant surgery.

"Don't worry, amor. We're going to be parents one day. You're going to be a mother, and I'm going to be a father. I'll mention this to Mamá. She'll know what to do."

Mihrta! Why did he have to bring her into it? What would she possibly suggest, electroshock therapy? I felt sorry for Rigo. What was it about men and their limited insight? Why did they think that the only thing that made a woman happy was having children and being a mother? Even Rigo was a typical male when it came to this. Would he now chalk up any anxiety or frustration, any pent-up energy or restlessness I had as the result of only one thing: that I couldn't have children? How to tell him I no longer wanted any children. I no longer wanted to be a mother. I had come to accept that I was too ambitious, and ambitious people did not make good parents.

Once the shock wore off and I digested the consequences of my plight, I wasn't sorry. Not one bit. Most young women would have found the news devastating, but I derived a sense of comfort, a sense of justice. At last I was being punished. At last I was being rebuked for my role in Pilar's misfortune. She would never see again, I would never have children. But I had other reasons to rejoice. I no longer wanted to bear children. I no longer wanted to bring life into this world, especially into Cuba. I couldn't be happier in knowing that my womb lay dead inside and harbored no chance of ever rising to life. I wouldn't be a mother—big deal! I'd be a writer, an underground rebel, an insurrectionist. That was the only parenting I wanted to do: the parenting of publishing; the parenting of politicking, the parenting of raising awareness for our true and dire plight in Cuba.

I'd had enough of this Periodo Especial and I wanted it to end, this *Periodo Trágico* more fittingly. The last several years had been insufferable for everyone. We all lived in a state of terror. Not knowing what would hit next or from where it would strike. We not only lived in a state of war, but a tug of war, a struggle between the physical and emotional. But nobody knew which side would prevail or if both would collapse. Would we further be crippled by additional epidemics or whither away from all the deprivation? Would we drown in the barrage of propaganda or suffocate from a dearth of intellectual stimulation? Would we perish from a lack of spiritual purpose or expire in this wasteland of want?

What a way to live. Functioning in a state of oppression *and* suppression. Where you longed to scream, but asked yourself why? What was the point? Nobody heard you and nobody cared. Yet we screamed anyway, futile as it proved, screamed and yelled and argued even as Rigo and I had been doing for the last three days. But no more. The rage had run its course and I wouldn't give Rigo one more thing to worry about—that is, my involvement in Nelson's group. Why say anything? Why complicate an already messy situation? How skilled I had become at compartmentalizing all the rooms in my life. How adept at keeping all content neat and orderly, but separate and hidden. Personally, I hated deception. I hated lying or hiding or any form of omission. But this manner of operation was necessary in Cuba, an element of survival in this Periodo Especial.

But not for long. After tonight, after this momentous and miraculous night of August 14, all the deceit would finally come to an end. Only after tonight would all the doors to my life finally swing wide open and could the contents of its rooms be free to mix and intermingle. Much of it thanks to my bespectacled friend, I might add, for a mere three days ago, on August 11, Nelson called together a special meeting of the Group Insurrection. We all discussed the situation at length and came to a unanimous decision: moving forward I would serve the cause better *outside* of Cuba than in it, this new technology of the Internet proving to be a great tool in the sprouting and scattering of news and information.

Then would I lay it all out for Rigo. Once we were gone, I would tell him about Insurrection and the group's goal of setting Cuba free. Once we were safely inside America nothing would stop me from spreading a message of truth and liberation. It was already happening. The message was gaining strength with this frenzied flight across the water, this forced and feverish escape. As thousands upon thousands of restless Cubans spilled forth and cast off, scrambling out to sea with its crisscross of currents and its seductive but treacherous straits, finally could the world bear witness to the unmistakable mess we were in. But it was time that someone took a genuine interest in it all and tried a hand in sorting the mess out. It was time that someone got the message and finally did something about it.

4

messes

august 14
late night

"Everything all right, compañera? *¿Todo bien?*"

I found myself face-to-face with one of the mongrels in blue, one of the Revolution's stern-faced guards in his black boots and belt.

"Yes," I replied calmly. *"Todo bien, compañero.* Why do you ask?"

The air felt cool coming in off the sea. Breezes along the Malecón were usually soothing and refreshing, but the one tonight had a mordant sting. And the sky had turned particularly black, without the moon or a single star anywhere in sight. Yet even in this disarming darkness, I could make out the mongrel's features quite distinctly, as if I were holding a candle right up to his face.

He was tall with short black hair. And despite the lack of

light, I felt his shadow fall upon me, his small gray eyes surging to hold my gaze. His lips were thin and pale. His face, in glistening bronze, bore a faint scarring of acne. The mongrel was strapped in his uniform and cap, and as he leaned against one of the miniature towers punctuating the seawall, I figured him to be in his midtwenties, Rigo's age.

"Out of concern, compañera, that's why I ask. You've been standing here for over two hours now, and I was starting to worry, starting to wonder if maybe something was wrong."

The tide lay low tonight, the water so still beneath the seawall that a mass of rocks rose from the surface like misshapen pyramids. I fixed my eyes on the water and these towering rocks, on the current moving across the harbor in serene undulations. I knew what the mongrel was wondering. I knew what he was after, and it had nothing to do with concern. How thoroughly he disgusted me, the way all policemen did. As always, the inherent arrogance in the voice, the underlying vibe that those outside of uniform were beneath contempt, and the probing eyes that pierced with suspicion. This had to be the only country in the world where standing stationary was branded a crime, which meant we must all be criminals since that was all anyone ever did around here: stand and do nothing.

"Two hours!" I declared. "No, compañero, that's impossible."

"I'm afraid so," he countered, a discomfiting smile accompanying his answer. "You were here when I arrived, and I've been on my shift for two hours now."

Precisely as I figured. Even while looking out to sea and minding my own business, I'd be targeted. Even in this arresting darkness, they saw insurrection all over my face. Had I really been at the Malecón for two whole hours ruminating over the events of the last several years? The mongrel was either lying or grossly mistaken. Or maybe he was sniffing for an opportunity. I looked around, and sure enough, bodies along the seawall had certainly thinned out; movement along the boulevard had definitely dwindled, and pedestrians along the promenade had all but dispersed. I honestly couldn't conceive two whole hours passing by unnoticed, but just in case he was right, I decided to take my leave.

"Buenas noches, compañero, and thank you for your concern."

I turned to go. There were times the Malecón was hardly a golden necklace on which to hang anything incandescent, even if it was all invisible. There were times it was a tarnished and heavy chain that tightened around one's neck. This was one such time. This mongrel had just ruined my last visit here and the sacrosanct moments of saying good-bye to one's homeland. If two whole hours had really lapsed unnoticed, Rigo must be worried sick and searching for me as we spoke. Not to mention Mamá and my sisters. I still had to break the news to them myself. A final bout of guilt assailed me and would not lessen its grip, and neither did this mongrel in blue have any intention of releasing me from his custody.

"What a disaster, huh, compañera? Tell me, what do you think of this huge mess we're in?"

His smile disgusted me more than ever. Did he really think I'd fall for the obvious? How I wanted to ram the speedboat of my disgust into the ferry of his hubris. How I wanted to pummel the vessel of his conceit until it split wide open. Exactly what mess was he talking about? The mess created by the man in green? The mess of being sprayed by the hoses of tyranny so that those on board wished to hasten their own drowning.

How much longer would it take? How many more decades before this Revolution radioed for help and stopped innocent citizens from disintegrating before its eyes? When would there be real concern for those who screamed in silent agony and covered their faces against the stench of our bearded leader in his green fatigues? Murderers. ¡Asesinos! The only mess I knew was that which Fidel Castro had made of Cuba for over thirty years now—*that* was the only mess! Every time I heard the clamor of his Communist clichés I needed to gasp for air. Every time I thought of helpless souls struggling to stay afloat in the dregs of this dictatorship it filled me with such rage I wanted to scream. But of course, I didn't. Of course, I couldn't. After all my silent wrangling I could barely utter a few paltry words.

"What do I think of this mess?" I began with newfound verve. "I think it's a miracle, that's what I think—an absolute miracle!"

This time I would not be deterred as I went to leave. Hopefully the mongrel got my message: Stop sniffing! I wasn't interested! Even if I weren't married, I still wouldn't be interested. Not in the least. Not with a mongrel. Without knowing or caring if he had uttered anything in response, I turned and crossed the wide boulevard that ran alongside the seawall, Avenida Washington as it was officially known, and slid into the narrow crevices of the city.

The streets had definitely thinned out, but I still encountered plenty of lost and lonely faces on the way home. I cared for only one thing: learning the truth, verifying whether I had really spent two hours at the Malecón. It couldn't be past eleven already. The streets remained buried in that suffocating blackness of our nightly apagón, and I quickened my pace. By now I was desperate to reach the house and have Rigo at my side, eager to learn of his family's reaction to our big news. How I longed to hear Mihrta's supplications that rather than leave his homeland, *I* be the only thing he leave: his own wife. But I would have to wait. Even before reaching the front door I could tell that no one lurked inside. Not Rigo. Not Mamá. Not Angélica or Pilar. I stood on the street and looked toward the front windows. No signs of life stirred anywhere within.

As I opened the door to the dark and empty house, my stomach churned miserably. This dull ache impeded all movement until I put all foolishness in check. What was the matter with me? I was leaving Cuba on a homemade raft tomorrow, on a raft called La Maloja no less! I was taking to the wide and open ocean and all its inherent dangers. In the face of so harrowing a scenario, how could a little darkness frighten me?

Somehow I cast aside all hesitation and stepped into the living room, nearly diving for the coffee table. I reached for our main source of illumination during the long and dreaded blackouts: a tall and sturdy candle that bore the scars of many a lighting. I lit the candle and picked it up from the wooden table. It illuminated my path softly down our long and narrow hallway.

I approached Mamá's room and looked in for a moment, catching sight of my father's tall bookcases and the texts that sat untouched these days. Shadows accompanied me as I pulsed anonymously toward my room. Anticipation swelled as I grew anxious to learn the truth. I finally walked in, but only to stare at the time in disbelief: *ten-twenty!* Not only was it past ten, it was ten-twenty! The mongrel had been right. It was true, and from my nightstand, the round-faced clock with its glowing hands taunted me in their candid incandescence.

How defeated I now felt, how spent. I couldn't take it anymore. I inched toward my dresser and placed the candle down on it, in front of a large mirror that hung on the wall in a dark wooden frame. I stopped for a moment until, in a wave of disgust, I gazed at my reflection. I stared at my pathetic face and the features that frightened me. What an absolute mess I was! My eyes looked back at me eerily and empty. My brown hair clung to my head in a sweep of lifeless strands. I felt dirty and grimy, and shadows shifted across my face to create a ghastly sight. Even my clothes stuck to my body in all their drabness, drenched in the dust and debris of day.

What was going on? Why was it so late and nobody home yet? If a surge of panic jolted me to go in search of my family, I simply lacked the energy. I was that drained. The events of the past nine days had caught up with me, and I thought I would drop to the floor from exhaustion. A pressure bore down on my temples and I needed to lie down. Wherever they were, I trusted in everything to be fine. I could think only of my bed and how I needed to rest. I wanted to clear my thoughts, but wondered if Amalia had left yet for

Cojimar.

But I needed to do something first.

Ever since the miracle of August 5, I had borrowed some prayer cards and votives from Mamá and arranged them reverently atop the dark-brown dresser in my room. There were six candles in all, ivory votives in orange-frosted crystal cups. I lit them one by one, and before lying down to rest, I blew out the larger candle from the living room. A trail of smoke snaked its way into the air in a twisting band of charcoal and ashen gray.

What a soft and pleasing glow the votives emitted. They stood firmly at attention too, like miniature kind-faced guards. And how gently they illuminated the saints adorning my dresser: Saint Barbara and Saint Lazarus, Saint Jude and La Virgen del Cobre. I even had a prayer card for Michael the Archangel, his sword positioned upward in the air. I didn't know what Rigo planned on taking with him in the morning, but these cards would accompany me as we pushed off from shore. I would clutch them tightly against my breast for protection along our journey.

How surreal a scene: casting into the ocean as the faint whispers of the water coaxed us away. It all seemed impossible, as inconceivable as being surrounded by so much silence right now. I wasn't used to it. In the past I would have cherished all this solitude, but I didn't want to be alone right now. I wanted to be surrounded by tears and laughter, by desperate supplications. All this quietude only hastened my fatigue, and I finally lay down. I needed to clear my thoughts if just for a moment, and my mind wasted no time in racing to the sights and sounds that greet us in our dreams.

To the water—that was where my thoughts fled. My strained and aching eyes hosted a rush of jumbled images, but the comfort of the water was where my spirit longed to go. The sights and sounds of the ocean had consumed me all week long, and now my dreams carried me there. Not to the cold untrusting water of night, but to the soft and sultry water of day. How I wanted that water to transport me, to thrust me into the tides of tomorrow and pull me along the currents of freedom. Yet it was not water I saw or felt, but air, a cool and tingly air. At first I was floating through air, then flying through air.

"It's because I'll soon be free!" I reasoned. "I'll know and taste freedom for the first time ever, and my spirit longs to soar upward."

This air lifted and embraced me, but as in most dreams, *things that aren't are and things that are aren't*, and my thoughts turned inside out and shifted in reverse. I was no longer flying through air, the air was flying toward me, that same cold air from earlier tonight, that mordant, piercing air so unusual for the middle of August. Instead of prompting me to clutch my arms though, it propelled me to bolt up in bed. The window! The window to my room must be open. That was how this pernicious air had insinuated itself into the house. But even as I jumped out of bed to close it, I knew I must be dreaming. I was planted firmly on my feet, but felt entrenched in some developing dream. What else explained the curious sight materializing before my eyes?

Air had snuck into the house, but it was not invisible as air should be. It was black and charcoal and ashen gray. It spiraled and spun before me, while deep in its center, a whirl of white and silver and a coating of vanilla radiated forth. I felt vibrations emanating from it, mysterious shockwaves that pulsated and undulated as if the swirl of light were trying to shatter the veneer shielding it. This peculiar sight seemed very real, but I knew I must be dreaming. My reflection in the mirror signaled I was awake, but I knew this must be a dream. Who in their right mind had ever seen air? Air that spun and whirled and turned furiously about so that it appeared more like water than air. Air and water. How similar the two were. No wonder one came from the other. No wonder one changed into the other.

I approached it cautiously. I needed to touch and feel this whirling plume of air. I reached my hand out, but it was not cold as I imagined. It was hot. This mass of energy throbbed with a heavy warmth while more shockwaves pulsated and bounced right off me. And this hot brewing air turned so dense I couldn't breathe anymore. I thought I would suffocate. I started coughing and choking and headed for the door because, surely, a fire raged inside the house and I must extinguish it. I must douse it with water before the entire house burned down and I perished. I turned to run for the door when, just as quickly, I came to a halt at the sound of a voice.

"Clara," called the voice. "Stop!"

I did exactly that. I no longer knew if I was dreaming or awake, but I stopped. I turned to face the mysterious voice and saw a bright glow. That whirl of white and silver and vanilla had pierced through the bands of charcoal and ashen gray, and in their place left a dazzling and arresting light. No wonder I had seen no stars or moon along the Malecón. They were all here, right inside my room in a constellation of blinding incandescence. The elements of air and water and light had coalesced into the rays of some wild and wondrous sun, all being fed by the flames of a white and whispering fire.

"No!" I cried out. "I can't stop! Can't you see there's a fire inside the house? Some raging white fire, and I'm in danger—we both are!"

"No, Clara. There is no fire. It is only I, and I come to you with greetings."

I shook my head in disbelief. *Greetings!* Had I just heard correctly? What type of foolish talk was this right now?

"What do you mean greetings?" I snapped. "Greetings from whom? Greetings from where?"

"From above, Clara. Greetings from above."

Greetings from above? What did that mean at a time like this? At a time of fire and flame? At a time of clear and critical danger? I certainly had to be dreaming. I had to be. Even if I felt myself perfectly alert in the glow of this pulsating presence, I knew I must be dreaming. And even if time was coinciding with reality, for I caught sight of the alarm clock and saw it was exactly ten-thirty, saw that only a mere ten minutes had elapsed, I knew this must all be a dream.

"From above!" I said. "What do you mean from above?"

"From your Heavenly Father, Clara. From *that* above."

It was then I peered intently at this presence, at this being that had materialized out of nowhere. It looked real, even human, but then it didn't. It possessed a familiar face, but again it didn't. Even its coloring kept changing, one shade one moment, another shade the next, a shifting blend of glistening bronze and shimmering white that almost blinded and burned. It seemed solid and impenetrable, but transparent too, bathed in some ethereal luminescence where, were I to thrust a hand at it, that hand would surely pierce through. A shimmer of white embraced it. A tingling silver surrounded it. Not only outwardly, but inwardly, as if some giant translucent candle lit it from its center and bathed it from within. It wasn't overly tall, but the presence towered over me just the same, engulfing me. Could it be that right before me stood a—no, of course not. I couldn't even finish my thought. Miracles were one thing, but this? This had to be my imagination. A hallucination. But a vision? Definitely not.

"From my heavenly father? Oh, I get it. You mean Papi. Yes, I understand now. It's because of the trip tomorrow. Papi knows that Rigo and I are leaving Cuba and wants to give us his blessing, wants to let us know that we're making the right choice. Well, you tell Papi that..."

I couldn't finish my words. As my voice trailed off, my thoughts dissolved in a vapor of sadness. Despite this soothing light that saturated my room and the pale-rust walls, any thought of my father, no matter how fleeting, still struck me with melancholy and regret.

"No, Clara. I don't mean your earthly father. I mean your Heavenly Father—that father!"

"Which Heavenly Father?"

"The Creator, Clara! You know, the one who created you, along with everything else in the universe."

His words dispersed in an echo, leaving me to peer at this being again, but suspiciously this time. I would always find it difficult to describe him, even now, this translucent, transparent, and incandescent presence. Even from those initial moments of its apparition, I thought it the most beautiful thing I had ever seen, natural or not. Yet there was something unnatural about it I had glaringly overlooked: a tremendous mass rising behind it, two white flames that emanated from its body that were tinged in bronze along the edges. There was no mistaking what they were, these radiant formations that glowed with a serene energy, these elegantly shaped masses as huge and magnificent as they were majestic.

"Who are you?" I asked. "*What* are you, and what are you doing inside my house?"

"My name is Gabriel," he replied. "And I'm a messenger, a messenger from God."

How I wanted to laugh at this. Even for a hallucination, it was too much! But if I didn't know how to ease back into consciousness, I decided to play along.

"Gabriel! Of course! Don't tell me, the Angel Gabriel, right?"

"That's right, Clara. That's precisely who I am."

I certainly wanted to laugh now, but I was too scared. This encounter had just taken a decidedly frightening turn, and I no longer felt at ease in its presence, no matter how soothing the light or how lustrous the luminescence. I should have thought his words were all the proof I needed that the events of the last week were indeed miraculous. But I also knew they signaled trouble. Unannounced visits often heralded unwelcome news, and this no longer seemed just a dream, but a bad dream—one from which I wished to wake up.

"Funny," I began, rather brashly and flippantly. "You don't look like an angel. Don't angels all have blond hair and blue eyes?"

"Oh, you mean like your friend here," he replied

flippantly himself, pointing to the prayer card on the dresser. "You mean Michael, our golden-haired boy wonder who can do no wrong. No, we all come in different shades and sizes, Clara—except for those little cherubs you see in pictures all over the place. I don't know who came up with that concept, but there no angels in Heaven that look like that."

"No?" I asked.

"No, Clara. And don't be so easily impressed by looks either. Michael may have the blond hair and blue eyes, but he doesn't have these. Just look at these, Clara. I bet you've never seen a pair of wings like this, have you? I've got the best wings in the whole universe—that's why I'm the messenger."

That he did. Those were the two masses I felt reluctant to acknowledge, too frightened to name—wings, beautiful bronze-tinged wings bathed in a white luminescence and larger than the expanse of his whole body. I could only imagine their magnificence as they spread in full flight.

"I just added the bronze highlights," he said. "It's only taken me since the dawn of time, but the Creator finally allowed it."

This was not happening. This was definitely a dream, and soon I would wake up. Soon I would find Rigo sleeping at my side and Mamá and my sisters asleep in their own rooms. Soon all this light that drenched my eyes would vanish, and I'd be back in the dark.

"Look," I said, trying to snap myself out of this irreverent reverie. "I know what's going on here. You're not an angel. You're an agent—an agent of the state. You've come to stop my husband and me. Someone has sent you to arrest us, and I know who."

"No, Clara. You're mistaken."

"I'm not mistaken. I know who's behind it: Mihrta, my mother-in-law. Well, it's not happening. We are free to leave and everybody knows it. The whole world is watching this miracle and you can't do anything about it, not even your 'father.' And you know which father I mean, don't you? The one there's nothing heavenly about, the one who created this mess we're all in."

The messenger gazed down at me with that blazing bronzed visage of his, and as he did so, more shockwaves swelled up again and lightly washed over me.

"¡Dios mío!" he said, shaking his head and flaring his fiery white eyes. "You're right, Clara. There is a miracle taking place right now, a far greater one than you can imagine, one in which you will even play a big part. But it has nothing to do with taking this trip tomorrow. In fact, you must not take this trip tomorrow, Clara!"

I was right! There it was! The trouble I had feared! The unwanted news I had dreaded. And I knew who was behind it: Mihrta. She had commissioned this creature to intimidate and harass me. That was why Rigo wasn't home yet. He had already been detained and now it was my turn. Had this concept come to Mihrta during electroshock therapy? Had she concocted the idea for all this fire and flame while her brain was being fried? Maybe this was the mongrel from the Malecón in some elaborate disguise. They looked to be about the same size, and even had that same bronzed complexion.

"What do you mean I must not take this trip tomorrow? Of course I'm taking this trip tomorrow, and nothing is stopping me—nothing!"

"Clara," he began, the hint of exasperation evident in his voice. "Weren't your words to Amalia earlier tonight, 'Si Dios quiere'? *If that's what God wants.* Weren't those your exact words to your friend?"

"Yes," I said.

"Well Clara, Dios no quiere."

"How did you know that?" I asked angrily. "How do you know what my best friend and I discussed earlier?"

All at once the messenger's demeanor changed drastically, and this Angel Gabriel, as he claimed to be, this translucent, transparent, and incandescent presence bellowed with such a booming voice that it sent even more shockwaves pushing hard against my body again.

"Hail Clara, thou are highly favored, the Lord is with thee; blessed art thou among women."

"Stop!" I cried out. "Stop this at once!"

"Fear not, Clara, for thou hast found favor with God. And behold, thou shall conceive in thy womb and bring forth a daughter. She shall be great and shall be called the daughter of the Highest, and the Lord God shall give unto her the throne of her father David. And she shall reign over the house of Jacob forever, and her kingdom there shall have no end."

"Stop!" I cried out again. "What do you mean a daughter? I'm not having a daughter. I can't even bear children."

"You can now," replied the messenger. "For remember, with God nothing is impossible."

"Out!" I ordered the messenger again. "I want you out right now, or I'm going to scream."

The presence looked up to the ceiling and flared his eyes.

"¡Hay mija!" he said. "You are nothing like Mary was. No wonder the Creator didn't brief me. Still, I can see why He's chosen you. You're feisty, aren't you? Quite rebellious. Yes, that Group Insurrection suits you quite perfectly. Look, Clara, you will not scream, and you must believe me. A great thing is about to happen—a miracle. You have been chosen to be the mother of God's next child, and this time it's going to be a girl. You will have a daughter and will name her Luz. You must name her Luz because, well, that's what the Creator wants. I think she's supposed to be the new light of the world, but don't quote me on that."

"Really?" I muttered to myself, prodding and prompting and pressing myself to get up, wondering why, despite all my efforts, this dream wouldn't end. Wondering why, as I looked around the room, I could see nothing beyond this dazzling, blinding light.

"That's original!" I said. "Luz of all names! Luz!"

"Well, let's just say your species isn't the brightest in the universe, Clara; humans needs as much of a hint as they can get."

"Wake up," I ordered myself, clasping my arms in a new round of restlessness. I even tried pinching myself. "It's time to put an end to this—wake up, Clara!"

"You are not asleep, Clara!" the messenger insisted. "And this is not a dream. Neither is it a hallucination or even a vision. It's a visitation, Clara. Do you understand the difference? I'm here to pay you a personal visit."

"Of course I understand!" I said. "And you're right. It's not a dream or any of those things. It's delusion, delirium. I'm delirious from all the rabidness and frenzy of the past week, and I've finally cracked."

"It's not delirium, Clara, and no, you haven't cracked. Look, I can prove to you that you're not dreaming."

"All right," I said. "Go ahead."

"Well, let's just humor you and say you were sleeping."

"Okay."

"Would you get up if you were to hear the phone ring?"

"Yes," I said. "Absolutely. I'm a very light sleeper."

"Well, Clara, get ready then. You're about to be *woken up*."

And it happened just as he said. As much as I wanted to scoff at his prediction, the phone rang just then—and rang and rang. But I knew it was a trick. My mother-in-law could produce great feats of deception, and she had conjured up a masterful magician with this messenger. Yet why was I not seeing myself springing up from bed? Why was I not groggy or creeping back into consciousness? I was still on my feet, alert as ever, and awash in all this dazzling luminescence.

"Well, Clara. Aren't you getting it?" posed the messenger. "Aren't you?"

The phone kept ringing and ringing from the living room while this Gabriel looked at me and I looked at him, our eyes never once wavering from each other. I tried disguising a round of trembling, but these tremors of disbelief could not be suppressed, would not be subverted.

"Get it, chica! It's your husband calling. Get the phone before he hangs up!"

"It's not my husband!" I snapped back defiantly. "This is all a trick, a practical joke, and once I answer the phone, I'll wake up and you'll be gone."

"Suit yourself," the messenger replied, shaking his head in exasperation.

I turned my back and slowly ventured out. That flush of white light bathed my room still, but the rest of the house remained frightfully dark, especially the hallway. I couldn't see my own hands in front of me, but those distant rings faithfully guided my way. By the time I reached the living room I could see everything with stunning alacrity, as if all power had been fully restored. I still had no clue as to anyone's whereabouts, but maybe this would provide an answer.

Our phone was an ancient relic, a rotary model that predated the Revolution and often acted up. But now its rings came in loudly and powerfully, as if shiny and brand new. I stood over that artifact hoping it would stop, but it rang and rang until it drowned my reluctance and I finally gave in.

"Dígame," I answered, my heart pounding so savagely I thought it might split open my chest.

"Clara!" said Rigo's voice on the other end. "It's me, amor. I'm still here with the family."

At the sound of his voice, I nearly burst into tears. I wanted to cry and release all the churning anxiety.

"What's taking you so long, Rigo? Is everything all right, amor? ¿Todo bien?"

"It's Mamá, amor. She's taking it just as we thought she would. She's inconsolable."

"Well, don't forget what you said to me, Rigo: no backing

out."

"Don't worry, amor. No backing out."

"Hurry back, amor! There's been a change in plans I need to tell you about."

"What happened?" he asked.

I dared not tell him. We had all had enough excitement for the week. As much as I planned on no longer keeping things from my husband—even when I only did it for his own protection—I couldn't tell him about our raft, La Maloja, having been dismembered. It wasn't quite time to open up the doors of my life and have the contents of its rooms freely intermingle.

"Nothing serious, Rigo, but you and I must go to Cojimar by ourselves in the morning. We have to meet Amalia and Henry there by eight o'clock. How will we get there, Rigo? How?"

"It's all right, amor. I'll be home soon and we'll resolve it then."

"Rigo!" I called out, my voice echoing, then pausing, then trying to revive itself in the quietude. "You're sure everything's all right, amor?"

"I'm sure amor, todo bien. But Mamá is a complete mess. She's having a nervous breakdown, and Papá is threatening to hook her up with the cord and lamp if she doesn't calm down. I think it's what she really wants."

"I'm going over there Rigo! I'm heading over right now!"

"No!" he whispered furiously into the phone. "Sorry Clara, but you're the last person she wants to see right now. Just stay home, and I'll be there soon." He paused before continuing. "I love you, amor. Don't worry about anything."

"I love you too," I said.

I was about to hang up when his voice sought me out a final time.

"Clara," he whispered tenderly. "I'm so glad you

convinced me, amor. You have no idea how thrilled I am."

"You are?" I said.

"Yes, amor, truly I am. Tomorrow will be the start of a whole new life for us and I can't wait. You were absolutely right, Clara. This really is a miracle and we'd be fools to pass it up! Absolute fools!"

I didn't know what to say. I was too stunned, too touched by so comforting a confession.

"I love you, amor. I love you with all my heart," I said.

The phone clicked, leaving the drone of the dial tone to hang endlessly in my ear. I stood in abeyance as everything fell dark again and I clung to the receiver. If I wanted to place it back in its cradle and cease that dreadful noise, I couldn't lift my hand. I couldn't move. And I knew why: *I didn't want to move.* I didn't want to go back to my room and face the truth—that is, if I could call it that. I knew *he* would still be there: the messenger, that translucent, transparent, and incandescent presence.

But it was time to face the music, so off I went. The hallway remained impenetrably dark, and I couldn't see my own hands before me. I was certain it had finally happened: I had woken up. Even as I approached my room, I saw nothing inside it: no faint light, no hint of a shine, not even a dim glow. But the moment I stood in the doorway and looked in, there it was: that constellation of incandescence lighting up the pale rust walls. No, he hadn't gone anywhere. He was very much there still, seemingly engrossed now in the contents of my room, leaning over the dark wooden dresser and examining the prayer cards delicately arranged there. He even had one in his possession, the one of Michael.

"What a ham!" the messenger muttered to himself, shaking his head all the while. "Look at how he always has to pose in that fighting stance of his."

"What was that?" I asked.

"Oh, nothing, nothing," replied the messenger, not bothering to turn and face me. "Just don't believe everything you read."

He placed the card back down and continued shaking his head distractedly.

"Don't believe what?" I asked.

"Never mind Clara, never mind. Well, was I right or was I right? Was it your husband Rigo or was it not?"

"Yes," I said in mild embarrassment. "It was him. But I still don't believe this is happening."

"And why not, may I ask?"

"Because!" I said. "It can't be! People don't talk to angels. Angels don't come down to earth, much less the Angel Gabriel."

"Of course they do, Clara. It happens all the time, and I should know, shouldn't I?"

"But it doesn't," I insisted. "It can't."

"It can and it does, Clara. Aren't you the one who's been talking about miracles all week long? Rapt with joy that you've been living through one? Yes, as I recall, you have. But now that you're actually faced with one, a real miracle, you don't recognize it for what it is. Why is that, Clara? Can you explain that to me?"

"I don't know," I said, shaking my head and grabbing my temples and applying a deep pressure. "I don't know."

"Well, I know, Clara. It's very simple: you're scared. And fear is filling you with doubt. The news that you'll soon be the mother of God's next child terrifies you. But it's all right, Clara. It's natural to be scared. You just have to believe and trust in the ways of the Lord."

"But this is a mistake!" I insisted. "For one thing, I can't have children. Last year I came down with a horrible affliction and the doctors said I would never bear a child. My husband and I have been trying, just to prove them wrong, and nothing!"

"Stop tormenting yourself, Clara," the messenger said.

"Who do you think has the last word in these matters? The doctors? Or the one who created the doctors?"

"But I can't be the mother of God's next child," I said. "You must obviously know that I'm not a…"

I struggled with the next word. I tried to find a less awkward term in the presence of this messenger and all his white flame and pure light.

"A virgin, Clara? Is that what you're struggling to say?"

"Yes! You obviously know I've had relations with a man."

"Of course we know you've had relations, Clara. Let's just say that no longer matters."

"No longer matters? How can it not?" I posed. "All my life it's been the Virgin Mary this and the Virgin Mary that and Mary Ever Virgin. So how can the mother of *any* child of God's not be a virgin?"

"Times have changed, Clara. What can I say? Besides, you are a virgin."

"I'm no virgin," I countered. "Trust me!"

"But you are, Clara! You are, and I'll explain why. Is a virgin not someone pure in thought and spirit? Someone innocent and pure of heart? You are those things, Clara, and much more—all of which makes you a virgin. That's one of the reasons why the Heavenly Father has chosen you."

"Really?" I said, surprised to hear the concept of virginity presented in such terms.

"Yes, and by the way, you don't really think Mary was a virgin forever, do you? I mean, that would not have been fair to Joseph *or* her, and if the Heavenly Father is anything, He's fair."

Fairness aside, I didn't really want to pursue the matter. Mary and Joseph's love life was really none of my business, and I preferred to change the subject.

"Well, what about being religious then? You must know I never go to church. Why, I only became religious this week."

"Well Clara, if you're not religious, why do you have all these little candles all over the place? And why all the pictures of all the saints? Which, by the way, I see mine is nowhere to be found."

I felt a slight but stinging embarrassment, fanned by the glare and the flame of an accusatory light.

"That's because they belong to my mother," I replied. "All these candles and prayer cards—she's the religious one. You see, I take more after my father, and you know which father I mean, right?"

"Yes Clara, I know all about your father, trust me. We have to keep a close eye on Alejo. Now, why don't you have one of me, may I ask? Am I not the messenger?"

"I don't know why Mamá doesn't have one of the Angel Gabriel," I said. "I mean, of you. You realize this is Cuba, don't you? You know about the embargo."

"Of course I know, Clara. But maybe it has nothing to do with the embargo and only because I'm the Messenger—you know, the one who bears good news as well as bad. Let's just blame everything on the messenger, why don't we? Let's just shoot down the messenger. But Michael, let's not forget that blue-eyed, blond haired Archangel who can do no wrong, Heaven's illustrious four-star general."

"Look," I said, trying to move past the vibe of hostility. "Don't get me wrong. I'm very flattered and all, but the Heavenly Father must know the contents of my heart. He must know that I don't even want to be a mother anymore, that I have no interest in parenting. I'm a writer. I'm an insurrectionist. The last thing I want is to bring a child into this world, especially into Cuba."

"You're going to make an excellent mother, Clara. I have no doubt about that."

"I'll make a terrible mother!" I said. "I've got terrible vices. I can't cook. I can't clean. I take the Lord's name in vain all the time. Why, I even follow the Zodiac."

"You do?" he asked in mock surprise.

"Yes, I try to read my horoscope every chance I get."

"Well, I'll let you in on a little secret, Clara—I follow the Zodiac too, but that's just between you and me."

"You do not," I said.

"Of course I do, Clara. You have to remember that we angels are not perfect beings. We are also swayed by temptation and give in to vices periodically. Besides, the Zodiac is just reading and deciphering the stars. What's more heavenly than that?"

"Please," I protested. "Go back and tell the Heavenly Father He's made a mistake. I'm about to embark on a big project in the United States: the liberation of my homeland. Tell him He needs to pick someone more holy, more spiritual."

"You just hit the nail on the head, Clara. You may not be religious, but you are spiritual, and the Heavenly Father has always seen that in you. Besides, He never makes a mistake. It may be hard to understand his reasoning at times, but He always knows precisely what he's doing."

"Spiritual? Me? I don't know anything about spirituality. I'm not spiritual."

"You are, Clara, and you'll come to learn that in good time."

"But I have no knowledge of spiritual things, especially biblical things. I know about the Garden of Eden, of course; about the Flood and the Exodus, of course. But I couldn't tell you whether something is in the Old Testament or the New Testament. Why, to tell you the truth, I don't even believe in a lot of what the…"

I stopped myself, suddenly realizing what I was about to say and cutting myself short before making a further mess of things.

"A lot of *what* Clara? A lot of what's in the Bible?"

"Well, let's just say there's nothing in there about this, about what's happening between you and me right now."

"There are many things in the Bible that have yet to be written, Clara, many. Do you honestly think the Bible stops with the book of Revelations? No, mija! What about when the Second Coming takes place? Maybe there will even be a Third Coming. Remember, nobody knows any of that, Clara, not even me, and it has yet to be recorded—all of it."

"It does?"

"Yes, it does. And don't forget there's a whole segment of the Messiah's life that has never been accounted for. You know, from the time He was about thirteen to thirty-three, 'the trouble years' as the Creator likes to call them. It's my understanding that these books are out there somewhere, but again, you didn't hear that from me."

As that serene luminescence continued blazing within my room, burning in its white and silvery brilliance, there was no refuting this messenger, no keeping up with him. My thoughts leaped to object and refute him, to critique him as I so loved to do, but he had an explanation for everything, a ready response for every objection I made.

"Well, what about being Jewish? You said something about the house of David and the throne of Jacob. Are you telling me I've got Jewish blood in me?"

"It's the throne of David and the House of Jacob, chica; and, yes, you do. Now *that* the Heavenly Father was insistent upon. You can say He likes to keep things in the family."

"I've got Jewish blood?" I asked in surprise.

"Yes, Clara, you do."

"Does Rigo?"

"No, Rigo has got Arabic blood, and plenty of it. But Jew, Arab, what does it matter? It's all the same, really. One day you will all realize that."

I had to find some way of disproving all this, of crashing through the mirror of this mirage. *That was it!* The mirror atop my dresser! I would do it that way. If I caught sight of this angel through the wood-framed mirror on the wall, I could finally expose this clever trick. Wasn't it common knowledge that spiritual beings did not have a reflection? That their images could not be captured or photographed? A raw exhilaration coursed through my veins. I turned excitedly toward the mirror, all the while hoping, expecting, knowing a reflection would reveal this chicanery when, much to my shock, nothing shone back—nothing at all! No reflection, no image, no nothing. Not even a white blaze of light that bathed the room. The only reflection I caught was my own, signaling to me that I was all by myself with my candles and prayer cards. Only when I averted my glance from the mirror was the messenger there again. No longer lost in a shuffle of shadow or in a shimmering charade, but right in the thick of things.

"Now do you believe me, Clara? Now that you've failed to catch my reflection?"

"Why is that?" I asked. "Why?"

"Very simple, Clara. You're made of dust, I'm made of air. And air, Clara, does not reflect."

"But please!" I persisted. "I don't think the Heavenly Father has thought this through. I mean, let's just say I take your word for it, that I've got Jewish blood and all; well, I'm still Cuban. Why would He choose a Cuban woman for a task such as this? Why not an American woman? A European woman? I mean, look at me. Look at my drab clothes and my dreary appearance. Look at this crumbling street I live on. All the buildings are decaying. Everything is deteriorating or falling to the ground. Why, the whole country is collapsing. How can any child of God be born in a place such as this? In circumstances such as these!"

"What about the Messiah?" the Messenger said. "Wasn't the Messiah born in a manger? If you think Cuba is bad, you should have seen Judea in those days—now *that* was bad. At least Cuba has one of the best healthcare systems in the world."

"But Cuba?" I asked. "Why would He choose Cuba? Why?"

"I can't be absolutely sure, Clara, but I know the Father

has a real soft spot for Cuba. He vacations here every year."

"Stop this!" I said. "This has gone far enough!"

"He does, Clara. Every spring, when it's not too hot."

"Varadero, I suppose?"

"No, Varadero is so passé. Santa Lucía, off the northern coast of Camagüey. His favorite beach in all creation, Clara."

"Santa Lucía? Why, that's where Rigo was supposed to…" my voice trailed off again.

"Design those luxury hotels? Yes, we know all about that."

I shook my head in earnest again, my thoughts throbbing in a dull disbelief.

"This is ridiculous," I said. "Absolutely absurd. Standing here and having a conversation with the Angel Gabriel about the Creator vacationing in Cuba. I know now this is a silly dream."

"And why is that, Clara? Explain it to me. Didn't He rest on the seventh day after He created the world? What's the matter with you, chica? Don't you think the Creator is entitled to some rest and relaxation? I mean, 24-6 He's with everyone all the time! And I mean *all the time*. Nobody ever leaves the poor Guy alone, Clara!"

I wanted to laugh again, really I did. I no longer felt this encounter bore the markings of some delirious dream. It bordered on the ridiculous, on the absurd. At any moment I expected a group of people to come out of hiding and start yelling "Surprise!" This had to be some intricately staged stunt with special effects and all.

"All right," I said. "All right. Tell me this is all a joke, a clever practical joke. Tell me that Rigo is even in on it. It's all been very funny, hilarious even, but it's not going to work. This stunt smacks of Mihrta, but it will not dissuade us from leaving."

Just then the angel's demeanor changed dramatically and I felt something familiar: those vibrations, those shockwaves throbbing and bouncing off my body again. I felt the whiteness of the flames leaping toward me, and he was no longer a messenger, but a sentinel, one of Heaven's stern-faced guards.

"This is not funny, Clara! And it's no joke! I can assure you that this is a very serious matter. I repeat, you must not take that trip tomorrow! I'm starting to lose my patience now. When I leave here tonight, the Holy Ghost shall come upon thee, and the power of the Highest shall overshadow thee: therefore, also, that holy thing which shall be born of thee shall be called Luz, Daughter of God. For behold that even though you and your husband have been trying to have a child and were told by learned men you would never bear children, that is no longer the case. For with God nothing shall be impossible—nothing!"

I didn't make a sound, and the angel stood perfectly still after so adamant a declaration, his right hand lifted up and pointing outward. He peered straight at me as I'd never been looked at before. I thought I might melt from so caustic a gaze. Did he know what he looked like? Had he ever seen himself at all? Maybe his reflection could be captured in one place: the human eye. I didn't know whether to respond or not, whether to look at him or not, but I felt my opposition starting to wane. Maybe from all the seriousness. Maybe from the authority in his voice. Or maybe going along with the pretense would force this dream to fade all the sooner.

"Fine," I conceded. "I believe you, I believe all this. But I'm still leaving tomorrow. My daughter can be born in the United States."

"No, Clara!" the messenger stated emphatically. "Your daughter must be born in Cuba! She will not be safe anywhere else, especially in the United States."

"But the United States is the safest country in the world," I said. "The safest place in the world."

"Do you remember King Herod, Clara? Do you remember when the Messiah was born how King Herod wanted to…"

"King who?" I interjected.

"Oh, just forget it, Clara. You really don't know the Bible, do you? Now look, all I know is what I've been told. Remember, I'm a messenger and my orders come from you know *Whom*. You must have the child in Cuba, and it must be raised in Cuba—those are the orders!"

"But what about Rigo?" I pleaded. "What about Amalia and Henry? We just finished firming up the plans for tomorrow. I can't ruin the trip for them. What shall I say? What shall I do?"

"What shall you do, Clara? You shall obey the word of God, the Father—your Heavenly Father—that's what you shall do! For your future is no longer in your hands. You have been chosen to fulfill a destiny far greater than your own, and you must submit to it! Now, silence, Clara! You're fortunate I don't strike you dumb the way I did Zechariah when he refused to believe Elizabeth would bear him a child. Unfortunately, I was not granted the authority for such measures at this time, but I wish I had been. Now go and rejoice, Clara, for you are going to be a mother! You are going to bear a child who will change the course of history and the entire world once again!"

"Rejoice?" I said. "You think this is something to rejoice about?"

"Of course it is, Clara! Go and rejoice, for I must take my leave. Oh, and one other thing before I go, so you won't have to keep doubting the veracity of this encounter or think it all a dream."

"What?" I asked.

"Look at the clock and tell me the time."

I walked over to the night table and looked at the alarm clock as instructed.

"Ten-thirty," I said in surprise. "But how is that possible? It was ten-twenty when I got home, ten-thirty as I was falling asleep, and it feels as if you've been here for hours."

"I'll tell you why it's possible, Clara. When I, the Angel Gabriel, Heaven's chief operating messenger, delivers a divine message from above, it's done in celestial time, not earthly time. That's the mode we're in right now, Clara: celestial time. This visit will barely register as microseconds on the clock of eternity, milliseconds at most. That's why, to you—and your husband—it's only ten-thirty still."

I didn't know why, but I suddenly thought of my family again. Maybe my thoughts had been trapped in some other sphere of time, neither earthly or celestial.

"Where are my mother and sisters?" I asked. "They're all right, aren't they? You know that my older sister is—"

"Yes, Clara, we know. But don't worry, they're perfectly fine. Todo bien. One of my underlings is keeping close watch over them."

"Underlings? A guardian angel, I presume."

"No, Clara. We don't go by that term these days. Security, that's what we call it now—security."

"You really are up to date, aren't you?"

"Yes Clara, and one more thing before I go. Speaking of your mother, when you finally see her, tell the woman not to waste any more time with what she did tonight."

"Visiting a great aunt?" I asked.

"If that were all she had done," the messenger said. "No, tell her not to mess with the occult anymore!."

"The occult? You must be mistaken. My mother is a very religious woman. She would never have anything to do with the occult."

"Your mother is an obstinate, strong-willed woman who always wants to get her way, Clara. I wonder who she passed that on to? Now, if you'll excuse me, mija, I need to get going. Just tell her to stay away from the occult. Oh, and one other thing: those bands of black and charcoal and ashen gray and all those swirls of white and silver and vanilla you saw along the Malecón tonight—that was me, chica, making my way down. Now, good-bye, Clara. It's time for me to make my way up."

They finally started moving, finally initiated their ascent, the two majestic masses emanating from behind his body, those bronze-tinged wings. Upon his arrival I had not even noticed them, but now they began to flutter and flame and emit their shockwaves as they stretched and extended.

"Wait!" I called out. "I need to know something."

"¡*Dios mio, chica!* You know, Clara, yours is not the only message I'm delivering tonight. I've got plenty more, even in terms of celestial time."

"Why is this happening? Why does the Heavenly Father want to have another child after so long, especially a daughter? Why not another son?"

"He already has a son, Clara. His one and only son, remember? That's also in the Bible. But trust me, mija, you don't want to know why or get involved in the middle of that."

"Of course I want to know why," the critic in me pressed.

"No, Clara, you don't. For one thing, it would take an entire millennium to explain—and this time I do mean celestial time, eternal time even. Just do yourself a favor and stay out of it. Don't get in the middle of that. Just keep out of that part of things—the *why* of it—and this matter will run much more smoothly. As it is—and this is strictly between you and me, chica—I envision this all turning into one giant mess. But that's just my humble opinion. Who am I to say anything? I'm just the messenger, remember. Good-bye now, Clara."

"Wait!" I interjected again. "What happens if I have any questions? Any concerns? Will I ever see you again? Will you ever come back?"

His entire being reverberated now, and those masses behind his back were no longer wings, but waves. They did not flutter or flap or extend as ordinary wings, but pulsated and throbbed. They were giant waves rising from the sea of his back, swelling and expanding in some rhythmic resonance that radiated warmth and resplendence.

"I'm not a guidance counselor, Clara. You'll have to figure it out on your own, just like everyone else. But you're a big girl. Rely on your faith, as you're supposed to do."

He must have seen the disappointment on my face. Not only because I suddenly felt I was getting a host of mixed messages from him, but because he was leaving. The messenger must have sensed I had grown fond of him despite only milliseconds together.

"Well, Clara, you never know," he added. "It all depends on you know *Whom*. Many of my assignments come at the last moment. Even I don't know what they're going to be. Think of it as security, chica, a sign of the times."

If I thought I had captured just a glint of emotion for the one and only time tonight—just the slightest hint of a smile—there was no question the messenger had completed his task, for in my room there was no longer a luminescence, but an evanescence. Off he was without another word, vanishing from my presence and leaving the house in a flurry of light and wind and water and leaving me to ponder, if not the why of things, then certainly my fate.

This time I did not pace the room in renewed solitude, but neither did I simply remain in a state of shock. I immediately looked at the alarm clock just as I had done before falling asleep. *Ten-thirty*. I looked and blinked and stared intently, but sure enough, ten-thirty the hands on the clock insisted on it being. *Ten-thirty earth time!* But how? Had the messenger not even been here one whole minute? Not even a full sixty seconds? It couldn't be. This visit, this visitation, it had felt like hours. Not a minute, but several hours. Also, it may have only been ten-thirty, but it was very late for no one to be home yet, especially Mamá and my sisters. If I suspected something wrong, especially after this admonition about the occult, I put my worries aside, possessing the peace of mind now that they were fine and secure. As for Rigo, that was another story.

"¡Dios mío!" What would I say? Rigo would think me crazy, insane. After hounding him for three days straight about leaving Cuba, how could I tell him I had changed my mind? It was inconceivable. How could I possibly do an about-face? How could I demand we call the whole thing off after the speedboat of my supplications had finally split open the vessel of his resistance?

I wouldn't do it. I would put a halt to this. I wouldn't waste any time or energy worrying about this either. This had all been a crazy dream, and the moment someone came home, I would wake up and banish it all from my mind, this dusk of derangement, this period of partial paranoia. For now I just wanted to lie down and rest. I felt spent like never before and could fight the exhaustion no longer.

Dejectedly, I walked over to my dresser. I went to blow out all six candles, but one remained lit. I blew it out and gathered up the prayer cards. I clutched them tightly in my hand and pressed them firmly against my chest. I didn't know how I would manage it, but I'd get one of the messenger, embargo or not. And I didn't know how, but I'd shake this delirium off as well. I just needed to clear my thoughts before I came crashing into consciousness. Yet if I foolishly believed I could finally rest, the most peculiar occurrence of the evening was yet to happen, the strangest visitation of all.

I finally lay down, but was no longer clutching those prayer cards, no longer able to. An intoxicating drowsiness demanded my defeat when, almost immediately, I began seeing shadows. I didn't see how this could be possible: shadows without any light. I also felt a pressure bearing down on my body, pressing in from both sides and causing me to curl up in pain. I felt hot too. Not only along my forehead, but across the length of my entire body, trapping me in some invisible, whispery fire. It reminded me of the year before when I got sick. A fever was whipping itself into another searing affliction, and I turned violently from side to side and thrashed about in my bed. If I wanted my body to cool down for just a moment, my mind wasted no time in racing to the sights and sounds that visit us in a feverish state.

Water. Visions of water consumed me. As I lay in my room

in the shadows of some unseen flame, I thought my delusions would transport me to the water. Not the soft and sultry water of day. Not that warm blanket fluffed by the sun, but the cold black water of night, those soaking wet sheets left damp by the moon. I felt certain this fever would transport me to the water that I longed to be submerged in, which would relieve my pain and force my body temperature to drop. Yet it was not water I saw or felt, but air: a warm balmy air that felt good. At first I basked in this air, feeling the raw exhilaration of its warmth.

"It's because of this fever," I reasoned. "It's because I've never had a fever this high and my spirit longs to be quenched by it, yearns to be purified by flame."

This air turned warmer and denser, but I didn't mind it at all; it felt good. As in all delusions, feverish or not, *things that aren't are and things that are aren't*, and I realized I was not burning from this air, but being comforted by it, glowing from it, even if, for an August night, it felt not warm enough, not hot enough, propelling me once more to bolt up in my bed.

The window! The messenger must have left some window open, and a breeze had caused my room to go cold. In my feverish state, I got up to close it. I wanted to lock all the doors as well, but it was too late. There was no time to act. This air was no longer cooling down but heating up, throbbing in intensity. Why could I not see it? Why could I only sense it? Air this hot was always visible, always! What with its waves of rising heat. With its rays of weltering warmth.

Why could I not see it and only feel the vibrations of its flames, the throbs of its shockwaves? Why could I only sense it whirling and spinning somewhere about me? It had to be another dusk of illusion, some partial state of insanity. Who in their right mind had never seen such a phenomenon? Air that spun and turned on itself and could be sensed but not seen. Air that almost felt like water as it overshadowed me even without light in the room. Air and water. How different the two elements were. No wonder one evaporated into the other. No wonder one repelled the other. I wanted to locate this whirling plume of air, but I couldn't find it and soon realized why. This air was not out in the open, but inside me, deep in the crevices within.

I wanted to seize it, to clasp and embrace it. But how could I? How could I grab a hold of this air moving within me? It was warm and thick, so hot and dense that, suddenly, I could breathe again. In and out it went, yet it was not my lungs inhaling it, but my body. The very pores of my skin expanded and soaked it all in, surging and leaving me to hope this feeling would never end.

I had blown out the very last candle on my dresser, but now another light took form within: a soft glow that circulated and coursed inside me and I needed to nourish this fire. I needed to fuel its raw exhilaration before it extinguished itself. As long as this force had insinuated itself inside me, I would not permit it to escape, not even from the house. Once more I sprang up in my bed, hoping to lock all the doors and windows when, just as quickly, I stopped at the sound of another voice, my own.

"Stop!" I ordered myself. "Just stop!"

So I did just that. Whether I was still feverish or whether my body temperature had finally quelled, I stopped. There was no need to lock anything in, no need to lock anything out. I felt the flames of one fire subsiding, the embers of another now simmering, some embryonic cinder smoldering and firmly being planted.

I could no longer move. I couldn't even think. The mystery embedded in this message had left me that siphoned, that spent, as if all the mass and matter of my innocence had evaporated into some perfect storm of disintegration. If I could make no sense of this right now, come morning I hoped to. By then I planned on deciphering the reason behind tonight's encounter and trusted in everything to be fine—*todo bien*. I knew one thing already. Miracle or not, mix-up or not, I was going nowhere tomorrow—nowhere at all!

The water—the one place where my spirit no longer

wished to go. The water—it no longer coaxed or cradled me, but swelled with whisper and warning. *Stop, Clara! Just Stop!* And I would do exactly that: stop everything!

Even if, by some other miracle, or even if by some otherworldly intervention my prospects were to change and, suddenly, I were presented with an airplane ticket or passage on a ship that guaranteed me absolute freedom without the slightest chance of any risk or peril, one thing shone incandescently clear within me and without. Come morning, I would not be leaving Cuba. I could no longer conceive of it. No matter what anyone said or anyone did, I no longer harbored any notion of departing from my homeland. Whether this had all been a vision, a hallucination, a dream or just delirium, for the moment I bore no concept of leaving—none whatsoever!

CONCEPTIONS

"*A sister!* Did I hear correctly, Father? I'm going to be having a sister? Why didn't you say anything earlier, Father? Why didn't you tell me?"

It was a beautiful night in the Heavens. A stunning but solemn celestial night. Glowing winds soared through the stratosphere. Galaxies far and wide shone in spiral incandescence. In all the infinite vastness of the universe, there was nothing as glorious as the radiance of outer space. Nothing as exalted as its luminous panoramas, or as soothing as its lustrous sweep of astronomical delights. But despite the grandeur and serenity of all this weightless splendor, the Creator of the Universe appeared baffled by his son's barrage of questions.

"Why, Son, I just assumed you already knew. I mean, you are the Son of Man, aren't you? That means you know everything I do."

If the Son of Man could tell by his father's tone he was being toyed with, he was in no mood for games right now and made it perfectly clear with his own tone—an angry one!

"No, Father, it doesn't mean that, and you know it! There's plenty you keep from me, plenty I don't know! And please, Father, if I've told you once, I've told you a million times. Do not call me the Son of Man anymore! You know I can't stand that name! You know how much I hate it."

Off in the near distances, Earth and her companions spun and orbited in quiet contentment around the tiny halo that was the sun. But off in the far distances, swirling galaxies tossed and turned; clusters of constellations formed towering volcanoes and giant pyramids lit up the skies. Despite the exhilaration from these invigorating views, the Creator of the Universe managed to keep Himself calm and constrained. The Son of Man was simply baiting him, but He would not take the hook. Not with tensions as strained as they had been lately between Father and Son.

"But Son, how can you hate that name when you were born for man's sake? When you were born to save him from his sins and offer him salvation? You know that, Son, just as you know you can't escape your destiny."

The Son of Man had no interest in any lectures right now. He'd been hearing the same outmoded sermon for the last two thousand years. Normally, he acquiesced to his father's notions and even bent to His will. But not tonight. Tonight the Son of Man was all charged up. He felt the eruptions of a thousand solar flares stirring within him and felt like challenging the Creator's views.

"His sins, Father? Man's sins? How about Man's stupidity? How about his selfishness? Or how about his complete lack of conscience, Father? Man has absolutely no conscience. Who's going to save him from himself, Father? Who?"

"Well...you are, Son, and you know it."

If the Son of Man didn't like being toyed with, he liked it even less when the Creator took a condescending tone with him.

"No, Father, I will not! I tried it once and it didn't work, and I'm not trying it a second time. Honestly, Father, I don't know why you made *anyone* for man's sake. What good did it do? I mean, look at the mess that man has made down there. Look at the mess that man is and always will be!"

Just then both Father and Son looked down toward pathetic planet Earth. In all the enormity of the universe and its bursts of boundless brilliance, plastic planet Earth seemed the only blemish in all of creation, a pimple on the face of the galactic sky. But it hadn't always been that way. Once, not long ago, Earth had shone too, quite luminously even, especially for not even being a star. But that was *before* man.

One glance at Earth these days revealed its true dismal state: the only heavenly body mired down in muck and misery and drowning in its own excrement. Earth had evolved into nothing but a conduit for consternation and conflict. While all the other heavenly bodies emitted a radiance of light and energy and glowed resplendently, Earth looked tired and tarnished, enveloped in a dusk of dirt and pollution, engulfed in more than a partial state of darkness. Even from light-years away, its many flaws shone shamelessly for all to see: all the conflagration, all the clashing and contamination. What a sorry sight. What a nasty shame to see the once-glorious Earth obscured by a thick nebula of petty narcissism and self-loathing.

Yet these days something more troubling worried the Creator: man's penchant for pollution, his uncanny gift for contamination. These dubious talents of man had extended to outer space; they had begun to soil the galactic sky with annoying contraptions that now junked up the Heavens and threatened to turn it all into a celestial cesspool: satellites and rockets, shuttles and space probes just to name a few; buzzing, floating insects that not only disturbed the weightless beauty of the universe, but spied and beamed down mysterious data back to man for his dark and malicious motives. Not to mention all the particles of dust and gas released by the exhaust and fuel for these gadgets. Where did man think it all went? That it just evaporated into nothingness?

How it broke the Creator's heart to witness all this desecration, the tons of floating debris both on the Earth and high above it. From its very inception, the Creator had taken great pride in Earth's potential and reveled in its beauty. But to see it now was to commiserate over beauty diminished, beauty disgraced. Why couldn't man accept his limits and be content with what he had? Why was man always defiling and defacing everything?

"Honestly, Father, I don't know why you just don't destroy the Earth and put it out of its misery. What's stopping you?"

The Creator looked aghast at such a suggestion. "Son, how can you say such a thing? How can you even think such a thing?"

"Don't feel bad, Father. It's no big deal. Why don't you just look at Earth as your one and only mix-up. There are plenty of other planets out there thriving and actually doing well. Earth was just a bad seed, Father—a weed. Pull it from the garden and destroy it! Snuff it from the garden of light that is an otherwise perfect universe."

The winds of the universe immediately evaporated. Sound itself instantly disintegrated. The Creator of both couldn't believe what He was hearing, even if He certainly suspected the source of such warped and wanton views.

"What's the matter with you, Son? Where in the world are these radical ideas coming from?"

"They're not radical, Father. They're quite sensible, actually. Remember my parable about the prodigal son? Well, Earth is the prodigal planet, Father. Except this prodigal planet seems destined never to learn and should not be welcomed back by you. Destroy it, Father! Get it over with and destroy it!"

Before responding, the Creator diverted his attention for a moment toward those great distances that, for Him, were easily within reach, but for everyone else stretched into mind-numbing infinity. He stopped and stared at a black pinprick in the central distance, a violently spinning abyss that sucked in and devoured anything light-years within its reach. Black holes, as man liked to call them. Vacuums of violent gravity.

The Creator couldn't quite put his finger on it, but He wasn't terribly fond of black holes these days, even if He had created them. These days they conjured up all sorts of unpleasant thoughts and images.

"Of course I won't destroy it, Son. How can you even conceive of such a thing? What's gotten into you?"

"But it would be so easy, Father. See that black hole over there? The one you keep looking at? That's exactly where you should send Earth: straight into the great garbage disposal of outer space. Isn't that what you created them for, Father? For ultimate annihilation?"

The Creator diverted his attention back on His son again, but in dismay and disbelief. What was going on with the lad? Even the Creator was shocked to hear such extremist thinking, and He had heard it all.

"No, Son. I absolutely *won't* do it! The Earth may be a prodigal planet, as you say, but underneath all that perdition and confusion is much promise still, and I won't abandon Earth—not with all the work I put into it."

"You put six days of work into it, Father—six days! Maybe that's what the problem's been. It was all a rush job."

The Creator of the Universe wanted to pray for continued self-control right now, but realized the only being He could pray to was Himself, and there would be no point.

"Yes, Son, but I'll kindly remind you it was six days of straight, tireless, nonstop work, and never once did I take a break. Besides, you know I made a contract with man. After the Great Flood I gave my word never to destroy Earth again, and I plan on keeping that word."

"Please, Father. *I* should ask what's gotten into you. You destroy and create and destroy all the time. Why should this be any different?"

"I just told you, Son. I gave my word and I plan on keeping it. Don't forget that, I not only *am* the Word, I *keep* my word."

Before contemplating his next volley, the Son of Man

turned his attention toward a dazzling shooting star arching wide across the Heavens. He certainly had no need for making any wishes, but he made one anyway.

"Well, good luck then, Father. I'd just as soon see you annihilate it all, but this is your baby, as they say."

The Creator of the Universe shook his iridescent and splendiferous head. He couldn't help but be astounded and shocked by so unrelenting a condemnation of that which he had fashioned in His own image: man.

"Where is all this coming from, Son? This sudden blood lust of yours. Don't forget you're the Prince of Peace, after all."

"That's a good one, Father! I am the Prince of Peace, but you want me to go down to Earth, launch the battle of all battles, Armageddon, and defeat the Prince of Darkness in the biggest showdown of the universe? Have you thought of all the bloodletting that confrontation will unleash, Father? Don't you find it all a bit ironic?"

The Creator of the Universe cringed, turning and looking his son squarely in the eye with a fierce and focused stare. It was a gaze so severe that even the Son of Man could barely stomach it.

"Son, if I've told you once, I've told you a million times. *Do not* mention that individual in my presence! Now, what's the matter with *you?* Up until recently you were all for the big bang. You couldn't wait to bring that Satan to his knees and get him to conform. All of a sudden you're scared of a little blood? Don't focus on the blood, Son. Remember what this is for, you just said it yourself: saving man from himself. That's the purpose of your going back down, Son—the purpose of the Second Coming."

The Son of Man kept his eye on that blazing shooting star he had finished wishing upon and commanded it toward him, bringing it spinning high overhead and making it burst in a refulgent shower of light straight above him.

"Sorry, Father. I've had plenty of time to reconsider things, and Man does not deserve to be rescued. I meant it when I said I wasn't going back down. So forget about any Second Coming, Father—just forget it! By the way, where are those scrolls of mine? What did you do with them?"

The Creator of the Universe knew exactly what the Son of Man was alluding to with mention of these scrolls. He simply ignored the question for, in addition to all His many greatnesses, the Creator could also be the Great Ignorer. Besides, He was too incensed right now to address anything other than his son's impudence and insubordination. It was one thing to mingle among man and challenge the authority of the high priests and scribes and the temple elders. It was another thing to challenge He who had created and would forever rule the Heavens.

"But Son, scripture has got to be fulfilled and you're six years overdue. You were supposed to go back down in '88, remember? You know that I wanted to wrap things up one generation after the homeland became a state."

"Too bad, Father. I've made up my mind. I'm *not* going back down."

"But you've got me seriously behind schedule, Son. The final conflict is long overdue, and you don't understand the gravity of the situation. You can't be serious when you say you're not going back down!"

"Oh, I've never been more serious about anything in my life, Father. I've had plenty of time to contemplate all that Man did to me, all that Man is *still* doing to me, and if you think I'm going down to sweep him up so he can enjoy a life of eternal happiness, you can forget it, Father. It ain't happening!"

The Creator of the Universe found himself doing the unexpected just then: tapping into His deepest reserves of constraint, which happened to run very deep. He did this only under the most extreme of conditions: when it became absolutely necessary to maintain an even-tempered tone with the Son of Man.

"Come now, Son, let's be fair about this, shall we? There's

no need to be so hard on man. Just be patient with your brethren. He'll turn himself around, you'll see."

"Patient, Father? Are you serious? Not even with the patience of Job will man ever turn himself around. Really, I don't know what was in that dust you used, Father. From his very inception man has been nothing but trouble, nothing but grief."

The Creator must concede that the Son of Man did have a point there. Still, nobody was going to order Him around, not even his son. Before responding, the Creator continued holding himself in check. He took only a shallow breath of that soothing celestial air which had taken him mere seconds to fashion from nothing. A deeper breath would have produced great disturbances far and wide.

"It's not man's fault, Son. You mustn't blame him. You know whose fault it is. You know it's the doing of that snake, that Satan. You know it's all his deception and trickery and constantly doing his best to confuse and tempt man. *That's* whose fault it is."

The Son of Man peered over at that black hole off in the central portion of the galaxy. He had to admit that, as much as it frightened him to gaze upon that violently spinning vortex, he also found something alluring and enticing about it, something mesmerizing about its fierce and fantastical force.

"I'm sorry, Father, but I beg to differ. It's time to stop playing the blame game, time to stop shifting fault. You need to call a spade a spade, Father, and man's misfortune has nothing to do with Lucifer. It's all man and his conceit. It's all his own doing and you know it."

That was it! At the mere mention of that name, the Creator's self-imposed constraint burst open into a cascade of spatial shrapnel, every last drop of it. It was clear why constellations of fiery volcanoes were the most prevalent visual in the Heavens, why He so inspired their image.

"*Lucifer!* Did I hear that correctly, Son? Did I? So now you're on a first-name basis with him? You actually call that

Satan by name? Listen here, Son. You don't like being called the Son of Man. I don't like hearing the name Lucifer. Do not utter that devil's name in my presence again. Especially on a night like tonight, on the night of your sister's conception."

While there was nothing more intimidating than the expression on the Creator's inscrutable face during the times He truly turned angry, His tone could be equally menacing. The Son of Man decided to tone things down a bit.

"I'm sorry, Father. I meant no disrespect, and you know it."

The Creator instantly calmed Himself down. As incensed and enraged as He could get at times, He could also un-anger Himself just as quickly. He could change his tack just as easily, and decided to appeal to his son's conscience.

"It's all right, Son; all is forgiven. You know I'll forgive anything as long as one is truly sorry. Now, why don't you try doing the same thing with man? Why don't you try understanding that man is a just slow learner, a little dull if you will. But He'll get it eventually."

"Eventually, Father? Hasn't two thousand years been long enough? How much more time does man need? You know, I learned something invaluable when I was down there, Father. Sometimes you have to cut your losses, and well, this is one of those times."

"That's perfectly fine, Son. Let's do exactly that. Let's cut our losses, as you say. But first you have to go down there. First you have to make contact and fulfill scripture."

The Son of Man shook his head vigorously. "Sorry, Father, it ain't happening. Not in my lifetime anyway."

The Creator tried His best to ignore the low-brow colloquialism His son had just employed.

"Really, Son? Are you absolutely certain of that? I mean, you are going to live forever, remember?"

Just then, the Son of Man felt what seemed like a pelting shower of meteors, a hail of asteroids rain down upon his spirit, realizing that, no matter what he did or wherever he went, no matter how far into the outer reaches or the outer limits or even the most remote regions of the universe, his Father would always be there right alongside him.

"Please, Father, no need to remind me. I know that already."

The Creator of the Universe shook His head in total dismay. So now the Son of Man was knocking eternal life—the very bane of his existence, the one gift he had presented and offered mankind. If the Creator couldn't believe such infernal flippancy, He was convinced more than ever of the source, of who had influenced this attitude: Satan, that snake. Something had definitely transpired during the three days before his son's ascent into Heaven; those three days when the Son of Man had descended into hell after being on the cross. Since then, he had lightened up considerably on Lucifer. The Creator couldn't quite put a finger on it, but Satan had planted some kind of kernel in his son's head.

"Why are you being so cynical, Son? Why?"

"Because I know you're up to something, Father. This ill-conceived whim of yours to have another child. There's some scheme behind it and you know it. Tell me what it is, Father. What are you up to?"

"I'm not up to anything, Son. What makes you think thus?"

"Because I know you, Father. I know you and your mysterious ways. After two thousand years, you can't conceal things from me that easily. You don't do anything unless there's some grand design behind it all, just like when you had me conceived."

"You assume too much, Son, way too much."

"It's true, Father, and you know it. Hadn't you had enough of man and his misdeeds when you concocted the scheme for attaining salvation and eternal life? Just look at my name, Father, the name Jesus. What does it mean? It means *God saves*. And look at the name you want to give this girl, Father. It means *light*. If you had a reason for creating me, you've got a reason for creating her. It's that simple, Father. I don't believe you just want to be a parent again. You're not exactly the paternal type, Father."

The Creator fell absolutely silent. Even for Him, He who had created the Universe, there was nothing that stung quite as much as the mordant recriminations of one's angry offspring.

"You're absolutely right, Son. You've caught me red-handed as they say down there. I'll admit that, when you were conceived, I did have a grand scheme behind it all: man's salvation. I made you the ultimate trade-off for eternal life. I wanted you to be perfect and become the ultimate overachiever. Not this time, Son. I'm older now, I'm wiser. I just want to relax this time around. I want to enjoy fatherhood plain and simple, that's all; and I've decided there's nothing more precious than a daughter."

The jabs from one's offspring could sting, but so could the barbs from one's parent.

"Thanks a lot, Father. So now sons aren't good enough? Is that what you're saying?"

The Creator smiled slightly and came over to put a consoling hand on his son's shoulder, a right hand.

"Now, Son, I didn't mean it like that and you know it. It's just that, well, thanks to man, daughters have always gotten the short end of the stick and I plan on rectifying that."

Despite so rare and tender a confession, the Son of Man remained skeptical and on guard. He couldn't quite put his finger on it, but he knew he was still being toyed with. Such were the drawbacks to being part of the Godhead. Sure, he and the Creator and the Holy Spirit all belonged to the Trinity, but there was still plenty the Creator of the Universe kept from him. He purposely arranged it so that, in the pyramidal structure of the Trinity, the Son of Man was not fully privy to all the designs and schemes that took place at the top.

"I don't believe you, Father. You're conning me. This is all some conniving scheme of yours, and you know it. Tell me what you did with those scrolls, Father. Where did you hide them?"

The Great Ignorer cast aside all mention of the scrolls again, focusing instead on his son's atrocious and foul use of language.

"I'm not conning you, Son. And please, must you use that type of language up here? What a foul mouth you've acquired: *con, ain't, cutting losses*. Remember where you are, Son. You didn't talk that way even when you walked among man."

"I was tempted to, Father, believe me."

"But you didn't, Son. You controlled yourself. And I know where all this filth is coming from. This must have been what you learned in hell those three days you were down there. Is that how Satan contaminated your head?"

The Son of Man could be a great ignorer himself, and decided to borrow a page from the Creator's book. He knew it drove his Father absolutely wild not knowing what had happened down there, what took place during those three days of his descent into hell. But as long as the Creator refused to hand over the missing scrolls, the Son of Man had no intention of making his own revelations. Yes, there could be certain advantages to the divisional structure of the Trinity: sometimes those at the top of the pyramid couldn't always see all the way down.

"Pardon me, Father. I didn't mean to offend you with my language. How's this for a compromise: you tell me what you're up to and I might reconsider, I might just go back down."

If the sheen of the stars and the glow of the galaxies should have flared up in the eternal light of the Creator's eyes, He was still Creator of the Universe and would not allow Himself to be tempted or toyed with, not even by the Son of Man.

"For the last time, Son—nothing! It's like I told you. I simply want to enjoy fatherhood this time around. It's difficult for me to admit this, but when you were growing up I was so wrapped up in all the matters of salvation that I missed out on way too much, on all the cute little things you said and did, on all your milestones. This time I'm not letting that happen. I plan on being there for all the important things in your sister's life: the sports events, the recitals, the birthday parties."

"Birthday parties? It's Cuba, Father. *What* birthday parties?"

"Oh, don't worry, Son. She'll have birthday parties like no other. You'll see."

"Well, that's great to hear, Father. In the meantime, what birthday parties did I ever have? Even now, when despicable man celebrates my birthday, is it even on the actual date? No, of course not. Let's see, man can figure out how to send rockets to the moon and space probes to explore the deepest recesses of outer space and he builds computers capable of performing millions of calculations per second, but he still hasn't figured out my real birthday."

The Creator patted his son's shoulder affectionately and in consolation.

"Let it go, Son. I know when you're real birthday is. That's all that matters."

"No, Father! I will not let it go! What type of celebration is it for me, anyway? The whole Nativity is only so man can give himself gifts and satisfy his own selfish needs."

The Son of Man suddenly brought his invective to a halt, his emotive countenance flaring in visible anger as he looked down with contempt on the third planet from the sun and wished it would just detonate into trillions of subatomic particles.

"You know what, Father? I've just reconsidered, and I will definitely *not* be going back down—definitely not!"

"Son, Son, just calm down, will you! You need to

understand that man celebrates your birthday with acts of giving, with the gifts of sharing, that's all. Believe it or not, those are the two main reasons I've decided to be a parent again—for your sake, for your own good."

"Listen, Father, I'm in no mood for any more of your games tonight. I've got things to do and places to go, and I don't feel like deciphering your riddles. What do you mean for my sake?"

"For your sake, Son, for your own good even. You see, you've been an only child for too long, and unfortunately, you've adopted many of the traits of an only child. Trust me, Son, you're going to benefit greatly from having a sibling. Not only will you have someone to share things with, but someone to talk to and confide in as well."

"Oh yes, Father, I'm really going to have a lot in common with someone two thousand years younger than I am, aren't I?"

"Two thousand years is nothing and you know it, Son. Besides, your sister will catch up in no time; I'm making sure of it. I plan on making her extra smart."

The Son of Man turned and looked straight at the Creator's iridescent but inscrutable face, the only other being in the universe who could do so without being singed to a crisp.

"Smarter than I, Father?"

"Well, let's just say she'll have different talents, Son. I made your primary gift the gift of healing, the gift of touch. Your sister will have the gift of tongues."

The Son of Man raised an eyebrow and crossed his arms.

"Isn't that a gift that girls *already* have, Father? You know it is. Besides, I wouldn't exactly call it a gift. It's more a curse."

"Son, Son, there you go again. When did you become such a contrarian? You love to oppose me these days just for sport."

"Honestly, Father, don't you know when I'm joking? You don't have a sense of humor anymore—if you ever did, that is. Why 'tongues' of all things?"

"Why tongues? Very simple, Son. Have you seen what's been happening down there lately? Technology is destroying man. It's sucking all the humanity and soul from him. Technology is terrorizing man and he doesn't even realize it. Man has got to get back to basics, Son: language, speaking, words."

"And you are not the least bit biased, Father, are you? Considering you *are* the Word."

"Well, I guess you could say just a little, Son."

"A little, Father? Well, I hate to be the bearer of bad news, but there's a reason why that is happening, why words and language are things of the past and nobody cares about them. They're boring, Father—boring!"

"And you're not the least bit biased yourself, are you Son? You, who've had two thousand years to master all the languages in existence, but insist on speaking only Aramaic and that little smidgen of Hebrew you know."

The Son of Man shrugged his shoulders casually, unaffectedly. "It's like you said, Father. It's not my gift. It's not my bag."

There he went again, those lowbrow expressions of his.

"Regardless, Son. That's not why language is dying. It's because of something else, something sinister that's awakened man's need for instant gratification, man's built-in desire for pushing the limits and hoarding knowledge. It's because of...of the *E* word."

"The '*E* word,' Father? Evolution?"

"Electronics, Son, *that* '*E* word.'"

"What's wrong with electronics, Father? First comes lightning, then electricity, then electronics. It's just evolution, Father, and not even you can do anything about it."

All at once, the Creator's tone and expression and his very essence fashioned itself into a force of cosmic fury.

"Of course I can, Son! I can bring it all down if I want! Electronics is the new Tower of Babel, and remember what I did with that, Son—I brought it all down! The Tower of Babel had man thinking he could accomplish anything he wanted, that he could be just like me. Well, electronics has given man the same illusion: except, now he thinks he's even *more* like me. Man needs to realize that anytime I want, I can flip the big switch off in the sky."

"Do it, Father! Flip it off! Start with that satellite over there. Just wrap your hand around it and crunch it into dust, pulverize it!"

"No, Son. I won't do it! Not until I've given man a chance to reconcile, to realize all the harm it creates and he turns away from it on his own. Not until man realizes where the 'E word' comes from and who is behind it all."

"Who is behind it all, Father? Who?"

"Who do you think, Son? The one and only enemy himself: Satan, the Great Tempter, the Great Defacer. He's behind all this technology and man has absolutely no clue. That's how great his final deception will be; that's how skilled a con man he is."

"Come now, Father, you can't be serious. What technology are you talking about? The Internet? That infantile mode of communication that man has just barely gotten off the ground? Why, I find it one of the most laughable and primitive things he's ever invented."

"That's because you're witnessing it in its infancy, Son, in its genesis. Just you wait. You haven't seen anything yet. Wait another fifteen years or so for YouTube, for Facebook and Twitter. Just wait for iPods and iPads and iPhones to rule and dominate every aspect of man's life."

"iPads, iPods, and iPhones? YouTube, Facebook, and Twitter? What language are you speaking, Father? What foreign words have you just uttered?"

"The language of technology, Son. A one-world language of terror that will connect man to his universal doom."

Son looked at Father in disbelief, not knowing whether to regard this as some latent prophecy, or what it really sounded like: paranoia, some implausible conspiracy theory. He tried his best to decipher the Creator's inscrutable countenance, but to no avail.

"See how you keep things from me, Father! See what I was saying earlier. What in the world are these ominous-sounding things?"

"Not *what* are they Son, but what will they be. They haven't even been conceived yet, but I can assure you they will be, and that Satan will utilize them as his last tool against man. It will be Satan's final way of tempting and distracting man. Most of the gadgets will even bear the mark of the beast: an apple, an apple with a bite in it, to commemorate man's disobedience and fall from grace, when man first ate of the fruit."

As much as the Son of Man hated to admit it, these sinister forebodings were arousing alarm and concern in him. The cold winds of the Heavens caused him to shiver and tingle as they moved through him and within him.

"I still don't get it, Father, what all these things will actually do."

"You'll see, Son, you'll see in due time, the way Satan will utilize graphics and visuals to bring about the destruction of Man. How these gadgets will employ images and sounds to defile the temple by actually rewiring man's brain. It's just Satan being true to himself. Isn't that what he's about, Son? The image? Especially when that image is a false one, when it deceives and misleads."

"Come now, Father. This is all too much, even for you."

"No, Son! Why do you think Satan has always steered clear of words and only utilized images? Why? There's clearly no disputing the written word, but images can take whatever form one wants, especially for enacting misdeeds."

As the Son of Man contemplated the Creator's apocalyptic warnings, he took a moment to fixate on a quaint and quietly shining quasar. Of all the heavenly bodies, quasars were his favorite: the most distant but luminous objects in the universe, the very last remnants of early existence. In some respects quasars seemed the outcasts of the universe, the dinosaurs of outer space. This one was particularly beautiful, a perfectly white sphere enshrouded in hazy mists of glowing energy and swirls of faint violet lights.

"Now, hold on a second, Father. There seems to be a slight contradiction going on here."

"Don't be silly, Son. There's no contradiction in anything I say."

"But there is, Father. On the one hand, you're all about the word. And you've just finished condemning what will be man's ultimate downfall: his obsession and worship of the image. Yet what did you do when you created man? You fashioned him in your own image!"

"Of course I did, Son. I had to fashion him from something, didn't I? Don't forget that man has never actually seen my image. Don't forget that the images of spiritual beings cannot be captured. That's because an image is not the least bit relevant when it comes to the essence of being. What does it matter what I look like? Of what possible importance are my looks? None! Man has yet to accept this, so I'm debating whether he'll ever be allowed to see my image—ever!"

The Son of Man desperately needed a breather. This was way too much to handle, way too much information to digest all at once. He focused his attention back on the sheerness of that primal quasar, on all its pulsating force, trying to draw insight from it even as he suspected the Creator's true motives in all this: simply trying to divert attention from the matter at hand.

"Listen, Father, I may have no clue as to what you're talking about, but I'll tell you this much: you need to stop pinning man's flaws on someone other than man. Why can't you accept that? Whether man decides to be ruled by false images or not, it's all his own doing and nobody else's. Man loves temptation, Father. He loves giving into it. It's just his nature, and he can't escape it. I should know, Father. I lived among man, I was man."

"No, Son! I won't accept that line of thinking. It's Satan. It's that felonious fiend down there. It's the Great Defacer himself! That's what all these gadgets and technology will ultimately prove to be: Satan's final way of enticing man, of entrapping man. You'll see!"

The Son of Man attempted to stay respectful, but he rolled his eyes in an orbit of speculation.

"Well, Father, you obviously have your way of seeing things, but I will continue to disagree with you. Man was a mistake, an experiment gone terribly wrong. I have no idea what Facebook and Twitter and all these strange-sounding names mean, but the only reason you keep investing in man is to save face yourself."

No mistaking or misreading the expression on the Creator's usually inscrutable face this time, no diffusing the constellation of fury that flared across his outraged countenance.

"No, Son! I do not need to save face! And man is not an experiment gone wrong. He just strays off course; he just needs to be reeled back in."

"Well, Father, you can be the one to reel him back in. And maybe you can get this new offspring of yours to assist you, but I'll have no part of it. And good luck, by the way. You know how accepting man is of woman."

"Son, I already told you. She's not going to be part of any grand scheme. I just want to be a parent again. And I'll remind you that this offspring of mine, as you refer to her, will be your sister soon enough, so please show some respect."

"No grand scheme, huh? Why Cuba then, Father? If you have no ulterior motives, why Cuba of all places?"

"Why not Cuba, Son?"

"You said you wanted to relax, Father, that you wanted to

take it easy. Yet you know that Cuba is always a lightning rod of controversy, a hotbed of turmoil. Why Cuba if all you want is to take it easy?"

"I said I wanted to relax, Son. I didn't say I wanted to be bored stiff."

The Creator deflected this inquisition quite easily, but the Son of Man wasn't buying it. Despite the insistent denials, this whole Cuba angle wasn't adding up. The Son of Man employed his innate gifts of calculating and theorizing and computating when it finally occurred to him *why* Cuba.

"I know why Cuba, Father. I know why. Because Cubans have been praying to you for the last forty years to liberate them from Fidel, and you've ignored them."

"No, Son, that's not why."

"Because their patron saint has been petitioning you for the last forty years and you've ignored her."

"No, Son that's not why either."

"Because the exiles have been begging you for the last forty years to liberate their homeland from Communism, and you've ignored them."

"No, Son, not at all."

"Then why Cuba, Father? Tell me why."

"All right, Son. I'll tell you why Cuba. Isn't it obvious? Just look at it down there. Cuba is wild and exciting. Cuba is bold and untamed. Surely you can feel its restless energy, all its raw exhilaration. It's like that raggedy and tattered quasar over there that refuses to collapse, refuses to die. I mean, look at all those Cubans risking their lives by taking to the water. That's what I like to see, Son, people willing to take risks."

Father and Son looked down for a moment, taking note of the alligator island and how almost fragile it looked; how its patch-quilt of rolling greenness rose gently from a blanket of burning blue; how the soft sultry slopes of its tropical terrain peeked bashfully from behind a crown of shining clouds.

"They're cutting their losses, Father, that's all they're

doing."

"They're fighting for their lives, Son, and that's what I like to see: a good fight. Just look at all those homemade vessels and all the rickety contraptions. You have to admit that some of them are pretty ingenious Son, especially the water taxis. Cubans do have a knack for contrivances, don't they?"

"It's a mess, Father, that's all it is—one enormous mess."

"It reminds me of the Exodus, Son. It reminds me of the parting of the Red Sea. And you know how fond of the sea I am. It was the first thing I formed out of the great abyss."

"Yes, Father, I know you love the sea. I love the sea too."

"I know you do, Son, I know you do. Oh, how I miss the days you used to teach along the shores of Galilee. It was mesmerizing to watch you, intoxicating. Nobody's ever held a crowd captive the way you have, Son."

"You mean that, Father? You really mean it?"

"Of course I mean it, Son. And just like your Middle Eastern ancestors, Cubans are attached to the sea. It's in their blood."

"Is that what you're planning on having her do, Father? Teach along the shores of Varadero?"

"Don't be silly, Son. I hope she never goes anywhere near Varadero and all those tourists."

The Son of Man didn't know what to think. He almost felt convinced by the seeming rationale of this all, but an infernal iota of doubt still plagued him.

"I don't know, Father. It seems to me you're still up to something and now I suspect it involves the sea. *Wait a minute!* Isn't their patron saint enjoined to the water somehow? Didn't she appear in a vision at sea herself? Don't tell me she crawled out of the depths?"

The Creator of the Universe adopted a perfect Cuban accent for his reply.

"No, Son. La Virgen de la Caridad del Cobre was found floating at sea by three Cuba fisherman, remember?"

"That's right!" declared the Son of Man. "Cubans are definitely tied to the sea. But why are you insisting that girl not take off on that dangerous contraption tomorrow? Why?"

"You just said it yourself, Son. I don't want her on that dangerous contraption because she's with child, because she's conceived."

"So, Father? You had my mother carry me into Egypt on an ass right after I was born; that didn't bother you any."

"Please, Son. Is it going to be tit-for-tat from now on? Is it? Your mother whisked you into Egypt to keep you safe, to spare you from the massacre that Herod had ordered; you know that. I'm keeping your sister in Cuba for much the same reason."

"Cuba is safe, Father? Is that what you're saying? The same Cuba that's under constant threat of invasion by its neighbor to the north? The same Cuba with a foreign naval base that the Cubans bitterly resent and can be used against them at any moment? I wouldn't exactly call that safe, Father."

"True, Son, but that's not the type of safe I'm talking about. You see, Cuba may be a Communist dictatorship, it may be under the rule of tyranny, but there's more faith in Cuba than in most parts of the world, and to be surrounded by all that faith *will* keep her safe."

"Not to mention she'll be on an island, which means she'll be surrounded by water. Is that part of her safety?"

"No, Son, that's just for my enjoyment. I really needed a change of scenery after all the dryness and dustiness of Judea and Palestine. This time I want water, Son, plenty and plenty of water."

The Son of Man reacted with mild indifference. "I know you love the sea, Father, but when did you become so obsessed with it?"

"I've always been at one with the water, Son, always, ever

since the very dawn of Creation. Don't forget that before I created light, my spirit moved upon the face of the waters. Why do you think three-fourths of the Earth is covered by it? I made water for my sake, for my inspiration. The water is mine, Son. I gave man dominion over the land and deserts and mountains so he'd leave the oceans alone, so he'd leave the skies alone. If I wanted man to have dominion of the seas, I would have given him gills. If I'd wanted man to have dominion of the skies, I would have given him wings. Those are my realms, Son, mine and mine alone. But look at what man has slowly been doing to them: infiltrating them, trashing them."

The Son of Man nodded eagerly in agreement, the persuasiveness of the Creator's words lighting the flames of his smoldering resentment.

"That's exactly what I've been telling you, Father. Give man enough time and he'll ruin anything he touches. You know that. You've seen it happen time and time again. But don't be fooled by the Cubans, Father. They're no different. Look at what a catastrophe they've made of their island. Look at the disaster they've made of both land and water."

Again, both Father and Son stopped to glance down at the alligator island. There it was—hidden and inconspicuous but stirring in the chaos of its turbulent beauty. Sure, it had its flaws, but nowhere near as many as the rest of the planet.

"And to think I gave them the loveliest land ever beheld by human eyes...just to think."

"It's a betrayal, Father, a complete slap to your inscrutable face."

"To think it was a veritable Garden of Eden. That's what the island was, Son: a second Garden."

Just then, the Son of Man felt the stirrings of another turbulence: a mental one, an inward one, the rays and waves and pulsations of analysis and conclusion shooting across the universe of his mind in a speed faster than light and only made possible by He who had actually created light.

"Wait a minute, Father! Now I get it. Now I understand *why* Cuba. Yes, it all makes sense now!"

"What makes sense, Son? Pray, tell me."

"Well," he began excitedly. "Isn't it obvious, Father? This is your way of finally getting back at…" The Son of Man stopped himself; he'd almost done it again, called the enemy by name. "Your way of getting back at Satan."

"I'm not following you, Son. How so?"

"It's very simple, Father. You just said it yourself. Cuba was a second Garden of Eden. Well, what did Satan do in the first Garden of Eden? He tempted man. He brought about damnation. Satan invoked the contamination of Man's own soul. Well, hasn't the leader of your precious Cuba done the same thing with his own people? Isn't he like someone else we both know? The way he tempted his fellow Cuban and deceived him? The way he ushered in the ruination of the Cuban soul. You've found the perfect way of getting back at Satan, Father, and I must admit it's quite clever."

For a Being that was all about the word, and always kept His word, and also cherished the word because He *was* the Word, the Creator of the Universe suddenly found himself in a position He rarely ever did: at a loss for words, a complete loss. When He finally summoned some words, He said: "Well, Son, I will admit that's quite an interesting theory of yours, but that's not why."

"Of course it is, Father, of course it is! I don't even think you're aware of your own motives. It's too much a part of your cosmic unconsciousness, but it all makes sense. Doubly fascinating is that, Fidel is not only like the Serpent, he's like man himself. He's man giving in to his own temptation, man relishing in the delights of the forbidden but turning around and shifting culpability. Doesn't Fidel love to blame the embargo for all his country's ills and woes? We both know he does, Father. And we both know the problem is not the embargo. The problem is him."

"Son, where do you come up with this stuff? Really!"

"You know I'm right, Father, you know it. Before you banished man from the Garden, or should I say 'embargoed' in this case, didn't he try to blame it on the Serpent's deception? Didn't he even try to pin it on Eve? He did, Father! He did! But we both know it was only his lust for disobedience that brought about his downfall and led to your 'embargoing' him from the Garden, if you will. It was only Man himself."

The Creator of the Universe had to admit that, on a certain level, He was quite impressed by the Son of Man's sharp insight and His keen abilities to make such abstract connections, no matter how radical the thoughts or how unorthodox the views. In the infinitely eternal span of all Creation, only once before had the Creator encountered such radical thinking, only once—by he whose name remained unmentionable.

"Listen, Son, you may find this hard to believe, but Fidel is an angel compared to that demon, a veritable saint. I understand where this is all coming from: he got to you. During the three days before your ascension, he injected you with his venom. Tell me what he said to you, Son. What idea did that Satan plant in your head?"

The Son of Man hardened his stance now.

"What did you do with the scrolls, Father? Where did you hide them?"

But the Creator of the Universe had finally had enough. He didn't need to be questioned or harassed about anything by anybody, especially his own Son, to whom He owed no explanations.

"Which scrolls, Son? Which scrolls do you keep referring to? The ones that Gabriel just mentioned? The ones that cover your childhood and adolescence?"

"No, Father, not those. You know exactly which scrolls I'm talking about, the ones that should have been found with the Dead Sea Scrolls, the ones I personally dictated and come *after* the Book of Revelation. Those scrolls."

The Creator shrugged His unshakable shoulders nonchalantly.

"I don't know what happened to them, Son. But shouldn't you know? Didn't you just say you dictated them?"

"You're toying with me, Father, and you know it. How can you not know where the scrolls are when *you know everything*. You're the Creator of the Universe, for...well...you know for whose sake."

Again with the inappropriate language, again with the flippant outbursts; almost taking his own name in vain just now, or...had he actually implied the Creator's name?

"Tell you what, Son. How's this for a proposition: you fill me in on what happened during those three days you descended to, *you-know-where,* and I'll consider sending an army of angels down to look for these scrolls that have you so riled up."

The Son of Man took a moment to weigh his options, still focused on events billions of light-years away: this time the very tail-end of a supernova and its intriguing lifecycle. It was a phenomenon of astronomical physics, watching the fiery and tempestuous nova return to a normal level of intensity after having burned a thousand times stronger than its own brightness. A nova was a giant match that someone had struck and lit then snuffed out in space.

"Forget it, Father. I'll find them on my own. And by the way, you're making a big mistake by getting a Cuban woman involved in all this, you'll see."

"Why, Son? Why do you say that?"

"Shouldn't you already know, Father? Didn't you create them?"

"Yes Son, but go ahead. Enlighten me."

"All right, Father. For starters, they're all hot tempered."

"I know that, Son, I know."

"And volatile."

"I know that too, Son."

"Fiery and tempestuous."

"Yes, Son, I know, but that's what I like that about them."

"Worst of all, Father, they love to argue and criticize and have to have the last word in everything—always!"

"That's all women, Son, all women. But regardless, that doesn't work with me. Remember, I enjoy the last word because I *am* the Word."

"There's only one redeeming feature about Cuban women, Father. They're...well...quite frankly, they're hot."

"Beautiful, Son. The word is 'beautiful' up here. But yes, I agree with you, they're quite stunning. Did you get a load of her mother, Son? I wasn't going to place much emphasis on the physical, but while I'm at it, I think I'll give Luz the gift of beauty too."

"Wow, Father, this girl is going to have everything, isn't she? The gift of tongues. The gift of beauty. Smart. What other gifts do you plan on endowing her with?"

"Well, let's see...I think that pretty much covers it."

"Just don't shower her with her mother's indecisiveness or temper, Father. That Clara may be beautiful, but have you seen what a little fireball she is? She isn't just a nova, she's a supernova."

"Yes, Son, but I like that about her."

"Well I don't, Father! She's a middle sister. And you know how middle children always have problems. It was so great seeing Gabriel put her in her place. I found it absolutely enthralling!"

"Son, Son, you need to understand that it's a different world from when you were down there. Back then women were second-class citizens. You know that."

"They're still second-class citizens, Father."

"True, Son, but that's one thing I hope to change. That's why I need a woman who can assert herself and who's sure of

| 157 |

herself. That's why a Cuban woman will be perfect for the job. There's no pushing them around."

"*Aha, Father!* You just admitted it! *Perfect for the job!* See! You are up to something. Now what job are you talking about?"

I didn't mean it like that, Son. What I meant is that sons and daughters are different, that's all. They have to be raised differently. They've got different sensibilities and…well…Clara will provide your sister with the proper nurturing and guidance she'll need."

"I don't see how, Father. It seems to me this girl has plenty to learn about herself. She's got serious trust issues that began with her own father and the way his work was more important than his children. Sound familiar?"

An absolute quiet settled upon and pierced its way through the Heavens, silencing both Father and Son. The Creator of the Universe had just been baited again, but this time He actually felt He deserved it, felt the taunt was merited. A contrite expression swept across His inscrutable face, and He knew there was no way out of this one.

"I know exactly where you're coming from, Son, and I couldn't agree with you more."

"Really, Father?"

"Yes, Son, of course I do. I know that, as a Heavenly father, I couldn't have been better. But I also know that, as an Earthly father, you needed a lot more interaction, that you never really bonded with Joseph."

The Son of Man grew momentarily moved by so disarming a candor, but this rare moment of tenderness also seemed a bit contrived.

"Why are you being so conciliatory, Father? Why?"

"Because, Son, it's the truth. Now please, just put aside all your doubts and fears and have a little more faith in your old man. You have to believe that I know what I'm doing."

The Son of Man felt sudden waves of contrition swelling

within him.

"But, Father, I thought *I* would always be your only child."

The Creator put another consoling arm around his son's shoulder.

"Come now, Son, sibling rivalry already? You know that you're my firstborn and always will be. No one can ever take that away from you, Son—no matter how many children I have."

"All right, Father, all right; I'll give you that much."

"Of course, Son. You will always be my one and only son. However, I never said anything about having a daughter, did I?"

The Son of Man had to concede that the Creator did have a valid point here.

"Well, I guess so, Father. When you put it that way, I guess you're right."

"Of course I'm right, Son. I always am and you know that. That's why I'm the Father and you're the Son. Now just trust and believe in me to set things right, will you?"

Miraculously, the Son of Man managed to pull himself out of that black hole of hostility ensconcing him all night and even perked up a bit, all the glowing in the Heavens invigorating him and making him take note of something.

"Just promise me one thing, Father—that You're not sending another savior down there, another Messiah."

The Creator shook his head and smiled with the rays of a thousand suns.

"See what I was saying earlier about learning to share things, Son. Well, part of sharing includes sharing responsibility."

The Son of Man's mercurial temper flared up again with doubt and speculation.

"No, Father. You can't be serious!"

"I honestly couldn't tell you, Son. I'm not getting in the

middle of it. I'm not meddling this time around. If your sister turns out to be another Messiah, so be it. Right now I'm just interested in expanding the family, that's it. Now go and rejoice, Son! Rejoice! Our family is growing and I for one can't wait for the blessed day."

In annoyance, the Son of Man shook his Father's right hand off his right shoulder and moved away from him.

"But, Father, how can you have such a cavalier attitude? You couldn't possibly be planning on going through the same thing all over again, could you?"

"Absolutely not, Son. You think I want to go through all that agony again? All that pain and suffering?"

"*Your* agony, Father? *Your* pain and suffering? What about mine? What about what I went through?"

The Son of Man's expression went blank. The light in his eyes faded like two dying moons, and the Creator of the Universe knew He should have quit while He was ahead. There was just no having a pleasant conversation with the Son of Man these days—none at all.

"Please, Son, must you dredge up all this unpleasantness right now? On so joyous a night as the conception of your sister?"

"Yes, Father, I must, and I most certainly will! I want you always to remember what I went through on that cross—always! Look at my hands, Father. Look at my hands and my feet!"

But the Creator of the Universe had no intention of looking at these and couldn't bring himself to do so anyway. He would rather strain His eternal eyes from peering countless galaxies away, than to gaze upon the black holes that still marked his son's hands and feet.

"Go ahead, Father, touch them! They still hurt, Father! Put your fingers right through my scars and maybe then you'll have an inkling of what I went through! Maybe then, Father!"

The Creator fell into an abyss of silence, a black hole of self-incrimination. Regret and embarrassment and the gravity of their combined force kept his eyes downcast. It seemed an eternity before He could lift them again and look his son square in the face.

"Son, I know what you went through. You make sure I know it every chance you get. Can't we let bygones be bygones? I was hoping for a fresh start, Son, and for your sister to be a major part of that fresh start."

But He who could accomplish the impossible was asking the impossible. Those two dying moons in the Son of Man's eyes rose again. They were filled with fire and fury. He had worked himself up into too much of a lather to let the issue go.

"I'm sorry, Father. But I just don't believe this is all as innocent as you're making it seem. For you to take so drastic a step means there's some monumental design behind it. What are you hiding from me, Father? And while we're at it, where are you hiding the missing scrolls? I hope you didn't destroy them."

The Creator shook his ever-splendiferous head with the force of a thousand winds, while brushing off his son's continued harangue.

"There's just no pleasing you, Son, no pleasing you whatsoever these days. Why don't you relax a moment and have a seat at my right hand so we can iron this all out."

But if Father hoped that Son would embrace the tender and paternal overture, the Son of Man remained too rattled and merely rebuffed him.

"No, Father, I will not join you at your right hand right now. We are not on official business. I've got other things to take care of at the moment—like finding the missing scrolls."

The Creator had had enough, and this time He cared not if His reply only exacerbated matters.

"All right, Son, suit yourself. Any idea where you'll start?"

The Son of Man was being toyed with again and he knew it.

"Yes, Father. I know exactly where to start: with the Holy Spirit. He'll tell me. He's part of both of us, Father, not just you. I'm going to find out from him, and while I'm at it, I'll have him tell me what this is really all about. He should know; after all, it was he who…you know…overshadowed that Cuban girl."

"Go ahead, Son. By all means, go ahead and find out anything you want. You'll see soon enough that it's simply what I'm saying: I want to be a parent again. I want you to have a sibling, Son. It wasn't fair to keep you an only child for so long."

"Well, Father, you're right about that. Just because I'm the Son of God doesn't mean I don't get lonely."

"I know that, Son, I know. And I'm trying to make amends, believe me. I know you've been lonely. I know you've needed someone other than your old man to talk to and confide in. I can think of no better way to remedy that loneliness than with a sibling."

"Really, Father? Well, I can think of numerous ways to remedy that loneliness, but they have nothing to do with a sibling."

The Creator's inscrutable face did not glow this time. It glowered, and in disgust.

"Please, Son, have some respect, will you? You know I don't like that type of talk."

"Respect, Father? What does respect have to do with it? It's just a fact of life, a fact of eternal life. You promised me I would get to consummate a union once I was up here, and I'm still waiting."

"Not now, Son, please! Now is not the right time for that."

"It's never the right time, Father. You never want to discuss *that* or anything else of importance to me."

"But Son, look at it this way: we've got all of eternity to discuss that; we've got 'til the end of time to resolve that issue."

"No, Father, I'm not waiting all of eternity, and there is no end of time, remember? I've waited long enough, and I want a timeline. I want to know when there will be a consummation, and I want Your word on it."

With all the pressing and truly important matters the Creator of the Universe had at hand, He couldn't believe this was first and foremost on his son's mind.

"But, Son, if you stop and think about it you'll realize we *have* discussed this before, and that you already have...well, you know...consummated."

"I have, Father? When, Father? Where and with whom?"

"With your church, Son, all the time, with those who believe in you and pray to you. Don't forget that you are the bridegroom and the church is your bride and that every time you save someone or anyone partakes of you, it's...well...it's consummation."

"No, Father. I'm not talking about *that* kind of consummation. I'm talking about the physical kind. Not the spiritual one, but the purely physical one—along with all the raw exhilaration that comes from it. And by the way, Father, that's not consummation either, it's Communion. So don't play your word games with me, Father. You're toying with me again and you know it."

"But Son, that's not what Heaven is about and *you* know it. If I made an exception for *you*, I'd have to make an exception for everyone who enters the pearly gates. I certainly won't have that going on up here—consummation that is; there's no way I'll condone it. You have to realize that along with technology, that's also been a tool the Enemy has used against man."

"A tool, Father? A tool? How about a gift? Your gift to man, remember? Now you want to brand it as one of Lucifer's tools."

"Please, Son! I told you, I don't want to hear that—"

"Lucifer, Father! Yes, Lucifer! There, I said his name. Stop giving him so much power, Father. He's just an angel. He's just a creature with wings who's starved for attention. He only has power when man gives him power—when you give him power."

Once again, the Creator of the Universe found Himself at a loss for words, so He merely sighed in exasperation. His breath expelled only the force of hundreds of gales this time rather than thousands. That was how enervated this exchange had rendered Him. That was how small and closed-in the vastness of the Universe felt right now.

"You want me to tell you why you want another child so badly, Father? You really want to know why?"

"Go ahead, Son. Pray, tell me."

"Because you can't handle the fact I'm growing up, Father. You can't accept the fact I want to be my own man. Not the Son of Man, but my own man."

"Of course I can accept you as your own man, Son. I'm as proud of you today as the day John baptized you. The day I cracked open the Heavens and told you how proud I was of you then. Remember that day? It's just that I've got other pressing matters right now, like making sure Clara's pregnancy goes smoothly and she gets enough to eat. Don't forget she's in Cuba, Son. There are severe shortages of everything there, especially food."

"What does she need food for, Father? She's going to be surrounded by faith, remember? Weren't those your words?"

The Creator of the Universe shook his head mildly, but it still generated enough energy to produce great solar flares and piercing gamma rays into the galaxies beyond.

"Look, Son, I've got a great idea to set your mind back on course. Why don't you be a good boy, a good older brother that is, and go down there and check in on your stepmother. Make some contact with her and make sure she's got everything she needs right now."

The look on the Son of Man's face no longer fell flat or went blank, or grew intense or even irritable. It turned rapt—rapt in white-hot rage.

"First of all, Father, don't call that girl my stepmother. She's no such thing! Secondly, I told you I wasn't going down there again! Now, less than ever, after two thousand years of being put off by you and having you brush aside that which most matters to me. Good-bye Father, I'm leaving! But it's not down there I'm headed; *that* I can assure you!"

"But wait, Son! We're not finished talking yet. And where are you going anyway? When are you coming back?"

The Son of Man was already halfway to another galaxy before he stopped and looked back in his Father's direction. He decided to turn the tables on Him.

"Do you really need to ask me, Father? I mean, isn't it fair to say you already know where I'm going? Wouldn't that be a fair assumption on my part? You are the Creator of the Universe, aren't you? That means you know everything I do—before I ever even do it!"

But the Creator of the Universe was not one to scare easily. In fact, He didn't scare at all—except on occasion with His son.

"All right!" He called out. "Just be careful and stay away from that black hole, will you? Trust me, Son, you don't know what you're getting into with that thing. I should know, I created them."

Without so much as another utterance, the Son of Man took off with Godspeed, plunging deep into that nebulous and dimly lit galaxy that Man had yet to discover or map out with all his high-powered gadgets and other technological marvels. That black hole continued churning and spinning and violently devouring anything light-years within its reach, but the Son of Man, like any rebellious offspring, came dangerously close to it on purpose, defiantly veering toward its path just to give his old man a good old-fashioned scare. No worries though, not really. The speed of light could not avoid capture by the enormous gravity generated in a black hole, but the speed employed by Father, Son, and Holy Spirit certainly could.

Still, the Creator of the Universe cringed and shook his

splendiferous head worriedly, watching his Son venture into the vicinity of that violently whirling vacuum in what any parent would regard as an adolescent show of exhibitionism. What was going on with him? Why the dogged defiance? Why the need to play the devil's advocate? Sure, the two were part of the Trinity, but Father and Son were different in so many ways and always would be.

Why couldn't he learn to make more concessions? Why was the Son of Man always chasing after the complex concepts of Creation? The quasars. The novas. The red giants and white dwarfs. Why couldn't he just take pleasure in the simple things of the Universe? The pale white moon as it hung in solitary beauty against a velvet black sky. A wild and wayward comet as its tail streamed and streaked and its particles of dust fired their way through the firmament. A star rising in the east or some planets hanging here and there. How about simple gravity or lack thereof. Why, after all, had the Creator fashioned Saturn's rings? Why had He created Jupiter's big red spot? For some local flair and color, for additional excitement. Was there really any need for more than that? No. But it was never enough. Not for man, not for the Son of Man. It was always more and more and more. Maybe one day both would learn that the answers to existence were found by looking inward rather than outward; that the keys to life were meant to be retrieved, not from the remote and unfathomable reaches of outer space, but from the infinite vastness of inner space, from the depths within.

But He who knew everything knew full well why this was happening. This was all the result of one thing and one thing only: His son being an only child for so long, two thousand years of pampering and patience and overindulgence. A parent should never wait so long before having his next child. A parent should never make the assumption that the period of adjustment will go smoothly either. And a parent should certainly never assume that just because he did *more* than his part, *more* than everything by the book—the Good Book in this case—the child would turn out exactly to his liking. That was definitely the wrong assumption.

"Well, Son!" the Creator bellowed out after him, knowing the Son of Man could hear him perfectly well, that all His thoughts would still reach him no matter what corner or nook or cranny of the universe the Son of Man tried escaping into and hiding in. "I have only one thing to add, but I assume you already know what it is: yes, Son, that would certainly be a fair assumption on *both* our parts. Congratulations, Son! Congratulations to you and congratulations to me! You're going to be a brother, and—once again—I'm going to be a dad!"

5

assumptions

august 15
early morning

"Wake up, Clara! Arise, amor! The car is going to be here in half an hour, and you need to get moving!"

I was awake—and been so for hours. I may have lain motionless in bed for the moment, but I was fully alert and been so all night. How could I possibly fall asleep after a visitation from the Angel Gabriel? Heaven's chief messenger. Telling me I'd been selected as the mother of God's next child, no less—and a daughter at that! How could anyone fall asleep after so preposterous a vision? *Impossible.* I had only feigned sleep. I had only tried sleeping the whole incident off, even if the strands of consciousness had never loosened their tightly woven grip.

Which had only given way to endless bouts of vacillation, flip-flopping, and indecision throughout the last vestiges of night. But now I knew exactly what to do. I was perfectly clear on it! I was going. I was still leaving Cuba as planned. Despite the admonitions from my winged friend, no silly hallucination would keep me from fulfilling my dreams. No product of delerium or exhaustion would deprive me of my goals. Within a few hours Rigo and I would set sail for America. And within a few hours more, we'd reach the golden shores of the United States.

"I am awake, amor, I am," I assured him, my focus renewed. "But you're right. It's time to get going. It's time to arise."

Rigo stopped for a moment at the side of the bed and shook his head in amusement. He bent down to run his fingers through my hair and then kissed my forehead.

"You really are something, Clara, you know that, amor. I thought you would have been up long ago. I've hardly slept any myself."

That I knew. When Rigo finally came home, long after the apparition's departure, he was a bundle of energy. After all of Mihrta's hysterics I expected to find him dejected and morose, ready to call everything off. Instead, he was rapt and jubilant. He couldn't stop moving, even if I felt like a zombie. So it went in this clash of motion. I could barely respond to his utterances, much less arise from bed, but Rigo had no intention of slowing down, even if it was two in the morning. He retrieved his green backpack with its black straps and pouches. He rounded up any essential documents we might need in the United States, like our marriage certificate. He looked for any tools that might come in handy along our voyage.

"Guess what we now have?" he announced proudly.

"What?" I asked.

"A compass, amor. Papá gave me his prized compass to guide us on our journey."

assumptions

"A compass?" I eked out. "We're not going to need a compass, Rigo. I told you, amor, the boats are going to be waiting for us twelve miles out. We'll be intercepted before we know it."

It was my last utterance before Rigo seriously faded out. Still, he persisted methodically, the expert now on fleeing Cuba.

"They're not always twelve miles out, Clara. And besides, twelve miles *is* a long distance, especially out at sea. We'll need this compass to stay on course, amor, trust me."

It was the architect in him, always needing to be precise and exact, always needing tools for guidance or measurement. At least we had my father-in-law's blessing for the trip, at least the compass signified that much. Whether it would actually come in handy, who knew? But I did know the moment of truth was finally upon us. I jumped out of bed and made haste, and sure enough, in the next half hour everything unfurled in a dizzying blur.

I moved about frantically and hurriedly, but Rigo shifted about our bedroom deliberately and cautiously, executing all his last-minute tasks with meticulousness and precision. It didn't seem he was about to venture off the island for good on some homemade raft, but merely packing up for the new school year in Camagüey. While my husband sat on the edge of the bed and carefully rolled and wrapped up our marriage certificate and IDs and the blueprint of his tower complex in plastic sheathing, I rushed to the dresser and gathered up my prayer cards and clutched them fiercely in my hand. As Rigo took the large water container and made sure it was sealed tightly before placing it securely in the green packpack, I suddenly wanted to shower. The day before I had never washed. I should have been covered in sweat and dirt and grime, but even in my nervous observations, I realized that wasn't the case. My body felt cool and refreshed, completely clean, as if I'd already showered and dried off. Even my hair looked thoroughly combed out, every strand perfectly in place. I made no sense of this, but it mattered not. I wanted to retrieve the one item I must absolutely take with me to the

United States: the letter my father had received from his friend in Iraq. The letter that made him weep right before he died and which I would finally have translated.

I rushed out of our bedroom to retrieve it, stepping into my parents' room down the hall and heading straight for the towering bookcases that housed all his texts, including the Arabic ones. I remembered exactly which book I had placed the letter in, what page number even. It was in that encyclopedia of leaves, that old mysterious book bound in leather and containing intricate and hand-tinted illustrations of all the leaves of the world. I treated it with more care and respect than ever now. As a child, how I remembered the way my father would peruse the pages of this book for what seemed hours on end. And given what Pilar told me after he died, I went and tucked the infamous letter away on the only page that seemed appropriate: page 609, which contained a whimsical illustration of the notorious leaf and its whitish wispy flower. Maloja, as it was called: the bad leaf.

Sure enough, there it was! The envelope and letter from Iraq pressed firmly between the pages of this sacred book. I plucked it out and closed the pages, kissing the cover before returning my father's book back to its shelf, letting my hand linger on it momentarily before jetting out to the hallway. I wished my heartbeat would settle down. But it raced and pounded nevertheless, even if everything around me unfolded in synchronized slow motion, especially in the kitchen, where I encountered Mamá standing over the stove waiting for her coffee to brew so she could pour me a *tazita*.

"Well, Mamá," I began in earnest, keeping that letter from Iraq hidden behind my back. "This is it, *Vieja*. The moment has finally come: I'm leaving. Well, we're both leaving. But I don't want you to worry, Mamá, because, one year—that's all it's going to take—one year for Rigo and I to become residents. And the moment we do I'm sending for you and my sisters and we're all going to be together again, you understand?"

I certainly didn't expect Mamá to break down and start sobbing. She wasn't the hysterical type like my mother-in-law. But I did expect *some* display of emotion from her, even if just a few tears welling up in her eyes or her voice choking up. But nothing. All she did was stand there in her drab gown and in her detached and distant manner, slowly and methodically pouring me my *cafesito* into a white porcelain cup and handing it to me.

"I know, mijita. I know," she said. "Now, here, drink up."

I normally loved coffee, especially Mamá's coffee first thing in the morning. But for some reason the smell of this coffee was so repugnant, I thought I would throw up if I took one more whiff of it. She kept holding the cup in my direction as waves of unexplained nausea swelled within me.

"Mamá!" I said in annoyance. "Did you hear me, vieja? I said this is it: we're going, Mamá. Rigo and I are leaving!"

"I heard you, mija, I heard you," she said, avoiding direct eye contact. "And I have faith that everything is going to be all right, Clara. I've prayed to the Virgin and to all the angels and saints and even to God himself to watch over you on your travels and keep you safe at all times, and I know that all of Heaven will do just that. So here, mijita, have your last cafesito before you go. Would you like some bread and butter too?"

As she finished, Mamá thrust the cup closer to my face, and I actually began to gag. Not just from the smell of it, but the sight of it too.

"Clara, mija. What's the matter? Are you feeling sick?"

I didn't know what I was feeling. And I didn't understand why so violent a reaction unless it was just a dose of anxiety and raw nerves. But neither did I like this cool and detached manner of Mamá's either, almost as if she were making a mockery of me or she were the bearer of some secret knowledge.

"Mamá," I pressed suspiciously, looking straight into her dark, inscrutable eyes. "*Ven acá chica*. What did you do last night? Why did you get home so late?"

She rubbed her hands for a moment along that drab gown.

"Why...you know what I did, mija. I was visiting your aunt for a while...that's all. I was just out visiting her. Now...here, take the coffee. I made it just for you and Rigo. Would you like some bread and butter or not?"

I shook my head. Now it was the thought of bread and butter that made me gag. I finally took the cafesito from her hand, but not to drink it, only to pour it back into the glass jar she used to store her morning supply. I tightened the lid on the jar firmly and placed it down on the counter as Mamá merely shrugged her shoulders and underneath her breath said, "Suit yourself, mija." She then turned her back on me, focusing her attention on the stove as she wiped away at its surface.

"Yes, Mamá. But what were you doing there? You never stay that long at tía's when you visit her, especially on a weeknight, and especially the night before your daughter is leaving the country for good. What were you doing there, Mamá? What took you so long to get home?"

My mother brought her slow and methodical wiping to a halt, wringing dry the wet rag in her hands and draping it over the kitchen faucet before turning to lock eyes with me. Whether she was finally ready to reveal the events of the prior night or simply maintain some carefully crafted pretense, I would never know. Just then—right before she seemed ready to formulate a response—our furtive encounter was interrupted by a brisk knocking at the front door.

"I'll get that, mijita," she blurted out. "You wait right here. Better yet, why don't you finish gathering up your things, Clara? You probably don't have much time before you need to get going, mija. Now hurry!"

How right that mother of mine would turn out to be. The knocking on the front door not only heralded the arrival of our much-anticipated driver—who happened to appear right on schedule—but my running out of time.

"Clara!" Rigo called out from the living room. "¿Lista amor? The driver is here—and we can't keep him waiting."

Of course I wasn't ready. It seemed there were a million

things left to do still, even if I couldn't possibly tend to them all or take everything with me I wanted. I would have to stick with the absolute esssentials: my birth certificate and carnét; my school diploma and copies of my grades; a few of my journals that I absolutely refused to part with, filled with some of the critiques and musings I was most proud of; the list of contacts Nelson had provided me with for our group Insurrection; my few beloved prayer cards, and of course, my father's letter from Iraq. That was it. All of it wrapped in plastic to protect it from the water. There was no room for anything else in that backpack, nor did I care about taking anything else.

Throughout this last half hour my thoughts and movements had struck with lightning speed and I could barely keep up with them. But now it was I, in some clash of motion, who could hardly move about the house. Now it was I who struggled with my steps as if moving along some invisible obstacle course, trying to dodge that repugnant smell of coffee so fresh in my mind. Somehow, I managed to complete the course and reach the finish line where I caught Rigo blithely waiting.

"Well, amor. Are we ready?" he asked.

I looked at the corner of the bed for the items I had set aside, but they were nowhere in sight.

"It's all packed," my husband informed me. "I've already placed your belongings in the backpack."

I smiled at Rigo. It was the architect in him: always organized and one step ahead when it came to storing things.

"Of course you have," I replied. "I wouldn't have expected any less of you."

"And now that we have Papá's compass to guide us, we're all set," he announced proudly again.

We stepped into the living room where all three sirens were standing there waiting for us: Mamá, Pilar and Angélica, along with the individual whom I took to be our driver, but who kept his distance from our group by situating himself near the front door. I noticed he was dressed quite stylishly in dark blue jeans and a tight-fitting shirt, short sleeved and the color of charcoal.

"I'm going!" Angélica announced unexpectedly. "I'm going with them!"

My youngest sister, Angélica, only sixteen years of age and so innocent. She thought she knew everything about life, especially love. She had acted this way for the last two years. Of us three, I had always regarded Angélica as the prettiest. She had a delicate little face with fine, dainty features. She possessed bright hazel eyes that were lively and playful. I especially loved her hair—light brown and wild—even if it was the one trait she unmercifully detested in herself: a thick head of curls so tight and coarse that she was forever cursing them and trying to straighten them out, all to no avail. No matter how much we reassured my sister that we loved her hair and told her how fortunate she was to have such a full head of curls, this would only further exacerbate Angélica, prompting her to declare her hatred for these curls all the more fiercely, rendering her all the more defiant in wanting to straighten them out.

"What was that?" Mamá turned and asked her. "What did you just say, hija?" It was the first time all morning my mother betrayed any hint of emotion.

"I don't mean it like that," Angélica explained. "I don't mean I'm going off with them. I mean 'acommpany' them. I want to go to Cojimar and say good-bye."

"Absolutely not!" Mamá shot back. "Forget about it!"

"Why not?" Angélica insisted. "It's my sister, and I want to say good-bye to her. Is there something wrong with that, Mamá? Is there? I'm sure the driver here won't mind waiting and bringing me back. Isn't that right, compañero?" she turned and asked the guy.

"Of course I wouldn't mind, not at all," replied the driver enthusiastically, using the opportunity to insinuate himself into our family dealings and even stepping away from the front door to inch himself toward us. I noticed the way he looked and smiled at my younger sister and I didn't like it one bit. Like the smell of coffee this morning, it filled me with utter repugnance.

"See!" Angélica declared. "It's settled. I'm going with them."

"Oh, no you're not!" Mamá countered. "You're not going at all."

"Señora," the driver boldly jumped in. "If you're worried about anything happening, please, don't be, there's no need. Your daughter will be perfectly fine with me. I have to come back this way anyway, and I'll bring her back safely, I promise you that."

But Mamá simply ignored the bold little man, disregarding every word he had just uttered; instead, keeping her attentions focused solely on my younger sister.

"You're not going anywhere!" she snapped firmly and with finality. "The next time you see your sister will either be in the United States or when she comes back here for a visit! That's it! End of discussion!"

Angélica fell into an embarrassed silence. She knew when to stop pushing Mamá, especially in the presence of strangers. My younger sister stood in place and cast her eyes downward, while the older Pilar lifted a comforting arm to drape around her shoulder. So typical of my older sister, always placing the needs of others before her own; always striving to comfort everyone else when she was the one whose needs should come first; she, the one truly deserving of comforting due to her blindness.

"It's all right, hermana, it's all right," she said soothingly, patting and squeezing Angélica's shoulder. "You need not go to Cojimar to hold onto Clara or keep her in your heart. She'll always be with us, no matter where we say good-bye to her, no matter where we last see her. Clara is with us and we are with her."

Upon hearing this, a surge of tears rose to my eyes and I stepped over to join them, the three of us forming a small circle where we held each other firmly, closely. As our arms intertwined and locked within the strands of sisterhood, we hugged each other lovingly, creating an impenetrable embrace until I could hold it no longer—until I began to weep and weep uncontrollably; it didn't take long for my sisters to join in. We sobbed in unison, letting all our pent-up feelings gush out. I contemplated my family and how much it had unraveled during this Special Period. Only a year ago my father had died, my sister had fallen blind, and now I was leaving Cuba. My family was rapidly disintegrating, and I could blame only one person for it, one thing for it: Fidel Castro and the tyranny of his evil ways.

"Now stop, you three! ¡Ya!" Mamá ordered, trying to keep her own maternal emotions in check. "This isn't a time for sadness. It's a time to be happy, a time to rejoice. Your sister is not leaving us. She's saving us!"

Of course, we only wept all the harder. But after a few more minutes of unfettered emotion, I felt a firm and steady hand on my shoulder. I knew it was Rigo reeling me back, trying to pull me up to the surface of reason. The moment of truth had arrived and it was definitely time to take our leave. I didn't want or need to take one last look at anything. Not at them. Not at the house. They were my one and only family and certainly we would always be a part of one another. This was my one and only birth home and there would never be any forgetting it. As much as I loathed Fidel Castro and what he had done to this country, this house would always remain my home and I would always cherish it.

How I ever made it inside the vehicle or what direction I looked in or what thoughts consumed me as the taxi pulled away and raced down our street, I could not recall. But I would always recall our driver and how the man never shut up. I tried ignoring his incessant prattle, but it was asking for the impossible. He simply could not close his mouth. I never knew his name, but that was fine with me. And I would meet him only once, during this brief ride from Havana to Cojimar, but I decided he must be the most obnoxious individual I had ever encountered. Never could I foresee the pivotal role he

assumptions

would play on this morning of August 15 and its turn of events.

He was short but muscular, albeit, slightly overweight; heavily balding with traces of dark hair; he possessed an abnormally low voice, and from his inarticulate diction and how fast he spoke, I could tell he hailed from the countryside, for he nearly swallowed his words whole. I figured him to be a complete illiterate, and was therefore dumbstruck when the absurd little man informed us he wasn't really a taxi driver by profession but a *Técnico Medio* in *Artes Plásticas*.

"Really?" I posed. "Well then, what are you doing driving a taxi?"

"What do you think I'm doing?" he shot off in his low-voiced, rapid-fire manner. "Same thing everyone else is doing these days: surviving, making ends meet, 'resolving' if you know what I mean. You think that anybody can make money in *Artes Plásticas* these days? During this Special Period?"

I kept silent, but only thought to myself: *I'm sure you could if you were any good, if you had any actual talent or were any kind of real artist.* But I simply kept my mouth shut. It wasn't worth it. I had to recognize that this impulse to lash out was just the critic in me, the cynic always wanting to find fault with things or needing to dissect everything. So I kept my mouth shut. At least I knew now whom I was dealing with: a frustrated artist. One more example of why I must leave Cuba and eagerly looked forward to it: so I didn't end up the same as this absurd little man; except, a frustrated critic in my case.

"Of course not," I replied with restraint. "You're absolutely right, compañero."

Rigo must have sensed my simmering unease, for he jumped in to give his two cents and diffuse the tension.

"Of course not, compañero. And I know exactly how you feel," he said. Why, I'm an architect myself. I'll have you know that I graduated two years ago at the top of my class from the Instituto Superior right here in Havana. But do you think I've gotten to exercise my talents even once? I haven't gotten to build so much as a cardboard box yet."

I cringed as I sat in the backseat of that car and looked out the window. We snaked our way through the streets of Havana and it seemed we were navigating through a familiar sea of blue, police blue: the mongrels were stationed everywhere, especially along the Malecón. I wished that Rigo would not divulge any aspect of our life to this absurd little man. I didn't trust him for one second in his dark blue jeans and tight-fitting designer shirt. I didn't know what had gotten into Rigo. He was usually so discreet, so reserved. But this morning he was markedly different, seemingly changed somehow. He was a running faucet of water that one could not force shut.

"Really?" said the bald little man. "I fancy myself as an engineer and an architect too. What have you been doing for the last two years?"

Just as the faint light of morning was cautiously tiptoeing and had yet to press its footprints upon the soft path of day, how I wished my husband would proceed just as cautiously. How I wished he had the sense to brush off this intrusive line of questioning since taxi drivers in Cuba were notoriously nosy, usually security people. But no, Rigo fell right in place with those steps by plowing and stomping full-force ahead.

"You wouldn't believe it if I told you," Rigo replied.

"Oh, I'd believe anything," the absurd little man shot back. "Remember, this is Cuba, compadre, where things that should make sense don't, and things that don't make sense do."

"You've got that right," said Rigo. "That's why they've had me in some remote, rural village in Camagüey teaching advanced math to kids who can barely read or write yet."

"¡Camagüey!" declared the absurd little man. "Why, I just drove through there a couple of weeks ago. Which town in Camagüey?"

"I'm sure you've never heard of it. It's this tiny little town called Rio Piedras."

"Rio Piedras? You mean where the cattle co-op is? *That* Rio

assumptions

Piedras? Why yes, compadre, I know exactly where that is."

I sank ever deeper into the backseat of that car, burying my face slightly as I brought a hand to my forehead and silently shook my head. Why couldn't we have any privacy? Just a few kilometers of privacy. I turned to Rigo to get his attention, signaling him to put a lid on it, but there was no tightening that spigot, no turning off that faucet.

"Coño, compadre. You're the first person I know who's ever heard of Rio Piedras. That's where I've been for the last two years, teaching calculus to fifth graders. It's called Early Exposure."

"Calculus to fifth graders!" declared the absurd little man.

"Yes, that's right. But do you know what they wanted me to do this year? What I would be doing if I were going back? Teaching mechanical engineering to fourth graders. That's what the project is for the upcoming year. It's called Intense Early Exposure."

The absurd little man shook his bald head, laughing uproariously in his abnormally low voice.

"No wonder you want to leave here so badly, compadre. I can't say I blame you in the least."

"No more!" said Rigo. "No more! I've wasted two whole years of my life with nonsense, but no more."

"Well, what is it that you do want to do?" asked the probing little man. "Design houses?"

"Definitely not!" said Rigo. "Growing up in Cuba has ruined that for good."

"And why is that?" asked the little man.

"Are you kidding?" said Rigo. "You think that after spending an entire life here surrounded by hideous Soviet-style apartment buildings built after the Revolution, I want to design anything residential? Not on your life. I want to design things there are of no use here in Cuba: tall buildings, skyscrapers, towers even."

"Towers?" said the little man.

| 181 |

"Yes, towers. You see, for the longest time I've been designing a very special tower. It's the first of its kind, and I'm finally going to make it happen when I arrive in the United States."

"In Miami?" asked the round little man. "I've seen many pictures of Miami and it seems to be nothing but towers."

"No, we're not going to Miami, compadre. Maybe for a couple of days, but that's it. We're going to San Francisco, in California. Now San Francisco is a city of towers. They've got this one tower that's completely round called Coit Tower. And they've got this other tower in the shape of a pyramid called the TransAmerica Pyramid. Well, my tower is going to be the perfect complement to these two. I call it the Tri-Tower Complex. You want to see it?"

"¡Coño sí!" he said excitedly. "I would love to see it! I've been designing something very similar myself. But mine is four towers!"

I didn't believe this for a moment. I straightened out in that backseat while in the grip of some silent terror. I reached over and grabbed Rigo's lap. He turned and looked at me as I shook my head furiously at him. *What's the matter with you? I wanted to scream out. What's gotten into you? Why are you confiding in this narcissitic little man who can betray us and denounce us at any moment? Who might even steal your idea and design?* Hadn't he heard the absurd little man say he considered himself an architect and engineer? Rigo must have read my thoughts because he suddenly did an about-face.

"You know what?" he said, changing gears and downshifting. "I don't think I can do that. The blueprint is all packed away. It will disturb everything else if I retrieve it."

"I understand," said the little man. "I understand perfectly, compadre. But coño, that's great. Congratulations on such a stupendous idea; a tri-tower complex. I imagine it's going to be three towers all in a row, right?"

"Yes!" I jumped in to save Rigo. "All in a row, side by side."

—— assumptions ——

Of course, I was lying. And fortunately this nosy driver was too narcissistic to wonder why I had suddenly answered for Rigo, which was fine with me. There were times narcissism actually paid off.

"Well then, it's a good thing you two are doing this right now," continued the narcissistic little man. "That's what I've been telling people all week: take advantage of this opportunity right away, the sooner the better."

Now he had *me* on the hook. Now it was my curiosity that was piqued.

"Oh?" I began. "And why is that?"

The narcissistic little man stopped to look up in the rearview mirror. Not to lock eyes with me, but only to steal a glance at himself.

"Well, I can't tell you with absolute certainty," he said, managing to strip his attention away from the mirror. "But I understand this exodus isn't going to be lasting much longer. In fact, it's going to be ending real soon."

How full this guy was of himself. What a delusional little narcissist. Not only a frustrated artist and balding fool, but a know-it-all. Typical taxi driver here in Cuba, always acting as if they knew everything. Not only because of their contact with foreigners, but because everyone knew they were agents of the state. No wonder being a taxi driver was one of the most coveted trades in all of Cuba: trained in tips, travel, and tourists. Except this guy had an additional degree: *tattler!*

"How soon?" I asked.

"This week, compañera."

"This week?" I said. "What do you mean?"

The taxi driver shot a glance over his shoulder. It was the first time he made direct eye contact with me. If I wasn't mistaken, he looked at me the same way he had looked at Angélica earlier. I really couldn't stand him or stand being in his presence any longer; in fact, I loathed him.

"Well compañera, you do know that your uncle...you

| 183 |

know who, right? The one who gives all the orders around here...that he's just doing this because it suits him, right?"

As he referred to our one and only *comandante-en-jefe*, the absurd little man gestured with one hand as if stroking an invisible beard, that silent but universal reference to uncle Fidel.

"Suits him how?" I asked.

"Do you need to ask?" the man fired back. "Certainly you don't think he's opened up the floodgates because of his generosity, do you? Because he feels bad for all the unhappy citizens he's created?"

"Of course, not" I fired back myself, defensive but determined. "He's doing this because he can't stop us. Because this time the forces working against him are too powerful and the whole world is bearing witnesss to it, that's why."

The *chofer* shook his bald head and laughed uproariously in his abnormally deep voice, trying to make eye contact with me in the rear view mirror.

"Don't be naïve, compañera, don't be so innocent. He's doing this because it creates a humongous problem for the Americans, because it forces them back to the negotiating table, that's why."

"Negotiating table? What negotiating table?"

"The negotiating table of immigration talks, compañera. *That* negotiating table."

"And how do you know this?" I pressed.

"Let's just say I have it under very good authority, compañera."

I settled down again in the back of that vehicle, but dumbstruck and deflated. I couldn't reply. Rigo sensed my churning unease because now he jumped in for me.

"That's Fidel for you," he said. "Never passes up an opportunity when he sees one."

"You know that your uncle is no fool," the driver continued, stroking that imaginary beard once more. "Didn't you hear him the other night on television? The veiled threat he made. What better way to force the Americans to bend to his will than by unleashing another exodus? Right now this is a mini-Mariel, but left alone, it could easily eclipse it."

I felt more and more disheartened as the absurd little man babbled on. The more he spewed his hot air, the more deflated I felt.

"What are you saying then?" I began. "Are you saying he planned this all from the start? This incident I've regarded as a miracle?"

"Well, I wouldn't go that far, compañera. He's not that ingenious. But your uncle definitely knows how to work things to his advantage. Didn't he do the same thing with Mariel? Wasn't Mariel a genuine revolt until he realized he too could make his move and clean house? Didn't he take advantage by emptying out his jails and mental hospitals?"

"So that's who's leaving now?" I asked flabergasted. "Convicts and mental patients? Is that what you're saying?"

"No, compañera, I'm not. But who knows? Who really knows? I think that if everyone were completely honest, they would admit that, in order to do what they're doing—what you two are about to do—you have to be a little crazy, wouldn't you? Be honest now. Risking your life at sea. Leaving behind everything you know and love. Everybody accuses Fidel of being old and crazy and blames him for Cuba being a mess. But Fidel is not to blame. *We* are. We Cubans are to blame. He's just an orchestra leader conducting this socialist symphony. He's just a chef preparing a major meal. You have to hand it to him. He always knows just when to remove the valve from that pressure cooker, doesn't he? He always knows exactly when to let the steam out."

There, in the backseat of that car, Rigo and I turned and faced each other to assume the obivous: this absurd little man *was* an agent of the state, he had to be. For the ensuing moments that followed, his words hung thick in our faces, their stifling force sucking out all the oxygen. We sat there deprived of all air until Rigo's voice pierced through the silence, but in a manner totally unlike him.

"Well," my husband began, "the whole damned thing can explode in his old, fucking face for all I care. Another thing, compañero: as far as that meal goes that our uncle is preparing, as you say, well, it's already been served, and it tastes like shit—pure shit! Who knows? Maybe we are crazy, as you suggest. But at least we're not cowards. You need courage to do what we're doing. Real courage. Just like the kid who threw the rock at the Deauville last week and made this all possible. That took more than cojones, and I will admire and respect that kid for the rest of my life."

"Oh no, compañero. I beg to differ. I couldn't disagree more. That was definitely crazy what that kid did last week, very stupid, actually."

"Oh yeah?" said Rigo. "And why is that?"

"Why?" the man posed rhetorically. "Haven't you been seeing the news reports lately? Haven't you been reading *el Granma?*"

"No," we both said in unison.

"Of course you haven't," retorted the bald little man. "How could you? You've been too busy getting ready for your trip. Well, they've got security images of the guy getting ready to throw another rock and they've been showing his picture in the paper and on TV. They're looking for him and anyone who helped him."

"Anyone who helped him?" Rigo asked.

"Yes, and believe me, I have it under good authority that when they find these guys—and they will—they're going to have a lot of time on their hands to think about what they did."

"Well, hopefully they'll never find him. Hopefully he's already escaped. Maybe he'll be in Cojimar this morning getting ready to push off."

Once again, I couldn't believe what I was hearing. What in

assumptions

the world had gotten into Rigo? If I was the one usually running off at the mouth, there was no catching up to that loose tongue of his this morning.

"And that's one of the reasons why you're going to be seeing so many policemen along the shore this morning. They're determined to catch him if he tries to escape. See what I mean?" he pointed. "Look over there!"

Rigo and I looked to our left, in the direction of his pointing finger. The prevalent color of blue stretched out like a dragnet: the blue of uniform, the blue of the mongrels. They were everywhere, it seemed, forming their own sea of blue.

More important, we had finally reached Cojimar.

"Where shall I drop you off?" the driver asked.

"Hemingway's bust," I said. "Do you know where that is?"

"Coño, who doesn't know where that is?" he asked. "It's right over there."

The narcissist pointed to the modest, yet respectable, monument that the town of Cojimar had erected in Hemingway's honor: a bust of him housed within a gazebo. It stood right across from the Spanish fort at the entrance of the harbor. The Malecón of Cojimar was tiny compared to Havana's, so we reached the monument in no time.

"This will do," Rigo said, taking charge. "You can drop us off right here."

I promptly stepped out of the taxi while Rigo thanked the absurd little man and paid him. I could barely bring myself to say good-bye, much less thank him. I could think only of saying good riddance. But he was a leech that would not let go.

"Compañera," he began. "Just one question, if you don't mind."

"What's that?" I asked, weary and exasperated.

"That sister of yours, the one who wanted to accompany you this morning. How old is she?"

"Sixteen."

"Sixteen. Oh well..."

"Why, compañero? How old are you?"

"Thirty-six."

"Thirty-six!" I declared.

"Yes, now tell me, from a woman's point of view, do you think thirty-six is too old for sixteen?"

"No compañero, not too old. *Ridiculously* too old!"

He fell silent and nodded erratically, almost talking to himself.

"That's what I thought," he replied. "That's what I thought. Well, what about the other sister then? The one with the weird eyes."

"She's twenty-three, compañero, and she's got a boyfriend. She's also blind, that's why the weird eyes."

"Oh," he said. "Well listen, good luck to you both and be real careful out there. The sea looks kind of rough this morning, much rougher than it's been all week. Not only that, I hear that in the last couple days a few corpses have washed up to shore. But don't worry about that. I'm sure you'll be rescued long before you know it."

He went to shake Rigo's hand before driving off, but my husband, so full of surprises this morning, unleashed one nagging question.

"How about you, compadre?" Rigo began. "Think you might be interested in leaving at all? In joining the exodus from here in Cojimar?"

"Me, compañero? Me? Why do you ask?"

"You must be frustrated, compadre, terribly frustrated. You're a Técnico Medio in Artes Plásticas, yet you have to drive a taxi in order to put food on the table. I can't think of a worse consolation."

But the absurd little man smiled and looked at Rigo with that half-crazed expression in his eyes. He would not be outdone, and he had the goods to prove it.

"Oh no, compañero, you shouldn't make such assumptions, not at all. I'm perfectly fine with my position, perfectly happy. You see these jeans I've got on?" he asked.

"Yes," said Rigo.

"They're Jordache. Not even Levis, but Jordache. And you see this shirt?" he posed again.

"Yes," repeated Rigo.

"It's Calvin Klein, chico, *Calvin Klein!*" he repeated. "The very best there is. All due to this job I have as a driver and the tourists who support me—I mean, my clients who care for me very much. No, compañero, I'm perfectly content," he added. "But remember what I told you now. Be real careful out there, real careful. The sea can turn on you in an instant, so it's always best to assume the worst, always! It's the only way to maintain control!"

With that, he was off! He slunk back into his taxi and drove away. I was a knot of nerves and couldn't think straight. Not as I caught sight of him for the last time, his dark blue jeans and Calvin Klein shirt, his balding head with its dull sheen glowing in the distance; meanwhile, Rigo and I were left to fend for ourselves within the curious scene unfolding along the waterfront.

The little sea village of Cojimar, just an extension of the eastern portion of Havana. I didn't know what to anticipate, what I would see or hear. Maybe family members making a last-ditch effort with some pleas and sobs, with hysterics even; maybe friends or neighbors who had come to say good-bye and offer well wishes to loved ones. More than anything, I expected an air of solemnity over the whole affair, a mournful silence draped over the canvas of this coast. Hardly. There was hardly anything mournful or melancholy about any aspect of the gathering here.

Sure, there were tearful good-byes and tight overwrought embraces. But the clamorous scene along the calm blue waters of Cojimar was not one of despondence or gloom. It was festive and brewing with energy. It seemed like carnaval time in Havana, as if these processions along sand and shore were the only *carnavales* being celebrated this year, these homemade rafts replacing the traditional floats. The floats of Cojimar were not the fancy flashing spectacles of a parade. They were the floats of some farcical fleet; a fleeing armada of vulnerable vessels, and where the most prevalent common denominator was the lowly everyday inner tube.

Inner tubes. *Everywhere!* Some inner tubes were single and solitary, their riders determined to make the voyage alone. But most inner tubes had been leashed like dogs, strung together in groups of two or three or even four or more; tied and fastened, saddled and harnessed for all their strength and might. Some had wooden planks; others had whatever floatable surface could be scrounged up; still others had material highly suspect—like ours, the only vessel woven together with stalks of sugarcane and maloja. All had been strapped like oxen to a cart, like chariots onto horses expected to gallop across the water. But this was one horse you could not whip to go faster or needle to giddyap. Not lest it pop or deflate or collapse under your weight and desert you in a watery grave. Some of these floating creations looked fortified and reinforced. Others appeared flimsy and precariously strung together. All came to life with the aid of the everyday inner tube—no longer a lowly object of disregard, but a true life-saver, a lasting friend.

And where did all these inner tubes mysteriously come from? This overabundance. During this Special Period we had shortages of everything in Cuba—food, energy, clothing—but certainly no shortage of inner tubes, the one item that needed no rationing, along with Chinese bicycles. Why was it that, suddenly, when a Cuban needed an inner tube, there were more than plenty to be found?

No, there was no shortage of these life-savers, just as there was no shortage of takers. As for the decorations on these floats or their visual themes, it was not pretty young girls or carnival queens who danced atop them. Thin young men adorned these vessels: stern-looking, hungry, fearless and

assumptions

brazen Cubans with a fierceness in their eyes and an angry intensity in their gaze. *Cojimar*. The town would forever be tied to the water. It was the setting for Ernest Hemingway's *The Old Man and the Sea*. Papa Hemingway had even docked his boat here. It remained a tiny fishing village of modest wood and concrete homes perched on a hill that overlooked a bay. But now, in this next chapter of the town's seafaring history, it was the launching point of Cuba's current exodus, later to be dubbed *El Crisis de los Balseros*.

I had only been to Cojimar once in my life, when I was twelve. My father had come here to conduct research and said we could make a family vacation out of it. He was writing a paper on the migratory patterns and language of the Cimmerians of Crimea: an ancient nomadic people now extinct and who were believed to have dwelled in perpetual darkness. Evidence suggested that, even though the Cimmerians had eventually settled as far north as South Russia, Asia Minor, and along the Black Sea, originally they had been colonists of Atlantis before it sank into the ocean.

And while it was generally believed that most of the Cimmerians who survived that cataclysm migrated to Northern and Western Europe, my father suggested in his paper that an offshoot of the group had headed south, never to be heard from or seen again. The Cimmerians who made it to the European continent went on to engage in centuries of warfare and conquests with rival groups; thus were they eventually expelled and driven out of Europe because of their affinity to the darkness. These embattled Cimmerians decided to head south this time, just as that small offshoot of their ancestors had done centuries prior. My father's research indicated that, sometime in the fifth century, this bellicose faction reached Cuba and modern-day Cubans were actually direct descendants of theirs. The newly arrived nomads happened to settle in Cojimar and the word Cojimar itself was a variation of the word Crimea, named after the Cimmerians.

I knew nothing of the linguistic correlations to the Cimmerians or their ancient language. But while my father and his colleagues hotly debated all these esoteric notions—

and at times their discussions grew heated and impassioned over cigars and shots of rum and servings of *guayaba* marmalade poured over cream cheese—I loved hearing all his description of the Cimmerians and the forbidden land of Crimea they once inhabited.

"It was beyond the ocean," he would explain. "A land of fog and darkness, at the edge of the world and at the entrance to Hades, along the edge of a dark and gloomy forest."

It was the last vacation we took as a family, and I would always recall it bittersweetly. My father could not relax. I remember our last evening in Cojimar as we sat along the seawall enjoying a rare treat of ice cream. How I wished Papi would simply savor and delight in that cool and sweet refreshment, along with the calming sight of the ocean, blue-gray and bleeding, and the blood-rust sun setting in the distance. How I wished he would tell me more about the mythical land of Crimea. But it never happened. He was too engrossed in his scholarly journal and his erudite thoughts. My father could never stop working. He could never just give of himself or give us his undivided attention.

I never knew what became of his research or whether his thesis about the Cimmerians ever got published. I doubted it; especially after what happened during his stint in Iraq and how his career in Cuba ended in such disgrace. But I certainly knew what became of the Cimmerians. They were alive and well, right here in Cojimar, all the messy multitudes of them, these modern-day Cimmerians who had been living in perpetual darkness at the edge of the world and the entrance to Hades.

It was a spectacular sight to behold, really it was. It seemed as if all the waters of the planet had funneled into the Bay of Cojimar and amassed into a shifting blend of oceans and seas. Seas of blue—the blue of the mongrels. Seas of bicycles—the Chinese bikes so prevalent these days. Seas of young people. Old people. Very Old People. Onlookers. Participants. Detractors. Curiosity Seekers. Adventurers. Most of all, seas of Dreamers. It was part parade, part procession. There were even shrines to La Virgen del Cobre

assumptions

set up everywhere. Some stationary. Some mobile. And we were all subject to severe food shortages during this Special Period, but there was even 'food to go' being provided for the multitudes: everything from pork *bocaditos* and *croquetas* to yucca and *chicharrones*.

Who were all these people and where had they come from? Why did they look so strange? Could it be true? Could that absurd little man have possibly been correct? Were the multitudes gathered here just everyday Cimmerians like Rigo and me, or some of Fidel's convicts? Fidel's mental patients. Loyalists and infiltrators going abroad only to gather intelligence for our great uncle. Was this really all a miracle or just a second Mariel? I regarded everyone with suspicion and mistrust now, as possibly having a secret agenda. Maybe I should come clean with Rigo myself, no matter how crazy the vision last night sounded. Who knew? Maybe he would actually believe in it. I should at least let him decide.

"Amor," I began in earnest. "There's something I need to tell you, something important."

We were standing by Hemingway's bust and Rigo turned to face me quickly, his eyes glowing with a brewing excitement. We may have been on land still, but his heart and mind were already on open water, navigating their way forth, tackling the peaks and valleys of the waves with the aid of that compass his father had given him.

"What is it, amor? Tell me anything you want. You know that."

But what could I tell him? How could I possibly relay the vision I'd had? The dream. The hallucination. The visitation or whatever it was. I'd take a stab at it no matter how tenuous.

"Well amor, you see, last night when you were gone I...well, I thought I was falling asleep when..."

But I could not continue. My words faltered in some crisis of motion. I could not weave the strands of language together to merge a sensible thought.

"Yes, amor," he urged. "Go on. You know you don't have to be afraid with me; you can tell me anything. What happened last night, Clara?"

But I couldn't shake this unwelcome pause. Not even as I struggled to ferret out the words from deep within. I couldn't unearth them; they refused to rise. I could only stand there mute as Rigo fixed his gaze on me, as this curious scene surrounding us kept unfolding in a clash of movement: from all the people shifting back and forth, to the would-be *balseros* putting finishing touches on their rafts; from those actually pushing off into the water, to those who came only to spectate, clapping and cheering vigorously each time someone launched off and set sail. Even Rigo joined in the applause when one such group took off. I, however, couldn't move or make a sound. I wrapped myself in a crisis of silence until, unexpectedly, I felt a hand tapping my shoulder.

"Coño, chica. Where have you two been?" asked Amalia. "We were starting to get worried about you."

How ecstatic I was to see my best friend. The mere sight of her released that tight chokehold over my thoughts and words. But if I embraced her presence like a dose of salvation, it wouldn't be that way for long; the morning was destined to unravel quickly. For the moment, however, I admired how stunning and alive she looked. She was dressed in tan shorts and a white top. Her hair was gathered back in a ponytail; two tiny earrings of gold hung from her ears. She looked like her old self again, brimming with life and energy, certainly not the motionless cadaver from the night before. Whatever had possessed Amalia last night, she had gotten it out of her system. The two of us hugged and greeted each other with a kiss on the cheek, while Henry and Rigo shook hands.

"We're on time, aren't we?" I asked.

"Sí, chica, sí. I guess I'm just a ball of nerves is all."

"Where is it?" Rigo asked excitedly. "Where's our ship?"

"Over there," Henry pointed out, some fifty yards away. "In fact, let's head over there before someone steals it. There have been several thefts this morning already."

─────────── assumptions ───────────

    I felt a sickening malaise unfolding in my stomach. It had to be the excitement, the nervousness that one feels before a race or a test. Pilar always told me that, despite years of running competitively, she always felt sick to her stomach right before a race. It had to be the same thing. Wasn't this just a race for our lives? I tried suppressing the feeling. But as we made our way through the throngs of people, it dawned on me what I would always recall about this morning of August 15: a clash of movement and motion.

    I didn't know what else to call it. A collision of the quick with the slow; a spar between the up and the down; a conflict between the forward and the backward, even a clash between that which circled and that which dispersed. Commotion and chaos, yet confidence and calm. These were the conflicting qualities of this morning in motion. But no movement caught my attention more than the water itself, and how, instead of rushing and receding, it flowed only in one direction, one motion: forward and outward. I was so mesmerized by this phenomenon that I never realized we had reached our famed vessel, La Maloja.

    There it was, finally before me. And I have to say that, the moment I laid eyes on this raft, all my anxieties dissipated, even about its name. It was beautiful, captivating—really it was! It was also the only raft of its kind there. La Maloja was three layers thick of sugarcane stalks, the most exquisite sugarcane I had ever seen: bathed in bright yellow and light-green and interspersed with hints of orange. But it was the shadings of green that dominated the palette: a textured translucent green that appeared to have been polished and emulsified. The paddles were sugarcane stalk too, but with the sturdy bark of royal palm attached as oars. The vessel sat like a silent flame of color shimmering in the sand. The paddles stood like two swords crossed in a regal and protective stance. Only the bottom layer was tightly wrapped and encased in the magical maloja that would guarantee the raft's bouyancy.

    "Well," Rigo asked without any hesitation. "When are we doing it? Is there anything we're waiting for?"

"That all depends," Henry said. "Do we want to take off by ourselves, or do we want to take off as part of a group? I was speaking to those guys over there and they said we could push off with them if we wanted."

Whatever Rigo's response, I never heard it. Just then I became aware of the only bodies, the only entities this morning, who seemed devoid of this clash of motion, the only group whose every movement seemed uniform and in sync.

"Why all the policemen?" I asked. "Are they stopping people? Or are they looking for someone?"

"Oh no," replied Amalia. "They couldn't care less. They're just making sure that anyone who leaves is over eighteen and is leaving freely, that nobody is being coerced."

"That's a good one!" Rigo scoffed. "What do they know about free will around here! Especially the police!"

I wanted Rigo to be careful. The mongrels still had the ability to mess with us if they so wished. They could still detain us if they wanted.

"Well, fortunately that's not anything we to have to worry about anymore, is it?" said Amalia. "This damned Communism, this stinking Socialist dictatorship. You know what?" she said, nearly foaming. "Let's not wait for anybody. Let's just go by ourselves as we planned."

"Yeah!" Rigo declared. "I'm all for that. But before we do, I want to pray first. I want to ask for God's blessing."

We all concurred with so excellent a suggestion, throwing our belongings onto the raft as it sat stationary along the sharp and rocky shore. The four of us then joined together and formed a circle. We clasped our hands in unison and closed our eyes reverently as Rigo led us in prayer.

"Father in Heaven," he began solemnly. "We gather here this morning to ask You for your blessing. We gather here to ask You for your protection and assistance. As we leave behind our homeland to embark upon a new life, please guide us safely across the water, please be with us the entire time we sail. Let us complete this journey safely, Father. Not just us, but everyone here. Heavenly Father, all-knowing God that You are, You know why we're doing this. You know that none of us want to risk our lives carelessly, that precious life you've given us and which we honor. But it is precisely because we honor and treasure that gift that we now commit ourselves to this choice. You know our desperation, Father. You know our suffering and misery and how life will never change here. You and you alone know this, Father, and have granted us this miracle. And so, Father, we petition you one last time: please join us this morning and light our way. Know that our intentions are pure and genuine and that we do this out of love for our families more than anything else. Thank you for your understanding and, once again, bless us and accompany us along this crossing. Thank you, Father. Amen."

As Rigo finished this prayer so moving, this invocation so eloquent, I could not release his hand. We all said *amén* in unison, but I could not open my eyes or look up. I didn't know about my companions, but I was still holding on, clutching Amalia's hand on one side and Rigo's on the other—clasping both of them tightly, fiercely—as it all came back to me, rushing but not receding.

I was back in my bed in Centro Habana unable to sleep. The apparition of the Angel Gabriel had just departed. Not only could I hear his words reverberating through my head, I was reliving the entire experience, bombarded with all his tidings and admonitions: the news that God Almighty, Creator of Heaven and Earth, had decided to have another child; that this time it would be a daughter; that I, a poor Cuban girl, had been selected as the mother of this daughter; that this daughter not only had to be born in Cuba, but raised in Cuba too. "Remember, Clara," the angel said to me. "*You must not take that trip tomorrow! Whatever you do, you must not take that trip!*"

I had to tell Rigo. No matter how ridiculous or crazy it all sounded, I had to make the confession. Why was I assuming he would reject the story? That he'd regard the incident as insane? He obviously had a spiritual side, latent though it may be. Look at how he had just anointed this undertaking with so inspirational a supplication. Clearly my husband was more profound a believer than he realized. I had to tell him then. I must give him the chance to know and now was the ideal moment if ever. I went to divulge this awkward secret of mine, but suddenly, without any provocation, another awkwardness crept into my mind: the sight of our driver this morning, the recollection of that absurd and narcissistic little man. Why could I not wipe his smug countenance from before me? Why could I not erase the imprint of his voice or block the impression of his words?

I felt my blood begin to boil. As the man's face hovered about me, and as his revelations about immigration talks and negotiating tables and Fidel's convicts and mental patients began to unfurl, all talk of angels and miracles no longer seemed relevant. It no longer mattered that God's chief messenger had paid me a visit about anything. In a clash of motion that demanded halting, a moment of truth descended upon me. The strands of a much higher truth were weaving themselves tersely and tautly, and ironically, I had the absurd little man to thank for it.

"I'm not going!" I blurted out, opening my eyes and releasing my hands from both grips to each side of me. "I'm not going anywhere!"

All three wasted no time in looking my way, and clearly, from their frozen expressions, they knew not what to think, knew not if I was joking or serious.

"Very funny, chica. Very funny," said Amalia. "Now let's go. I really want to push off now."

"I'm not joking, Amalia. I'm not leaving."

A crisis of silence wrapped around those three faces now. The shifting collage along that shore swirled all about us and collided unabated, but in this little corner of Cojimar we couldn't hear a sound or detect any motion. My companions continued staring at me, not knowing what to say or do or unable to determine whether I was playing a joke or in the throes of a panic attack, but Henry spoke next, figuring my nerves needed soothing.

"Clara," he began calmly. "It's all right, chica. I can assure you our vessel is going to be just fine; it won't sink. The only reason there might a problem is if the weight is unbalanced. You know that it needs four people on it to float safely, don't you?"

"Yes, Henry. I know that. And I'm sorry, chico, but you're going to have to find two other people to go in our place, ¿verdad Rigo?"

Another round of silence, much sharper silence, punctuated now by a clash of confusion and recrimination and total astonishment. The clamor and commotion of Cojimar kept feeding a steady stream of rafters answering the lure of the sea, but the silence enshrouding Rigo and Amalia and Henry only served to starve my companions of any hope. They stared hungrily at me as any notion of this being a joke clearly evaporated.

"Why are you doing this, Clara?" Rigo asked. "What's the matter with you?"

"I'm sorry, amor, I'm sorry. But look around you and see what's happening here? Why are we doing this? Why are we letting him get away with this?"

"Letting *who* get away with *what*?" Amalia shot out. "What are you talking about, Clara?"

"Letting Fidel get away with it, that's who."

Amalia volleyed back, this time injecting a sharp venom in her tone that threw me off guard.

"Fidel? Are you crazy, Clara? We're not letting Fidel get away with anything. He's the one letting *us* get away! He's the one allowing this to happen, remember?"

"Yes! And why? Why is that?"

"Who cares why, chica? What does that matter as long as it's happening?"

"It matters a lot," I replied. "For over a week now, ever since this all began, I've been thinking it was all a miracle, some act of God. But now I feel like a complete fool, an idiot. This isn't a miracle, it's manipulation, a charade. It's nothing but Fidel's latest ploy and we are all his pawns."

"Clara," Henry began softly. "Why don't you sit down a second and relax, chica? You're frightened is all, which is only natural."

I could see why Henry was an artist. He was sensitive and sensible and seemed to be the only level-headed one among us.

"I appreciate that, chico, but I'm not frightened, really I'm not. What I am is angry, mad that I've been fooled."

He didn't know what to say, but Amalia's eyes sure did. I had never seen such fire in them, two black and raging fires that could not be contained. Unlike the night before, she was back to her old self, filled with all the verve and vigor I knew her to possess.

"Say something to her, will you, Rigo? See if you can make her come to her senses."

I couldn't take the venom in her voice. It stung me deeply. She and Henry stepped off to the side, confering and gesturing in private, while Rigo and I did the same. I followed as he led me by the arm, escorting me a few feet away so that, we too, might talk in private.

Privacy. The one thing I had craved all morning: just the chance to talk alone with my husband without some extraneous presence or intrusive force coming between us. Yet a new presence seemed to be looming. I detected it from the corner of my eye. I turned to the side to look, and there it was, rather close to us too: a policeman, one of the mongrels in blue. One of the officers assigned to patrol the beach and ensure that anyone leaving from Cojimar was not being coerced. He appeared young, and carried himself with that brash air of confidence of someone who hailed from the countryside. No doubt one of Fidel's goons bussed in from the interior to beat down us haughty Habaneros. This young *guajiro* made no attempt to disguise the vigilant eye he kept on our exchange.

assumptions

"Amor," Rigo began. "What's the matter with you? What's going on, eh? You were going to tell me something earlier. Something that happened last night while I was gone. What was it, Clara?"

But I no longer wanted to delve into this matter or indulge in any part of it. What would I possibly say? "*Listen, amor. We can't go to the United States because, you see, last night I had a visitation from the Angel Gabriel, and even though the doctors have told me repeatedly that I cannot bear children, you and I will indeed be having a child together. Well, kind of together. You see, the child—a girl—will not really be yours. She'll belong to God. She's to be named Luz, daughter of God. I will be the mother, naturally, and you're going to help raise her just like Joseph helped Mary. There's one catch,*" I would add. "*Now, don't ask me why, amor, but the Angel Gabriel told me I could not leave Cuba. He was quite emphatic about that. He said the child had to be raised here in Cuba. You understand now why we can't leave? You get it?*"

But I stopped my thoughts cold in their tracks and shuddered at this ludicrous scenario. Was that what I would say? Was that how I would present it? So that Rigo could stare at me in disbelief and think I had completely lost my mind? No, I wouldn't do it. I'd do nothing of the sort.

"It was nothing, Rigo. Nothing happened last night. Nothing at all. It's what happened this morning, just now. I can't stop thinking about all the things that absurd little man told us. I can't get it out of my head."

"Who?" Rigo asked in earnest.

"The driver!" I replied. "That preposterous little know-it-all."

"What things, Clara? What things did he say?"

"You know what things, Rigo. You heard them yourself: that Fidel is the one engineering all this, the one who conceived this whole plan. What if all these people fleeing are just his minions? What if they're spies going over to infiltrate? Or what if they're convicts and mental patients and we'll be seen as nothing but Marielitos?"

"You don't know that, Clara. You don't know that for a fact."

"Of course I do, Rigo. It all makes sense now. How else do you explain all this? How else?"

"It's a miracle, Clara. You said so yourself and I believe it now. You were right, amor."

"No, Rigo. I was wrong, dead wrong."

"Stop it, Clara! You're just scared, amor. Henry was right. You're scared."

"I'm not scared, Rigo. I was simply wrong. I made the wrong assumption and I'm not afraid to admit it. All this commotion and chaos is no miracle. You want to know the real miracle? It's what happened the day of the revolt, the rebellion on the fifth. It was the brave people who stood up to our captors. It was the chants of freedom that rang through the streets and the defiance along the Malecón. It was the breaking of windows at the Deauville and the throwing of rocks at those mongrels in blue. *That* was the miracle, Rigo. Not this. Don't you see that, for the first time in our lives, we felt courage and conveyed it? *That* was the miracle, Rigo This is just cowardice, compliance with Fidel's plan. He's got us exactly where he wants us, and we're playing right into his hands. Hasn't this been his goal all along? To get us out of here, all those who hate this? Of course he's only too glad to discard us. Each time one of us washes up on the beach or perishes in the ocean, he's only too thrilled for it. We're nothing but thorns in his side, weeds to pluck from this caged garden. I'll tell you one thing, Rigo: the only ones not going anywhere are the two who started all this, the two who ignited the revolt. Those two guys now labeled as delinquents and derelicts. God help them, Rigo. Why do you think all these policemen are here? They're not here to check ages or ensure that no one is being coerced. They're here looking for those two. They're hunting them down and God help them when they're found. Now tell me you agree with me, amor. Tell me you understand all this and no longer want to go."

I strove to stay focused on Rigo and his reply, but I

couldn't. That damned mongrel kept distracting me. He wouldn't budge from where he stood some ten feet away. *Privacy.* I couldn't find privacy even here, among the chaos and clutter of Cojimar. The mongrel and his partner were on their radios seemingly checking someone's carnét, but I knew it was just a ruse. He kept stealing furtive glances our way, clearly focused on our exchange. Maybe he thought Rigo was one of the rock throwers. Maybe he thought I was the rock supplier. I didn't know. I just knew that, the longer I waited impatiently for my husband's response, the longer it took for him to say something, the worse it fared for me.

"No, Clara. I'm not," he finally replied. "I'm not."

How heartily I embraced him just then, immediately thanking God and the Virgin for answering my prayer.

"¡Gracias, amor! ¡Gracias! Thank God you agree with me. ¡Gracias, Señor! Now let's go tell them we're not going, Rigo. In fact, let's get Henry and Amalia to see the light."

"No Clara," he uttered impassively. "You don't understand, chica. What I mean is *no,* I'm not telling them that. What I mean is *yes,* I'm still going."

I couldn't have heard correctly. I couldn't have. For me to have heard what I thought I just heard could only be the result of one thing. It was all catching up with me: the exhaustion, the delerium, the strain and stress of the last ten days. How badly my whole body shook. How savagely the strands of stubborn disbelief pulled at me from both ends, scouring away at my very constitution as that mongrel in blue continued eavesdropping on us, continued looking our way as if to determine whether he should intervene, as if perhaps Rigo and I might be on Fidel's Most Wanted list.

"No, amor, you can't be serious."

"I am, Clara! I'm dead serious!" he said, grabbing me firmly by the arms and looking me squarely in the eyes.

"Remember what I told you last night, Clara. Remember what I said: make sure you were commited to this, make absolutely sure because there was no turning back. I would not be changing my mind once I moved forward. Remember that?"

My shoulders collapsed as I cried. Of course I remembered. Of course I did. But no matter how much I sobbed or shook my head or my entire chest caved in and heaved, I could not accept or believe this was happening. It was all some horrible dream and I could only feel the mongrel's presence stronger than ever, as if he were getting ready to intervene and get to the bottom of our altercation. Privacy. Why was there never any privacy in Cuba? No time, nowhere.

"I was wrong, amor, I was wrong. Say you're staying with me. I'm your wife, chico. You're my husband. What about all the people in Rio Piedras who are counting on you? What about the library project in Camagüey? You're going to abandon that too?"

But Rigo's eyes held fast to mine, their expression stern and intractable, yet eerily calm.

"This is what you haven't told me about, isn't it, Clara? This is what happened last night while I was gone? You had a change of heart. You decided not to go through with this, didn't you? That's why you hardly packed anything. Why you stayed in bed so late this morning and took your sweet time moving about. You planned this all along, didn't you, Clara? Yet you accuse Fidel of engineering things!"

"No, chico, that's not true. I swear that none of this occurred to me until right now, until the words of that absurd little man sank in and made sense to me. I had an epiphany, Rigo, a revelation of some sort."

"What do you mean an *epiphany*, chica? What do you mean *a revelation?* You know that this whole religion thing has really gone to your head. What made sense to you? That all these people here this morning are not courageous? That they're just fools falling for Fidel's latest ploy? Don't you be a fool yourself, Clara! They *are* courageous; they are brave. And for you to think otherwise is an insult, a slap to their faces. What difference does it make if Fidel is playing one of his

assumptions

tricks or not? Who cares if the end result is freedom? *Freedom, Clara!* That is all any of us cares about—libertad! Freedom and being able to eat. Is that so bad? For the last time, Clara, are you going with us or not?"

I finally had my answer. If there was ever any chance I might reveal what transpired last night, Rigo's words just sealed his fate. How had he just put it? *This whole religion thing has gone to my head. This whole religious thing!* Now I knew how receptive he'd be to last night's visitation. I turned from him and looked toward the water. I didn't know if it was my imagination, but the tide seemed higher, the current much stronger, and I could hear the words of the Angel Gabriel galloping toward me from across the waves, all his tidings and admonitions..

"No, Rigo!" I said definitively. "I am not! I can't go, and I'm not going. And I'm begging you to do the same, chico. Don't leave me, Rigo. You're my life and I love you."

"What do you mean you can't, Clara? Why can't you?"

I suddenly felt such anger at my husband that I refused to answer him. No, I felt anger and defiance. If now was the perfect time to divulge the visitation from the Angel and reveal the admonition that I stay in Cuba, I refused to do so. I would not share this with him in any way. Not with what little regard or respect he just showed me. Courage indeed! Of course, I didn't know—nor did I assume to know—the driving forces behind all those gathered here, those who had been coming for ten days now and would surely keep coming. Frustration, of course. Desperation, for sure. A hunger for freedom, no doubt. But there was also an element of opportunism here, of pure adventure and wanderlust, and these were the forces now catapulting Rigo to flee: a lust for adventure, a lust for escape. He had to keep in mind that, as of yesterday, I *still* had been battling him, I *still* had to persuade him to leave. Had it not been for all my pleas and supplications, we wouldn't be standing here right now; instead, he'd be getting ready to return to Rio Piedras. A craving for action. A greed for excitement. These were the forces truly driving him and I felt betrayed. Not only was he choosing adventure over me, he was willing to sacrifice our love and marriage for it.

"Answer me, Clara! What do you mean you can't? What happened last night while I was gone, chica? Why did you have a change of heart?"

"Nothing happened, Rigo, nothing at all! But I won't allow you to strand me. I won't allow you to abandon me."

Still, Rigo persisted.

"What happened last night, Clara? Tell me, chica. It was something serious, and you know it. You were on the brink of telling me right before Amalia showed up."

"For the last time, chico, nothing! Nothing happened! I was lonely is all. Lonely and scared."

But the look in Rigo's eyes said he wasn't buying my explanation. It was the architect in him, always needing to inspect every nook and cranny and account for every morsel of detail.

"So you're not going to tell me? Is that what you're saying? You know something, chica, I don't know you. For the first time in my life, I can honestly say I don't know you."

"You *do* know me, Rigo. You *do* know me, and if you loved me, you wouldn't leave me. That's all it boils down to."

"I'm not the one doing the leaving, Clara. I'm not the one doing the abandoning. You're abandoning me—you are, chica! So I'm going to ask you one final time. Are you joining me? Are we going together, or am I going alone?"

My body wept heavily and uncontrollably and even shook from convulsions.

"I'm not abandoning you, amor. I love you, Rigo. You're my life and you know it."

"Well, if I'm your life, you'll come with me, won't you?"

But I could only keep sobbing and shaking my head 'no' as the salty taste of tears invaded my senses. He *was* my life. Since the age of twelve I had loved him. But for the first time

assumptions

ever I was seeing that he truly didn't love me. He couldn't possibly love me and the tightening strands of this realization wove themselves so arduously around my heart I thought it would explode. How could he? How could he love me anywhere near what I loved him? When you loved someone, you didn't give that person an ultimatum. That was only when you loved excitement more; when you were choosing a foreign land and all its tarnished allure over the person you had vowed to share your life with. What purpose would it serve to tell him about the visitation? If it was true that, soon enough, I would be with child and needed Rigo by my side, what difference did that now make? Now that I knew how he felt. What would such a man possibly care about fathering a child not even his? *No!* It was settled. I knew what I must do and how I must act. I decided once and for all—right there along the black and rocky shore of Cojimar—that I would not say anything about my predicament—not one word. Never would I divulge to Rigo the visitation of August 14 or what the Angel Gabriel had revealed to me.

"No!" I uttered firmly, resolutely, that salty taste of tears finally evaporating from my senses. "I won't go, I won't."

"Well then, Clara, I guess this is good-bye. Good-bye, plain and simple."

"Don't tell me you're serious, Rigo. Don't tell me you're going through with this."

"Listen to me, Clara! And listen to me good! I *am* doing this! And I'm doing it for the two us, amor, because I love you. You're not thinking clearly. You've panicked at the last moment and it's all right. I understand. You're scared and I can't fault you for that. Believe me, now that I'm standing in front of this enormous ocean, I can see why anybody would be scared. You think I'm not? Our brothers and sisters are leaving in groups, and we hear the stories of everyone making it across safely, but all that changes when you're standing in front of this endless ocean face to face with it. How quickly hope withers when its vastness stares you down. I'm terrified, Clara. Deep down I'm terrified. But something else terrifies me more: the prospect of what will happen to us—what will happen to me—if we both stay behind. Understand what I'm going to tell you, amor: I'm leaving. I'm going ahead and sticking with the plan—*our plan*. I'm leaving for the United States. Not for me, but for us. I'm going to San Francisco to find work as an architect, and after just one year and one day, I'm sending for you. How's that, amor? That way you can arrive by plane and won't have to *touch* so much as a drop of water. Think about it. If I leave right now it won't be so bad. It will be no different than my going to Rio Piedras for the school year. You won't even notice my abscence. The months will fly by, and before you know it, I'll be sending for you. As for Amalia and Henry, don't worry about them. I'll explain it all. They'll understand and forgive you, just as I understand and forgive you."

"Rigo," I uttered in disbelief, a disbelief so profound there was no navigating its depths. "Are you telling me you're actually going? You're actually taking off?"

"I am, amor. I am."

If I should have fallen to the ground hysterically, and begun sobbing and pleading like a typically wounded female, I stood firm and resolute and my heart even hardened.

"Let me have my things, chico. Take my things out of the backpack right now."

There was nothing left to say. Rigo turned and headed toward the vessel. Amalia and Henry sat there anxiously, in abject abeyance awaiting their fate.

"What's happening?" Amalia asked. "¿Qué pasa, chico?"

But rather than diffuse his focus by uttering a single word, Rigo remained stonily silent, resolute, on course as he reached for the green backpack and proceeded to retrieve my belongings. Amalia and Henry both knew what this meant. My best friend immediately buried her face in her hands and cried while Henry embraced her and tried to soothe her. After a few sobs she attempted to break free of him and head toward me, but Henry clutched onto her firmly and would not let her go.

assumptions

"Here, Clara," Rigo said. "Here are your things."

I didn't say a word. I numbly accepted my belongings, but with barely the force to hold them. I could only focus on the sight of Amalia downcast and crying. Rigo had the audacity to embrace me. Worse, I had the audacity of wanting to embrace him back, of wanting to hold onto him so tightly my body might meld into his and he physically couldn't leave me. But I quickly tamed this audacious urge, this sickening sentiment of mine. I simply let my body go limp until I felt dead again, as I had for so long. Something was quickly scooping out all my false hope and my blind belief so that my entire body felt hollow. For so long I had felt dead inside. Now I felt empty and lifeless from the outside in.

"I love you," he said, unclasping me from the audacity of his embrace, even kissing me lightly on the lips. "I love you, and we'll be together again, amor, I promise you."

So it all ended. That simply. That uneventfully. Rigo turned and headed back toward La Maloja, that beautiful green vessel that would pull him out of my life forever. I couldn't believe it was actually happening. It had to be a dream of some kind or some cruel prank. A visitation from the Angel Gabriel seemed more real than this. As Rigo's steps took him farther and farther away from me, I kept thinking I would awaken from this nightmare and a soothing illumination would bask my heart once more. I even found myself taking a few steps and following numbly behind until, again, I felt some intrusive presence. I stopped. It was that damned policeman again! That mongrel in blue who had glued himself to us. He kept lingering and looming out of the corner of my eye. Why wouldn't he leave us alone? Why wouldn't he just get lost?

Rigo didn't turn around. As he reached the raft I knew what he was thinking. I could feel it. He was hoping I'd call out to him, hoping that I'd have a final change of heart, hoping that I'd run toward him and admit I had momentarily lost my mind, but now fully regained my senses. I knew this had to be his silent hope. I still knew his heart and mind. But it wouldn't happen. I would not give in and now I felt doubly betrayed. Not only had he chosen adventure over me, Rigo had robbed me of the right to be angry with him and unleash my fury. How could I possibly be mad? As gentle and loving as he had acted, how could I be angry? Abandoned yes, angry no.

I stayed put as he conferred with Henry and Amalia, breaking the news that I could not be swayed. The moment he finished Amalia broke away from their huddle and advanced toward me. I braced myself. She either intended on pleading with me one last time, upbraiding me for my selfishness, or physically dragging me onto the raft whether I liked it or not. Whatever her intentions, I would never see them realized. I would never see or talk to Amalia again because, just then, our friend the policeman, that mongrel in blue, blocked her path and brought her to a halt.

Good, I thought. At last the mongrel had found a way to make himself useful. Maybe *he* could stop the three of them. Maybe he would arrest and detain them for coercion and Rigo would be charged with attempted abandonment. I couldn't make out their peculiar exchange, but the mongrel suddenly accompanied Amalia toward the raft. In a matter of seconds this new foursome began speaking and nodding and gesturing vigorously. I kept an eye out for any hint of trouble. Maybe this mongrel had mistaken Henry and Rigo for the rock throwers of August 5. Maybe they would be paraded as *elementos antisociales* and counterrevolutionaries on State television. But if I expected the mongrel to radio for assistance while he inspected their carnéts, little did I envision what happened next. It was truly inconceivable, not to be believed. Yet it unfolded before my eyes in the strands of stunned disbelief. Rigo, Amalia, and Henry had just procured my replacement, had just secured the fourth passenger they needed so badly. I stood and watched in astonishment as the mongrel in blue took off his uniform, removed his black boots, belt and gun, stripped down to his shorts, and became the fourth passenger on our raft, La Maloja.

It produced nothing less than a thunderous applause, the most boisterous response of the morning in Cojimjar by all who had witnessed this unlikely apparition: one of Fidel's own, in some moment of crisis, stripping down to his underwear in desperation and climbing onto a raft to join the exodus. If only our great uncle could have been there to witness it. Only then would it have completed so perfect a portrait.

This sight alone clinched the spectacle of Cojimar for the carnival it truly was, with La Maloja winning a prize for the most memorable float of the morning. Unforgettable. Indelible. Unstoppable. So it marched on, this parade of sorts, gliding with a momentum that could not be reversed. But instead of marching and stomping and waving batons along a planned route, this parade drifted slowly upward and floated every which way into infinity, jabbing the currents of those unpredictable waters with paddles and oars as they lifted into oblivion. Only one of the revelers from that winning float managed to wave good-bye at me: Henry, who seemed to bear no ill will despite what I had done. Even the mongrel, no longer in blue, waved enthusiastically my way, his smile so bright and glowing it looked like whitecaps riding the waves. Amalia, however, kept her back to me as the float drifted away and I couldn't blame her. I had stranded her, stranded our friendship. I too would have felt betrayed—destroyed more like it. I would never talk to Amalia again after that morning in Cojimar, even when, years later, she returned to Cuba to visit her family.

As for Rigo, his eyes never wavered from mine the entire time he faded from view. Even as the water drew him away from me and he became smaller and smaller in that swallowing ocean, I could feel the pull of his eyes upon me. I could feel his eyes searching and seeking me even when, surely, he could no longer distinguish me from any of the others gathered along the shore.

"Rigo!" I cried out. "Rigo!"

I couldn't help myself. I knew he couldn't hear me, but I cried out anyway. I had to stay connected in some way. The image of Rigo floating off would haunt me forever, the sight of him vanishing into nothingness while I stood there helpless. All the days of my life I would recall the events of Cojimar, of how and where they occurred with the precision of some internal compass. The commotion. The contraptions. The consequences. All these unwelcome recollections would rip through my mind with the force of some savage storm, a criss-crossing of images along the straits of memory to be played back and forth over and over again.

He was leaving for good. I didn't need to assume it. I knew it. As for me, I also wanted to leave. I wanted to run and hide. I felt as if everyone on that beach knew who I was and what I had done: chickened out, discarded my husband and stranded best friend, committed a horrible act of betrayal. I felt that everyone standing there looked at me and regarded me a traitor, a coward. Not only an hoja mala—a bad leaf—but maloja itself: that which must be pulled off and discarded, that which must be burned alive out in the fields. I wanted to run back home and hide within the pages of my father's text. I wanted to jump onto page 609 and have someone forever snap that book tightly shut. No wonder Hemingway had chosen this spot as the setting for his famous novel, except I had just rewritten it. *The Foolish Girl and the Sea*—that's all I was. I had done exactly as Santiago had: captured the big fish only to throw it back into the water and have it vanish forever. I also wanted to vanish. I wanted to disappear even though I had no idea where to go or how to get back to Centro Habana. A bus maybe. Walk even. But a taxi? Never. I just wanted privacy. I wanted to be annonymous. Most of all, I wanted to move away from the water, far away from it.

Water. As much I had always loved the water, from that moment on I avoided going anywhere near it. Never again would water hold any more magic for me, any more mystery. Never would I walk along the shore of any beach again or sit along the Malecón to wonder and dream and gaze at the infinite expanse of horizon. Water would come to terrify me. No wonder I had thought of nothing but water all week. No wonder it had haunted my dreams. I'd been issued a warning, but had failed to recognize it: a foreshadowing of the betrayals water would bring. The ocean. From a distance so silky a surface, so alluring. Up close, a dark and deep

assumptions

monster constantly in motion, constantly swallowing things up.

No longer did I yearn to be near the water, but wanted Rigo near me. How I ached to be at his side. The farther he drifed away, the closer I felt him to me. The more invisible he became to my eyes, the more visible he grew in my mind. I envisioned him before me and could hear his parting words: *he was carrying on with our plan; he would go to the United States and send for me after a year; he was doing this for the two of us because he loved me.* For a fleeting moment I entertained his ideas. I longed desperately to believe in them. This future he had carved out for us. This illusion of living blissfully in the land of freedom and raising our daughter. Both families living nearby and everyone existing in Capitalist contentment. Deep down I knew this would never come to be. Deep down, in that monstrous ocean that can be the human heart, where the waters of doubt dampen all our dreams, I knew this would never happen.

For one thing, I would never dream of going to the United States again. Not in a year. Not in two years. Not ever. If I still hated Fidel Castro for this prison he had created and the misery he continued to inflict upon his own people, how betrayed I now felt by the United States, stabbed in the back by all its pretense and promises. America. So much like the ocean. So silky and alluring on the surface. So deep and dark a monster underneath. Constantly stretching, spreading, hunting new prey. America and its Eagle. Not a bird of might or majesty—but a bird of prey. Uncle Sam. Just as crotchety and incorrigible an old man as our own great uncle. Both men always having to assume control of everything. How much a hand had the United States played in all this? How much had they engineered this all themselves? *Back to the negotiating table.* Wasn't that what the absurd little man had said? Had the Americans walked away from that table on purpose? Had they deliberately simmered that pressure cooker to the point it would explode? How much had Uncle Sam possibly conspired with our own Cuban uncle?

I had to stop myself. I was assuming too much. How

betrayed I felt by the United States now and all it represented: the ambition and consumerism, the greed and illusion. That was all it stood for. Land of blinding delusions. Land of cruel separations. I decided then and there I would rather starve in Cuba and dream about freedom than be a slave to the United States of Avarice. No wonder the angel had admonished me not to go there. No wonder. God's next child had to be born anywhere in the world except that dangerous place.

Freedom. How I savored that right now. How free it felt to know precisely where I stood. Determined never to step foot on American soil—how liberating it all felt. I would do it from here. I would fight Fidel Castro from within the walls of this inferno. Surely another miracle would strike, a true miracle like that of August 5. A rebellion. A revolt. This time I'd partake in the uprising. I'd weave myself into the insurrecton and gladly give my life if necessary. I believed this as Rigo got sucked into the hunger of that horizon. I presumed I'd lose my life long before seeing him again. As that float made of sugarcane evaporated into the mists, I was certain I would die and go to Heaven long before we locked eyes again. But I was wrong. Even as I stood there, myself dissolving into a tiny grain of sand within all those endless grains of sand, I may have believed all this, assumed all this, but I was wrong.

In the remaining days of my life I would indeed see Rigo once more. Only once. It would happen many years later, long after this morning of August 15 in the year of our Lord 1994. By then, however, so much would be changed, so much would be different, his presence would have no effect on me whatsoever. No sadness. No hopefulness. No sense of loss either.

If one had ever taken solace in the notion that love could pick up where it left off, what a mistake to assume that. If one had ever taken solace in thinking that love could always revive its step along that endless parade of marvels and intimacies and the infinite wonders that it delights in creating, what an incorrect assumption.

By the time Rigo and I were to see each other again, so

assumptions

much would happen, so much would transpire, it seemed as if the world had already ended and started anew, that the Earth had simply been obliterated and been newly reborn. By then we would be such completely different people that one would safely assume we had never loved each other at all. By then we would feel so completely foreign to each other, one would assume we had never even known each other at all. But none of that mattered for the time being. At present I took no solace in anything. I simply wanted to move away from where I stood and step off this rocky shore, overcome by that sickening smell of coffee again to the point I began to gag.

What was the matter with me? Why did I feel seasick even though I clearly wasn't at sea? And why could I detect the odor of greasy food from what seemed miles away? Was this the result of not eating anything all morning? I didn't know. But I did feel a new clash of movement taking place internally, inside me, some kind of motion sickness though my feet were planted firmly on the ground. As the waves of some vile and advancing nausea swelled deep from within and brought everything rushing upward, I felt my head turning and circling, spinning furiously into some dusk of uncharted disgust. I felt grimy from the spray of sea salt, and every strand of hair on my head felt wildly out of place. It may have been midmorning, but I no longer felt alert or awake. Sure enough my legs gave way so that, next thing I knew, I lay motionless on the ground.

I had fainted. In a spectacle within a spectacle, I crashed down near the shore. How could I not have? Rigo had just stranded me. The one and only love of my life had just vanished beyond the ocean for good. Into a land of fog and darkness guarding the entrance to Hades. Telling me he loved and cherished me, but casting me aside. For no less than a year at that! When already we had spent so much time apart in our brief marriage. How could anyone not feel sick and weak after so inconsiderate an act? *Impossible!* I struggled to stay alert. I battled to remain fully awake, trying to brush the incident off and fight the criss-cross of emotions.

But I couldn't do it. I had not the force. I had not the will.

As the soothing strands of unconsciousness undid their tight weave and fully came undone, I felt relief in knowing I could no longer fight anything. I simply lacked the strength as my body hit the ground. I may have only fainted for a matter of seconds, but I took solace in knowing that it felt like hours upon hours.

6

solace

*august 15
mid morning*

"Wake up, compañera! But, please, be careful! You may have a concussion, so please, don't move any!"

I couldn't move if I wanted to. I couldn't even budge. As my eyes fluttered open, and I came to with a start, I found a face looking down on me, sturdy and strong. I didn't know this face, yet it looked vaguely familiar. Its clear brown eyes seeking to comfort me; its gentle smile trying to assure me. The expression on this face gave such warmth, I didn't want to move. It was only upon realizing exactly what I looked at, that my body stiffened and I slightly recoiled. It was nothing less than one of the mongrels in blue, crouching down right over me just inches from where I lay.

"¿Qué pasó?" I asked startled. "What happened?"

"You blacked out, compañera, right here along on the shore. Are you all right? You think you're hurt?"

What a question! Did the mongrel really need to ask? Couldn't he tell? Of course, I was hurt. Of course, I wasn't all right. Not only was I light headed and nauseous still, I was disconsolate, dejected, drowning deep in a dusk of despair. But more than anything, I felt repulsed, disgusted to have one of the mongrels in blue crouched down so close to me.

"I blacked out?" I asked. "But how? I...I don't understand. I don't remember anything."

By now it wasn't just the mongrel in blue hovering over me but a crowd of spectators swarming about, all the countenances of Cojimar: the curiosity seekers, the caregivers, the clowns—they had all gathered round to partake of the spectacle. For a moment the focus was off the water and onto the sand; off those fleeing and onto those fainting. And a mongrel sat huddled in their midst, but whispers abounded about the other spectacle everyone had just witnessed: the officer stripping down to his shorts and jumping onto the raft, the very same raft I should have been on. Nobody knew what to make of it, whether it had all been real or some kind of stunt. One thing was real: how quickly his remnants had been collected, how swiftly a responding pack of mongrels rushed over to whisk away the uniform, baton, and gun.

"Don't worry, compañera! Don't you worry any!" said the mongrel crouched over me. "I've radioed for assistance and a car is on its way. Just stay put. Make sure you don't move any, please."

Had he just said car? As in police car? Now I wouldn't stay put even if I wanted to. Hopefully he'd meant ambulance, but I doubted it.

"That won't be necessary," I said. "I don't need a car. I'm perfectly fine."

I finally began to move. I even managed to switch from sprawled on my side to flat on my back. But the moment I went to prop my elbows up underneath me and hoist myself up, the onlookers leaped into action and launched into a litany of advice.

"¡No, chica! ¡No!" they urged in near unison. "He's right.

You may have a concussion! You shouldn't be moved."

"Quick! Get her some saltwater," someone suggested. "It's the best thing for fainting."

"That's smelling salts, chico! Not saltwater," another countered.

"I meant for her face!" explained the prior person. "I meant to throw on her, not to drink."

"Look!" someone chimed in. "She's passing out again! What she needs is CPR! What she needs is resuscitation."

"I can do that!" some guy eagerly volunteered. "I'm certified in that."

As the crowd burst into laughter, I took notice of this individual and his grungy appearance. He reminded me of a mangy street dog, like the ones so prevalent throughout the streets of Havana, abandoned and neglected animals scrounging around for whatever scraps they could find. The sight of this flea-bitten creature revolted me. He too looked familiar, even if I couldn't figure out why. Regardless, I was not passing out again. I needed no resuscitation. What I needed was to be left alone. As the crowd swarmed and swelled about me that was all I wanted, but there was no getting through to the onlookers or quelling their solicitude.

"Thank you all very much, really," I called out. "You're all very kind, and I appreciate it, but I'm fine now and I'm getting up."

The crowd protested at once. They objected vigorously that I knew not what I was doing, that I was in grave danger of seriously hurting myself. But I proceeded anyway. Only the mongrel seemed to respect my wishes. He extended a hand and pulled me to my feet so that, at last, the crowd stepped back and cleared the path.

"I believe this is yours, compañera," he said to me.

I looked down. In his hands were my belongings, the items that Rigo had wrapped up neatly in a plastic sheath.

"Yes," I said. "Thank you."

I reached out to retrieve them, but the mongrel held onto my possessions like a dog with a bone.

"That's all right, compañera," he smiled. "I'll carry it for you. I don't want you exerting yourself any."

"It's no trouble," I insisted. "I'll take it."

He relented, handing me back what were probably the most important possessions I had in life: my journals, the prayer cards, the infamous letter to my father from Iraq, my birth certificate and carnét. How grimy I began to feel, and itchy too. Sand covered me in patches, and with my back to the ocean, I dusted myself off. Several in the crowd tried lending assistance, looking for a towel I might use as they peppered me with questions. *Where are you from, compañera? Where do you live? Do you want to go to the hospital? Do you want anyone to accompany you? Are you hungry or thirsty at all? Surely you must be thirsty.* No! I screamed inwardly. No! I wanted to be left alone, not pried or picked at. I wanted to block out everything surrounding me. But despite the deafening screams inside my head, I couldn't drown out the clamor of Cojimar, especially the whispers of this swarming crowd that: *I was the one, the girl who had backed out at the last moment as my companions took off.* I thought I might black out again. I felt my legs giving way until that slimy individual, the one who had offered to resuscitate me, brought me crashing into consciousness, the full throes of it.

"It's all right, compañera. There's still time if you want."

Before I could ask *time for what*, an unnerving scream punctuated the moment.

"¡Mire!" one of curiosity-seekers yelled out excitedly. "Look over there!"

The crowd quickly reset its sights, shifting its focus from 'all things sand' to 'all things water,' from fainting maiden to fleeing men. It swarmed toward shore to a raft resembling a horse cart—yes, a horse cart of all things! It was called *el Caballo del Mar*, which they had painted red and gray. Seven passengers boarded as the craft prepared to push off. My caregivers had gone to cheer this group of rafters on and their slightly worrisome vessel. Only two mongrels remained faithfully at my side: the mongrel in blue and the mongrel in rags—that grungy and disheveled animal that made me disgustedly uncomfortable.

There was something odd about him, something vaguely reminiscent. It wasn't until I took note of his eyebrows and how they connected in the middle that I realized what: he looked just like the driver from this morning. *Este tipo* reminded me exactly of the preposterous little man who ran tirelessly at the mouth. But *este tipo* was not short or muscular or balding. He was tall and thin, and he had a full head of hair. He had a broken front tooth and another one entirely missing from along the top of his mouth. He wasn't dressed in Jordache jeans or a Calvin Klein shirt, but he had exactly the same face as the driver! He even had a similar voice, low and gruff, with those eyebrows that connected in the middle like two cockroaches joined at the head. He drove no taxi. His only mode of transportation seemed to be a Chinese bicycle. But he might as well have been the driver's fraternal twin.

"Hurry, compañera! Hurry, so you can go and make it!"

"Make what?" I asked perplexed.

"Over there!" he pointed out. "Don't you see what's happening? The group in the horse cart is getting ready to push off. Look! They've got room for one more. Why don't you see if you can jump on and join them? You've still got time, compañera. It's not too late to catch up to your companions. ¡*Dale!* Move!"

Even if someone had jolted me with volts of electricity, I couldn't move right now. What a foul and disgusting animal stood before me, a true mongrel. He really was the incarnation of the taxi driver, the man's malicious twin. Clearly, I was being haunted. Some horrible curse had befallen me: the Curse of Cojimar, where all my failings and weaknesses would forever be examined and exploited. How had this perfect stranger managed to zero in on the most vulnerable moment of my life and rub my face into it? How had he succeeded in peeling back the layers of my misfortune to make a mockery of it?

I didn't answer this mangy animal. Not because I didn't want to, but because I couldn't. I was that numb, that stung with inaction. Plus, I suddenly felt sick again. Being on my feet summoned forth those brutal waves of nausea. They rushed violently upward until I finally released the contents of my stomach, little as it may have been. I vomited and retched unable to stop. But rather than be repulsed by my retching, the toothless and mangy animal seemed amused by it all, watching me as if I were entertainment. It took the other mongrel, the one in blue, to finally get rid of him.

"*¡Dale tú chico!*" he said. "Why don't you jump on the raft yourself and *you* get the hell out here! You're not wanted here. You're not needed here."

The animal stood silent for a moment as he licked his wounds.

"Ey," he finally said, shrugging his shoulders. "*¿Qué pasa,* chico? I haven't done anything for you to talk to me that way."

The mongrel in blue wasted no time in growling and barking back.

"You want to see what you've done, chico? Do you? Maybe arresting you will show you. Maybe *that* will do it. Don't forget you're still in Cuba and I can haul your ass to jail for anything I want. Get lost now, chico! *¡Lárgate!*"

I straightened myself up. I tried regaining my composure as that taunting toothless animal walked off while pushing his bike in hand. But it wasn't to join the cheering along the shore. He simply vanished into the chaos and clutter of Cojimar never to be seen again. There had to be a reason why this kept happening, why I kept drawing all this negative energy to myself. There had to be. I had no idea of anything at the moment and knew not where we went, but I followed along as the mongrel led our way. How punishing the midmorning sun. How searing its ascent.

"Where are we going?" I asked. "I thought you said a car

was on its way."

"It is, compañera. It's right over there."

My eyes followed in the direction he pointed. No, it couldn't be. The Hemingway Monument again. Where this horrible ordeal had all started and unfolded. Wonderful. Just wonderful. More reminders, more negative energy.

"All the way over there?" I asked. "That's what you call the car coming around? Why don't I just walk home?"

The mongrel in blue ignored me. We strode in silence toward this phantom vehicle and the monument which the town of Cojimar had erected in honor of Hemingway. What must they all be thinking? All the faces of Cojimar. With each step I took I felt their probing, questioning eyes. *Who was the girl being escorted by one of the mongrels? Was she being arrested or assisted? Was she being detained or deported?*

How I wished this were the ancient city of Crimea rather than the tiny sea village of Cojimar. How I wished I were an ancient Cimmerian rather than a modern-day Cuban. That way I could hide in a shroud of darkness. That way nobody could track my movement from shoreline to street or see me walking side by side with one of the mongrels—except, I was not walking the mongrel, the mongrel was walking me, leading me on some invisible leash to *who-knew-where*. How desperately I wanted the clouds overhead to dissolve into the mists of a black Cimmerian fog where nobody could identify me or point me out as the girl who had cravenly stayed ashore while her companions had risked their lives at sea. Even the mongrel's colleagues threw nasty glances my way. Every few steps they would stop us and inquire suspiciously.

"You all right, chico? ¿Todo bien?"

"Sí, chico, sí," he would answer. "Todo bien."

Mongrels. All of them. It figures they were only worried about him. I was the damsel in distress, yet their concern was for the mongrel in blue. I tried disregarding it all. I still felt weak and dazed, stung from the encounter with that toothless freak. Nevertheless, I managed to catch plenty of snippets swarming all about; snippets of speculation but with one central topic on everyone's tongue: the policeman who had stripped down to his shorts and jumped aboard the raft. *Had he planned it all? Had it been spur of the moment? Had anybody else been in on it? Might it happen again? How could it be prevented, and who could be trusted now? What about his partner? Had his partner known anything about it?*

What did it matter? Why should anyone care? Hadn't Fidel said that *anyone* was free to leave? Including his own mongrels. Who cared whether the guy had stripped down to his shorts or taken off naked. The Americans would easily figure out why he had floated in half-clothed. But it wasn't until I caught even more of their snide speculation that I truly began to worry. *Who were those people he left with? Was it a random choice or planned? Did he know them intimately, or was it a last moment encounter on the beach? Who were those people? Where were they from?*

We neared Hemingway's bust. I felt weaker than ever from the brief but troubling walk. Worse, I felt ill at ease knowing that some anonymous mongrel and I would forever be linked by the morning's turn of events. I felt naked now, thin and threadbare and wishing I could wrap myself up in the strands of anonymity, wishing I could plunge deep into some Cimmerian darkness rather than be exposed by Cuba's specular sun. What a scolding castigating sun hung high overhead. How I wished that we, all those in Cojimar this morning, were ancient Cimmerians who dwelled in perpetual darkness rather than Cubans under the constant light of a microscope. Cubans whose actions were always exaggerated by some monstrous magnifying glass and whose every move was grotesquely amplified by the aid of some giant government crystal, like all the shiny crystals spread out before us now: microscopes and magnifying glasses in the form of row upon row of parked police vehicles—all meant to establish a presence in this crisis, all designed to send a message that, despite the desperation and disarray, there was still going to be order in the disorder, that all those who paced and kept constant watch could still see right through everyone.

"Here we are," announced the mongrel. "Here's the car."

"But where are we going?" I asked apprehensively. "Where are you taking me?"

"Why, to the nearest polyclinic," he replied. "Don't you want to be seen?"

"Seen for what chico? I only fainted. It's nothing more serious than that. What I want is to go home, that's what I want."

"I'm sorry, compañera, but I can't do that. I've only been authorized to take you to the nearest polyclinic."

"In a police vehicle?" I posed suspiciously. "Why not an ambulance? Why didn't you radio for an ambulance?"

He grew quiet for a moment, those clear brown eyes of his capturing an abundance of the ambient light.

"Compañera," the mongrel began. "I don't like having to discuss this, especially with a young girl such as yourself, but fine, I'll tell you why *not* an ambulance. You see, there's currently a shortage of ambulances here in Cuba. Ever since this Maleconazo of ten days ago, we need all the ambulances we can get here, and we need them available at all times. Every day, for the last ten days, bodies have been washing up, compañera: the drowned and mutilated bodies of our countrymen. That's what we need ambulances for, compañera: the corpses, the cadavers. Everything else is being handled in police vehicles, especially minor incidents. Everybody in Cuba may hate the police, but you certainly don't think we should drive around with dead bodies in our back seats, do you?"

I didn't know whether he was being serious or trying to comfort me. Those clear brown eyes of his glowed incandescently, but I didn't know whether he was trying to inject humor into this morbid affair or telling me the truth.

"All right," I said. "Fine, chico, I understand. But I'm not going to any clinic. I want to go home."

"And where is home, compañera?"

"Centro Habana," I said.

"Centro Habana!"

"Sí, chico, near the Malecón. Close to the Deauville, as a matter of fact. You do know where the Deauville is, don't you? The site of el Maleconazo!"

What had gotten into me? Why was I mouthing off to one of the mongrels? Especially now that I wasn't leaving? I guess Rigo's behavior from this morning had rubbed off on me.

"I think the whole world knows now where the Deauville is, don't you, compañera?"

"Let's hope so," I said. "Let's hope the whole world not only knows *where* it is, but what led to it."

Again, what had gotten into me? Why was I being so brash and openly hostile? I could easily be arrested and I knew it. Hadn't the mongrel just threatened that mangy animal with arrest? But maybe it was time I threw some rocks, even if only in the form of words.

"You don't trust me, do you, compañera? You think I'm up to something, don't you?"

"Well," I said. "Would it be that unlikely a supposition?"

"Fine, chica. Fine," he said. "I'm not only going to show you I'm not up to anything, I'm going to show you that you can trust me. Get in the car!" he ordered.

"Where are we going?" I asked.

"Where do you think we're going, chica? Centro Habana, that's where—Centro Habana, off the Malecón, near the Deauville itself. I'm sure I'll be fired, sanctioned severely, thrown in jail and never work in Cuba again, but I'm taking you to Centro Habana and dropping you off right on your doorstep just to show you that you can trust me. How's that, compañera? Now get in!"

I didn't know why, but without so much as another word or thought, I slid into the back of that police vehicle. The mongrel in blue held the door open for me as I melted into the backseat. He wasted no time in closing the door and walking round to the front. I may have been making the biggest mistake of my life, but what did it matter? Wasn't I alone now? Wasn't Rigo gone for good? What was there for me to look forward to? I had no one or nothing. What did it matter where this mongrel took me? Whether he was transporting me to Villa Marista or some other interrogation center. Whether I would be beaten or tortured or locked up for good. They could do whatever they wanted with me. How would anyone even find me since I was supposed to be gone?

Could I really rule out such a scenario? Hadn't I just heard with my own ears they'd be looking for me? The people who the mongrel had run off with. Wasn't I the only remnant of that group? The sole and stranded survivor of it. This mongrel knew something and his kindness was all a ruse. He had witnessed some portion of my exchange with Rigo and planned on delivering me into the hands of his superiors. I'd be pumped for information. I'd be coerced into providing names and addresses. If the government didn't already know, it would soon learn about Nelson and the group Insurrection and my involvement in it. Just as it already knew whose daughter I was and the disgrace that ended my father's life and career. My fate with the university was well-documented and now they would connect this incident to Rigo. I was cursed, really I was. And it wasn't just the Curse of Cojimar. It was the Curse of Cuba.

How wrong this mongrel had summed things up. He was definitely carrying a corpse in his car, definitely riding with a dead body in the backseat. He just didn't realize it. I was dead, just as I'd been dead for so long. Nothing I saw registered through my eyes. Nothing I thought penetrated my head. I felt nothing and the mongrel was simply transporting me to be buried, interred in some secret cell. Just in case I was wrong, just in case he really was dropping me off at my doorstep, I planned on carrying forth alone. Whether locked up in some facility or holed up inside my house, I was withdrawing from the world and going into seclusion.

That was all I felt grateful about with this mongrel: the seclusion and isolation in this backseat. The way he left me completely alone and rendered me solely unto my thoughts. The way he let me relive those last moments with Rigo as I delved into some inner space and lost all track of time. I kept expecting my captor to launch into some preliminary interrogation, to trick me into divulging information on the others. But my expectations went unfulfilled. Nothing of the sort took place. No probing or prying. No insinuations or innuendo. Nothing at all. Just calmness and quietude. Just a Cimmerian silence.

And how peculiar too, that here of all places, in the backseat of a police vehicle, as my head drooped lifelessly against the car window and I cried in silence in the presence of a total stranger, I finally felt alone. I could finally embrace the privacy I had craved all morning. The mongrel only asked for my address. No more than that. He obviously knew Havana with all its twists and turns. Only one commentary broke through the dispassionate daze of my despair, pulling me out of myself.

"That was my friend, you know…my partner."

"Who was you friend?" I asked obliviously, my tone midway between dazed and detached.

"The one who left with your companions."

I was no longer dead. My head shot up like a bullet in the backseat of that car. But that bullet was not taking my life, it was giving me life, especially as my eyes shot two more bullets right at him. *So that was it! Why he looked so familiar!* This was the mongrel who'd been hanging around the other mongrel, who'd been shifting back and forth and hovering in the background. For the first time that morning I took note of his physical appearance.

If he was younger than Rigo it couldn't have been by more than a few years, midtwenties certainly. He was taller than Rigo, thicker and sturdier too, probably from the much better diet afforded the mongrels, all the generous morsels of meat thrown their way to keep them well-fed and happy. He was fair complected. His eyes were a stunning clear brown, small but sharp. He had thick black hair he combed back and to the side. I had to admit that, for a mongrel, he wasn't bad.

"You knew him?" I asked.

"Knew him? He was my partner, chica, my best friend. I had no clue, no idea that he was going to do what he did."

The mongrel not only shook his head seemingly in disbelief, a chord of distress rang out in his voice. I, in turn, had no idea what to say. I was that astonished, that dumbstruck. But might this be a trick? Might this sudden revelation be some technique to loosen me up and get me to spill my guts? The thought crossed my mind, but his demeanor pointed to the contrary. He was being truthful and fell silent after the revelation. His eyes even reflected a mild hurt through the rearview mirror.

It was I who wanted to offer some solace now, to suggest he move vigorously and shake it all off. But I stopped myself. I remained leery of him, as I did of anyone in uniform. No wonder he had fixated on me. No wonder he had stayed readily on hand after I fainted. It all made sense now: his best friend and partner had taken off with my companions. If I might be interrogated, he definitely would he.

That silent ride in the backseat was no longer soothing, but a struggle, a swaying and a tossing about, a crosscurrent of images that receded and revived themselves repeatedly. But one particular image kept coming back to life in fiery defiance, haunting me, harassing me, stalking me: that of the absurd little man being right. This *was* all a game: a politically motivated game, a series of carefully executed maneuvers made from both sides.

I wanted to offer him some words of reassurance, but what good would it do? Nothing I'd say would change anything. Nothing I could offer him would have any transcending effect. I drooped my head against the window and gazed out to the streets. By now we were passing those hideous Soviet-style housing units in the eastern section of the city, those post-Revolutionary eyesores that Rigo had always loathed. We passed them quickly, zipping along as the car disappeared into *el túnel de La Habana*. The tunnel not only cut underground but underwater also. We looped around and emerged above ground. What a striking view of the city's skyline.

"I'm Manolo," he introduced himself. "And you, compañera?"

"Clara," I replied flatly, not caring if revealing my identity might be some fatal misstep. "My name is Clara."

"Clara, ey? That's a beautiful name. Nice to meet you, Clara. Think you can trust me now? Do you, Clara?"

I was neither dead nor alive now. I lay somewhere in the middle between life and death, between silence and sound, in a state of dispassionate abeyance that I noticed not where we were at the moment. Not near the Malecón. Not even close to the Deauville, but at my front door. The mongrel indeed made good on his word, dropping me off on my doorstep as promised. So then, *Did I trust him? Could I trust him?* Before I could think of answering this, I contemplated one thing. I heard but one thing: the sound of his voice saying my name. It too struck a tone between life and death. It too hit a chord between light and dark. How soothing to hear my name being spoken. What solace the sound of that voice gave me.

But this state of calm died as quickly as it came to life. I would now have to walk into my house without finding Rigo. He would no longer be there to greet me or embrace me and I came crashing into consciousness, the full throes of it, stripping me of any false comfort or unsatisfying solace so that I screamed inside my head: *What did it matter whether I trusted you or not? What earthly difference could it possibly make? It's not as if we were friends or neighbors or even acquaintances. We were nothing, nothing at all to each other, and would forever remain that way!*

All these bullets sat poised on the tip of my tongue, ready to fire off in rapid succession. But I never got the chance to shoot any of them. The moment that fierce and feisty falcon who was my mother spotted a police car in front of her house, she immediately flew into the street to look and investigate, to find out why it had planted itself right outside her door.

That soothing voice of Manolo's never got to hear my own voice in return. Before I could tell him whether I trusted him or decide *if* I should trust him or not, another voice punctuated the moment with every exclamation point and question mark she could fling.

"¡Clara!" Mamá cried out. "¡Clara mija!"

Upon seeing my mother plowing toward the vehicle, I thought she might throw something through the back window. I even thought she had some rocks in her hand. Fortunately, she did not. She merely flung the back door open and lunged for me in a fury.

"What in the world is happening, hija? Why are you in a police car? And what are you even doing here? You're supposed to be on your way to the United States. Where's Rigo, mija?"

I was still adrift in that sphere between sound and silence. I managed to exit the vehicle, but at the mention of Rigo's name I thought I'd pass out again. All I wanted was to hide, to seek the seclusion I had vowed to give myself. Angélica and Pilar might have been present in the living room, but I never knew it. I saw no one or nothing. I merely slid through the rust-colored walls of our house as if being sucked through some secret tube in the hallway, some hidden tunnel that cut through both ground and water. I shot straight to my room. Upon entering I closed the door and bolted it shut.

Right away, I could barely stand it. I could barely tolerate occupying that space and knowing Rigo would not be coming back. I threw myself on the bed and began to cry. Meanwhile, the mongrel had actually entered the house. I could hear him through the door as he explained to Mamá all that had transpired this morning. His muffled, distant voice no longer had that caring or soothing quality.

"But what in the world happened?" Mamá asked. "What is she doing here?"

"I couldn't tell you exactly what, señora, but I think she got scared."

"Scared? And Rigo just took off?" Mamá asked.

"Which one was Rigo?"

"Her husband, that's which one."

I didn't know if it was my imagination, but it seemed the mongrel lost his footing momentarily, that he struggled to formulate his next words.

"Oh, her husband? I guess that's the one she kept talking to for so long. Well, yes then, señora, he left."

"I can't believe it," Mamá said. "I just can't believe it."

I continued lying face down: my head buried in the mattress; my arms and hands clutched tightly underneath my body. The spheres of sight and sound briefly intersected as I pictured Mamá shaking her head in dismay and disbelief.

"Don't feel bad, señora," the mongrel said. "My partner took off too, totally unexpectedly. I had no idea he was going to do it. Why, he even took your daughter's spot on the raft."

"Your partner?" Mamá asked.

"Yes, my colleague," he explained. "Another officer. Before I knew what was happening, he had ripped off his uniform and jumped aboard the same raft as your daughter's...well, her husband's, I guess."

Even from my back room, and with the door tightly closed, I could hear Mamá and my sisters gasping. I could visualize them shaking their heads, stunned and appalled. What I didn't know was that Pilar had actually begun to cry for me.

"I can't believe it," Mamá said again. "It just doesn't seem possible."

"How I wish it weren't, señora, but it is. And then, just as the raft reached the horizon, your daughter blacked out right along the shore."

"She blacked out?"

"Yes, but don't worry, señora. She wasn't out for long, maybe three or four seconds! I happened to be nearby and revived her immediately. I also made sure she didn't move her head any, just in case she was hurt."

"Well, thank you so much, mijito. Thank you for taking such good care of my daughter. You even brought her home in a patrol car. Are you even allowed to do that?"

"Not really, señora, not really. But you won't say anything, will you?"

"Of course not mijito. Of course not."

¡Mijito! Had Mamá just called the mongrel *mijito*? I couldn't believe it. How I wished I were adrift again, deep within some sphere of silence, but I wasn't. I tried unplugging my ears from this watered-down version of events, but I couldn't do it.

"Don't mention it, señora. It was my duty."

"What's your name, mijito?"

"Manuel, señora. But, please, call me Manolo."

"Manolo. Why, what a nice name," she said. "Tell you what, Manolo. If you're ever this way again, I would like to repay your kindness, show you my gratitude."

"No, no, señora. Please, there's no need. It was my pleasure, my duty."

"But I would like to cook you something, mijito. I would like to invite you over for a wonderful dinner."

"Gracias, señora, but please, you need not go to any trouble, really."

"Oh no, mijito, no trouble at all. You're the one who's gone to all the trouble, and I insist on repaying your kindness."

If a moment of silence had finally ensued to seal the sanctity of this exchange, I couldn't make it out. Maybe I had finally tuned them out.

"Well, señora, thank you then, that's very kind of you. First chance I get, I promise I'll be by."

"I'll be expecting you, mijito. I'll be waiting."

"Gracias señora, gracias. By the way," he added. "I believe this belongs to your daughter. She left it in the backseat of the patrol car."

I tuned back in: sharp and clear and receiving every signal. My things. The mongrel had my things. My journals and prayer cards. My father's letter from Iraq. For a moment I almost got up and zipped into the living room.

"Yes, those are her things," I heard Mamá say. "Thanks again, mijito. I'll take them."

I wanted to rush out there, to make sure he had not ransacked my possessions or confiscated anything. But I quickly abandoned the idea. I didn't want to see him. I didn't want to see anybody. Besides, he had finally left. Not only was there no response, but a car took off, the front door closed, and moments later came the knocking I expected.

"Clara mija, let me in, mija. Please, let me in."

"Leave me alone, Mamá. Just leave me alone."

"But mija," she persisted. "What happened? I have a right to know, don't I? Not to mention you must be starving, hija. Let me bring you something to eat."

The mere mention of food made me gag again. Even as I lay in bed I thought I might throw up. How typical of my Cuban mother. Food was always the solution to life's ailments. No matter what the ill, no matter what the predicament, life's turmoils could all be tempered with food, particularly her food. And true, she may have been a great cook, and a great mother, but food would not do the trick this time. Food could offer me no solace at the moment.

"I'm not hungry, Mamá! What I want is to be left alone. Please, can you respect that?"

If I expected a fierce and protracted battle, I didn't get one. She mysteriously relented. Whether the urgency in my tone prompted a retreat, or the locked door commanded respect, Mamá acquiesced, yielding to my request for solitude. Too little time lapsed, however, before she came knocking again.

"Aren't you hungry, mija? Can't I bring you something to

eat?"

"No, Mamá. I'm not hungry. Just leave me alone, will you!"

Even Angélica and Pilar knocked on the door periodically, asking if they could help at all, asking if I wanted to talk about anything, but I only turned them away as well.

"I'm fine!" I called out. "I just want to be alone!"

And it was true. That was all I wanted. To be left alone and suffer in solitude. To ponder my fate in silence and endure it all by myself. I would do it too. And just to make sure that no one snuck into my room unbeknownst to me, I took a chair and wedged it underneath the doorknob, lodging it there as hard as I could. I did it. I secured my withdrawal from the world as hermetically as possible. Only one force intruded on that solitude, which I could not shut out—Rigo.

How do I explain what the hours of my days were like after that morning of August 15? What the hours of my life were like after Rigo? Only one word came near to describing them. *Intolerable.* Only one feeling remotely captured them. *Insufferable.* The emptiness I felt. The worthlessness of my existence. I already felt dead inside, but there were hours I wanted to die all over again, hours I prayed for a new death. The thought of water asphyxiated me and I no longer wanted anything to do with it. But there were hours I yearned to throw myself deep into the ocean and end my life there. The face of the water mocked me. It resurrected the memory of Rigo's departure from my life and the horrible moment he stranded me on the shore. I was so distraught I thought of nothing else. Not the visitation from the night before. Not the tidings or admonitions from the Angel Gabriel. I could think of only one thing and recall one thing only—Rigo.

I was a zombie again, numb and paralyzed, and each passing moment transported me to thoughts of nothing but my husband. Memories. Visions. Imaginings. I pictured him constantly before me. I heard his voice at all times. During our life together I never dreamt of Rigo at night. Not even during his time in Camagüey. So secure was I in our love for each other, so rooted in the bond that cemented us. Now he came to me on a nightly basis and I dreamt of him constantly. Some dreams I understood. Others I didn't.

Some dreams were simple and straightforward, reliving things we had done and places we had visited, but most dreams were of people we knew not and unfamiliar locations. These were accompanied by a sense of incompleteness, by feelings of wrenching abandonment. There were times Rigo came home and walked through the door, but mostly I sat in my rocking chair waiting and waiting for him, rocking back and forth repeatedly, while Rigo never returned.

I had strange dreams too, nightmares really. Not just nightmares, but night terrors, where I woke up screaming and gasping for air. The worst involved curious high structures and peculiar tall buildings. I dreamt that Rigo went to the United States—not to build that tri-tower complex he had worked on so long—but to erect the same hideous eyesores so prevalent on our island: our towering tenements and unsightly *solares*, those depressing housing units that could only be called Socialist slums. I dreamt that he went and transplanted these dreary buildings onto American soil, but the Americans only crowded around these to burn them or tear them down. Many times I dreamt of Rigo trapped in the Deauville, yelling and screaming for help, but with nobody lifting a hand to help him. Nobody throwing a rock through the windows to shatter them and set him free. Once did I dream that, finally, at long last, my husband completed that tri-tower complex he had designed for so long. But only to have it collapse on him, to have it crush him to death in an avalanche of steel and glass. They were horrifying images, terrifying scenarios. Yet the water and its many faces inspired just as much terror.

I dreamt of underwater caves and strange pinnacle formations that jabbed and stung me as I looked for Rigo along the ocean floor. I dreamt of tiny pins of light that lured me forward and beckoned me to slip through its luminous cracks, but only to sear my eyes and cast me permanently into a Cimmerian blindness. I even dreamt of Rigo falling to the

solace

depths of the sea and rising again, but only dead. In all these dreams how I wept for him, how I cried with worry as to whether or not his journey had ended safely. But the answer was forever kept from me. Each time he answered back and tried comforting me, tried consoling me, nothing would give me solace. Nothing.

So I alternated between sobbing and sleeping. For hours on end I sobbed. For hours on end I slept. I knew not if I sobbed in the middle of the night or if I slept in the middle of the day. The hours brought a timeless maze of agony and misery, a mangled morass of clouded emotion. Good thing I didn't work. What type of job could I possibly hold? What capacity could I function in? Instead, hours went by before I'd get up. But I didn't want to get up. Not with Rigo's smell embedded in the sheets. Not with his scent still surrounding me. This only made things worse: feeling him next to me and sensing his physical presence. But that was all I wanted: to feel him, to hold him, to envelop him completely.

"Rigo," I called out over and over again. "Rigo," I cried inwardly.

What would I tell people? What would I tell Mamá and my sisters when I finally faced them? I didn't know. I couldn't bring myself to talk about any part of this ordeal—just as I couldn't stand to look at myself. At one point I jolted up from bed and caught sight of my reflection in the mirror. How horrible I looked, awful. My face red and blotched from crying, my eyes swollen and half-dead. I relived the events of the last twenty-four hours like a recurring nightmare, a dream that would resurrect itself even though I wanted the images dead and buried. Why had this happened? Why? Less than twenty-four hours ago I had pleaded with my husband to leave Cuba. I had begged him to join me. Now, less than a day later, he was the one gone and I was stuck behind.

Why? I repeatedly asked myself. *Why?* I drilled myself over and over again. But I knew why. The answer resonated clearly. As crazy as it sounded, I believed in the visitation. Or I wanted to believe in it, even if the Angel Gabriel hadn't answered any of the *whys: Why* I couldn't leave? *Why* this child must be raised in Cuba? *Why* this was all happening? I didn't get this part, but I would now seek out the answers. I would now hunt them all down.

This was the precise moment I felt hopeful again, when I decided to embark upon this quest. Maybe I was snapping out of it. Maybe I'd had enough, saturated with thoughts and images of all things Rigo. But I felt some force guiding me. I felt it beside me and I felt it inside, an impulse of energy, a jolt of power. For so many hours the strands of time had tightened and twisted me up in a knot of torment. But now I felt my spirit freeing itself, rising up as I sought out the *why*. *Trust me,* the angel had warned. *You don't want to know why. Stay out of that part of things. Matters will run much more smoothly.*

Hardly a consolation. It only motivated me to want to unearth things all the more. And so, without knowing the time of day or whether afternoon had melded into evening or evening had merged into night, I set out on a mission in the solitude of my room. A journey I would not turn my back on. This morning I'd forgone a trek across the water to a land of the future. Now I would embark upon a journey into the wavelengths of the past, a passage across time and space into world I knew not. Some regarded this world as archaic and obsolete; others viewed it as vibrant and alive. To me it was a fervent strand of hope in the endless stretch of hours. But despite this newfound resolve, it seemed fate wished otherwise. Just as I was about to launch upon this exciting new journey, everything went black.

Apagón time, our nightly blackout. It had to be eight o'clock or so. An unnerving blackness pressed down upon the room so that I couldn't see my own hands in front of me. I took this as a sign, a warning to stay put and call off my quest. But I would not let a power failure stop me. Nothing would. I was tired of letting doubt rule my heart, tired of allowing fear to cloud my judgment.

I rose eagerly from my bed and took some hasty steps. A pitch blackness had descended upon me, but I needed no compass, nor did I stumble. I was engulfed in total darkness, but I could see more clearly than ever. I sensed everything perfectly fine. Just as the blind navigate an unseen world with deftness and agility, so did I head to my dresser with equal acuity and to where all my answers lay.

I felt around for a box of matches and found it easily, right next to a small vase made of white porcelain. I kept three votives on top of the dresser and lit the candles one by one. Their glow swelled up the room and I glanced in the mirror again. How horrible I still looked. What a drawn and deathly specter I made, frighteningly thin and frail, fraught with stain and shadow. Not to mention my eyes red from crying and my face blotched and blemished. I did not recoil from this image; it only strengthened my resolve. Nothing would stop me from retrieving my answers. Not even my own deathly reflection.

Given all the turmoil and chaos of the last couple days, I should have been spent. I should have collapsed from exhaustion. Yet all the contrary. The yearning to find answers rendered me awake and alive. Not mildly alive, but dangerously alive. For the first time since the unfolding of this fiasco, I finally felt some solace.

There it was. On my dresser. Next to the candles. The passport to my journey. Not only the passport, but the visa and ticket all in one. I rested both hands on it reverently. The book that would supply me with all my answers. The Holy Book, as it was known. *La Santa Biblia.* The Angel Gabriel might never visit me again, so I would visit him. Sadly, my prayer cards were missing from this threadbare shrine, but I decided to do without them. I presumed they were still with my belongings, but I would not leave my room to retrieve them.

Tonight was like any other night when it came to the usual antics accompanying an apagón: the rowdiness, the restlessness, all of it loud and boisterous. The streets swelled with life during our nightly blackouts. Voices grew louder. Pots and pans turned into conga drums. Even the neighborhood street dogs grew more animated: snarling and growling louder than ever, yelping and barking more vigorously as they fought one another and ran back and forth in packs. It was no longer a sphere between sound and silence we inhabited, but between noise and nuisance. But you couldn't blame them. They were only trying to comfort themselves, only trying to find solace, both Canine and Cuban. It was their way of affirming that life still existed in that Cimmerian darkness. But I needed no such connection. I had something wondrous to look forward to and rejoiced at the prospect. I kept myself entombed against all the clamor and commotion. I sealed off these distractions from the present as I prepared to venture into the past.

As already stated, I had never been religious. Not the least bit. Yet anyone seeing me right now would have figured otherwise. I had always loved to read, and like all Cubans, decried the lack of reading material available here. Our cultural censors deprived us of anything engaging or entertaining unless it had to do with the exploits of Fidel or Che, which were neither. So why had I ever wanted to be a critic? What was there to critique here? Sure, there was plenty to *criticize*, but not critique. Admittedly, the Bible had never appealed to me as an alternative. It was simply too long a book, too daunting a text. But this was no longer the case. No longer did the sheer size of the book intimidate me.

Those three votives swayed with a tantalizing but strong glow, their flames fluid but fierce. I picked one up from the dresser and brought it to my nightstand; in my other hand I carried that Santa Biblia. I don't think I had ever opened a Bible, much less read one. But I would read it now, eagerly so, expectantly, all by the light of this one devout candle. And not merely read the book, but devour it. For I did not merely embark upon a journey, but leapt upon one.

The Old Testament. I didn't start there. No need to go back that far in time. I needed my answers *now* and went straight to where they lay: the New Testament, the gospels in particular. The Gospel of Matthew. The Gospel of Mark. The Gospels of Luke and John. How surprisingly easy they were to read, how inviting and enticing the text, starting with the first of them, Matthew.

It amazed me how, already, given my very recent visitation, I had such insight into what I read, especially the account of the Angel Gabriel appearing to Mary. I couldn't help but smile wistfully. How different her visitation had been from mine. Gabriel was right. Mary had not acted the least bit impertinent as I had. She never doubted his word, and instead, accepted her fate obediently. She truly was blessed among women and I would never come anywhere near her. *But why?* Why was this happening? And why had I been chosen for this task?

I would find out. I kept reading. I kept studying. I analyzed any nuance in the text that might illuminate my circumstance. I lost all track of time and had no idea whether minutes had crawled by or hours had marched on. I knew not whether Mamá and my sisters had retired to their rooms or if they had left the house.

I did note that, after a while, everything acquired a palpable stillness: my room, the house, the air I breathed. Even the flames from those votives burned in a fixed and frozen stillness. Surely now, given all the events of the last twenty-four hours, I expected to conk out. But I didn't. I read long into the hours. I read vigorously, voraciously, submerged in the glow of that frozen candlelight, wandering deeply into a biblical landscape as if, finally, I too had pushed off from the shores of Cojimar, a parallel Cojimar. Finally, I too had become a balsera. Really I had: a biblical balsera. I too had acquired an inner tube on which to float upon. That is all this book was. Not an inner tube that floated along the face of the world's seas and oceans, but an inner tube that took you traveling deep inside yourself, in search of some inner truth and peace. Not an inner tube that would ever puncture or toss you about or you could slip and sink through, but one that offered constant companionship, a hand that would not let go. Amazing. All of it. Even if I never attained the answers I set out to find, what an education I received. How much I learned and soaked up as I floated inwardly upon that inner tube and wove through the strands of one gospel to the next.

Jesus Christ. Jesus of Nazareth. I had never really

understood him, never known the intricate details of his life. But how I learned those details now. How astonishing a man he truly was. There were so many sides to his personality. So many facets to his life. There were his teachings and ministry. His miracles and healings. There were the parables and prophecies and all his travels across the ancient world. There was the Jesus in the text whom the whole world thought it knew, and the stereotypical images of him as well. But it was the Jesus underneath the text I began to discover, a Jesus I never would have encountered had I not climbed aboard and clung to this inner tube.

Glimpses into his personality. Insights into the shifting shades of his character. A peek into his temperament. Even his likes and dislikes. Such as his obvious love of water and a profound affinity to it. How many times had Jesus ministered seaside or healed by the water? How many times had Jesus even addressed the multitudes from a ship on the water? How many times did Jesus command a tumultuous sky and sea? Many. Numerous. Even his most famous miracle involved water and assuming control of it—walking on the water. Something nobody had ever done or would ever do again. Jesus not only conquered the waters, he derived comfort from it, solace.

An inner glance. A deep illumination. I felt I possessed that now. Like a true understanding of his compassion, a compassion so profound it made him seem more vulnerable than his human brethren. If everyone expected the Son of God to show nothing less than compassion, his was far more than average. It sprang forth from some metaphysical inner source, some inner well that enabled him to understand human frailty in a way others could not; that allowed him to embrace weakness and forgive mistakes where others never would; and that easily allowed him to overlook flaws and failings where others refused. How many times had Jesus healed people or made them whole again simply because he took pity on them? Simply because he was moved to compassion by their faith?

There was the teacher in him too. How Jesus loved to

teach. He felt it his very calling to educate. How many times did he illustrate the mysteries of life and Heaven by the use of parables? Those rich and living analogies used to make comparisons between the earthly and the sublime. There was the healer in Jesus too. How many times did he cause the blind to see or enable the lame to walk only because they touched his garment and he felt their faith? Felt their belief. Whether he spit into clay and rubbed his hands into a stagnant pair of eyes, or someone in need simply asked and truly believed, his healing freed them of their chains. The abundance of his miracles ran the full gamut. Whether he was feeding the five thousand or feeding the seven thousand or turning water into wine or even raising the dead, Jesus managed it all. Not only was he the ultimate showstopper, but a one-man show.

On and on the miracles went. On and on his teachings went. On and on my travels progressed so that I lacked all sense of time. Still I kept reading. Still I kept searching. What did this have to do with me? Why was I being selected to have God's next child? What in here indicated that God would be having another child, much less one born in Cuba? Nothing so far, nothing. So I kept reading and traveling and scouring through the scripture with a tireless and abundant energy. I was not the least bit fatigued. Not with the education I was getting. Not with the insight I was gaining. I couldn't put that Bible down. I couldn't release my grip from that inner tube—how it coasted and guided me along. And how ashamed I suddenly felt, embarrassed even, recalling what I had told the Angel Gabriel about never really believing in the...well...I couldn't finish my thought. But I believed now. Truly I did. And for the first time since Rigo's abandonment of me, I was finding peace and comfort. I knew this because a long stretch of time elapsed when I thought nothing of him. Rigo did not enter my mind or cross my thoughts as that inner critic in me swelled and sprang to life.

No, Rigo no longer existed. Not as I read through the Gospel of Matthew and noticed how he wrote from the Jewish point of view. Matthew depicted Jesus as the royal Messiah. He frequently cited Old Testament prophecies and concentrated on Christ's teachings regarding the true kingdom of God.

No, Rigo no longer mattered. Not as I raced through the Gospel of Mark and flipped easily through his matter-of-fact style. Mark seemed to be writing for the Gentiles and possibly even the Romans, and concentrated on Christ's power to save as shown in his miracles. His account was surprisingly short and even seemed rushed at the end. Still, I learned much. Still, I enjoyed it. But not as much as I enjoyed the Gospel of Luke and his lush, lyrical writings.

No, Rigo no longer meant anything as I easily sailed through the narration. I must admit that Luke's was my favorite. His Gospel was a pure joy to read. How rhythmic I found it, how smoothly it flowed. I lingered through the pages of Luke lovingly, meandering through them much as a person strolls along the shore just to hear the lull of the waves rushing back and forth. Luke depicted Jesus as a gracious savior who exhibited his favor to the fallen, the outcast, and the poor. How I longed for this journey to continue. I didn't want any portion of it to end. Not even when it meant encountering several of its wonders more than once. Each time an account in one gospel resurfaced in another, I found it not repetitive, but reassuring—comforting and familiar.

On and on I read. On and on I critiqued. I finally felt I was enrolled at the university. Not the University of Havana, but the University of Heaven. I didn't know whether morning had come, or whether I lay encased in some plush eternal night. I didn't know if I had read through the insomnolent layers of darkness, or their slow unmaking of the dawn. I cared not whether morning had emerged in the sultriness of sunlight, or whether afternoon had sprinkled the faint droppings of dusk. If I cared about time at all, Mamá functioned as my clock, my calendar and compass even. Our daily apagones alerted me to eight o'clock at night; Mamá's voice to eight o'clock in the morn. But I cared not about time. It no longer mattered or existed. Rigo no longer mattered or existed. Every so often came the familiar knocking outside my door. Every few hours or so came the faintly familiar call

solace

from outside my vault.

"Clara!" the voice began. "Open the door, mija! When are you going to eat something? Stay in there as long as you like, but please, let me make you something to eat! How about some coffee hija? You must be dying for a cafesito."

But I wasn't. I cared not for coffee or anything else. I wasn't the least bit hungry, and I didn't understand why. The very thought of food turned my stomach; the mere thought of coffee repulsed me.

"No, Mamá, I'm fine. Just leave me alone, please."

"But Clara," the voice still pleaded, in what seemed minutes later but was hours gone by. "Open the door, mija. Do you know how long it's been since you've eaten anything? Let me make you some *arroz con huevo*, hija. You know it's your favorite."

But the thought of that swollen egg yolk, punctured and bleeding and mashed into a blanket of white, and only to turn into a sticky yellow concoction, revolted me like nothing else.

"*No, Mamá!* I'm fine, I told you. Just leave me alone, will you!"

"But what's happening, mija? What are you doing in there? What are you accomplishing by locking yourself in there all this time?"

Good question. And I wished I could tell her. It seemed that, if anybody would understand, Mamá would, being as religious as she was, given her devotion to the Virgin and the saints. But I knew the hour had not yet come, the time to involve her or share any of this with her. How could I possibly convey all the wonders of this sacred journey? All I was understanding and learning for the first time in my life? Mamá may have been a woman steeped in religion, but this was more revelation than religion. This was more epiphany than explanation. How would she understand this personal quest to conquer my own inner demons and embrace courage? How could she comprehend embarking upon a path that offered no passage back? And how would she understand the inner peace I knew now simply from encountering all the lives this man had touched?

There was no explaining it, no elucidating the effect of a charisma that mesmerized and entranced and left me basking in a new awakening. I could explain none of it, especially this new understanding of life itself, and how, suddenly, my everyday foibles and petty concerns meant absolutely nothing in the large scheme of things, in the realm of some mysterious master plan.

Mamá was caring and sensitive, but she was not spiritual. She would understand none of this. Not when all she cared about was feeding me physically. And true, I had not eaten anything in who knew how long, but I remained not the least bit hungry. Nor was I tired. How could I be hungry or tired when I was being supplied with a food that nourished, if not the body, then certainly the mind and spirit? So she need not worry. I not only knew exactly *what* I was accomplishing, but what I *hoped* to accomplish: something she could not yet understand, something beyond her curative Cuban cooking. I had some questions of my own for her. What had *she* hoped to accomplish? Where had *she* been the night of the visitation? I hadn't forgotten the Angel's admonishment. *"Tell your mother not to waste time anymore with what she did tonight."* But I shrugged this off. I was sure that, in due time, I'd discover that, just as I'd discover this.

It was not sustenance I needed then, but answers. So my quest continued. The critic in me pored on, studying and scouring and scraping my way through the scriptures, pondering their content page after page, analyzing the characters of each and every chapter. Dissecting the subtleties of verse after verse and trying to memorize one memorable quote after another. My eyes traveled feverishly down one column and darted up the next. My fingers turned one page after another and resumed the process all over again.

How profound his ability to sum up a situation. What precision Jesus employed in cutting right to the heart of a matter. He was the architect of argument, the master of critical thought. All the while, I overlooked certain details

solace

that would hit me later on, even crucial observations, one might say. But that was all right. For now I was too caught up in the hunt for clues, too wrapped up in uncovering every inlaid hint. On and on the journey unfolded, and for endless stretches of time, for an infinite array of hours.

I had begun with the highest of expectations, but by the end of that lyrical Gospel of Luke I was no better off than when I started. After all the hours of self-imposed exile and contemplation, I had unearthed nothing, no viable reason as to why God would possibly be having another child. Not when the Creator had already fathered so perfect a child. Not when Jesus of Nazareth had made such an exemplary son. And not when "son" was anywhere near *all* that he amounted to. Minister and Teacher. Miracle Worker and Healer. Protector and Philosopher. Rebel and Revolutionary. Yes, even revolutionary. And Brother now too. But where was it in the text? Where was it in the scripture? Nowhere I could see. Nowhere. Yet what a wonderful older brother Jesus of Nazareth would make. If some miracle child really did emerge from this, what a marvelous role model for a younger sister.

I had come against a brick wall, but only from my own inner obstacles, my own private demons. The answer was in there; I just didn't know it yet. I couldn't see it. I would later on, after much else had happened. For now there was no scaling this wall or knocking it down. Not since my journey took a disarming turn when I came to the Gospel of John. This fourth gospel differed completely from the first three, its emphasis being on the words that Jesus spoke and on those intent on destroying him.

Before I begin on that, let me explain what a completely different image I now had of this Jesus of Nazareth. How much more real he became in my heart and mind. How all the more palpable. For so long, the little I knew about him rested on a foundation of the perfunctory and superficial, underscored by those mild storybook images that parents usually fed their children—that of a holy being who, although he walked among man, was far different from man, set above the ordinary mortal and perfect in every way. He was the Son of God, after all—delegated extraordinary powers here on earth, granted boundless insight and knowledge. These traits remained firmly rooted as I galloped across the open fields of the Gospels, but this persona of mild pacifist was the first notion to be dispelled.

Jesus may have been a miracle worker, but he was neither meek nor mild. He preached a philosophy of forgiveness and "turning the other cheek," but his words could be cutting and offensive, openly confrontational, especially against hypocrites. How he loathed hypocrisy. Jesus called things exactly as they were, and if the recipients of his diatribe didn't like it, too bad. This was where the Gospel of John opened my eyes and made me apprehensive.

The first three Gospels were marked by a pervasive image of 'the multitudes': the multitudes who flocked adoringly to Jesus and followed him in throngs; everyday people in awe of his every act and word. But John painted his Gospel in adversarial brushstrokes, where the focus shifted to the chief priests and the church elders, to the scribes and rulers who hated Jesus and forever challenged him, constantly trying to trap him with his own words and even conspiring to kill him. They liked it not that Jesus defied their views and authority. They found it not amusing that he had torn through the strands and seams of their sanctimoniously woven society. And certainly they grew irritated that, this Son of God, as he claimed to be, delighted in ripping apart their laws: laws they painstakingly adhered to and which wove together the frayed fabric of their ways. Jesus not only seemed to relish undermining these laws, but in undoing each and every stitch.

I'd had no idea. Honestly, I hadn't. He was an insurrectionist, an upriser and rebel, truly he was. No wonder he made so many enemies. No wonder so many men felt threatened by this Jesus of Nazareth, Son of God. I had no idea of his boldness and bravery, that he could be so candid and blunt. I knew that, even in his lifetime, his influence had been wide and far-reaching. But I had no idea of just how extensive the plots against him, how fierce the determination to do him in. Now I understood why. How many times had Jesus heaped scorn and contempt upon those in power? Upon the Pharisees who relied on custom and ritual more than spirituality. Upon the scribes and elders who were interested only in maintaining their high station in the synagogue rather than being at one with the people. How many times did Jesus single out such hypocrisy right to their faces? In how many ways did he threaten social status by challenging narrow interpretations and misguided views? And how many times were those in authority forced to remain silent because, in answering Jesus, they betrayed their own falseness and ignorance?

It happened during this last Gospel of John, when I saw the light about Jesus and the story of his life: how political he was, how political a tale this all was. Yes, political. Not only the politics of governance, but the politics of getting along. Not only the politics of spirituality, but the politics of status quo. What a twist in the tale. What a turn in this journey. All this time the inner tube that was this Bible had coasted along smoothly and safely. But now I was slipping through its center, sliding into the depths. I knew that Jesus had made enemies, and I knew these enemies had orchestrated his crucifixion, but never had I seen his death through the prism of politics. I had always viewed it as strictly religious and preordained, a criteria for salvation and the ultimate punishment for the commission of blasphemy. But now I saw his death in full light. It had less to do with blasphemy and betrayal than the preservation of order. His death was all about the subjugation of the spirit, both human and divine.

I couldn't stop reading now even if I wanted to. More than ever all sense of time twisted and tossed and turned on itself so that I couldn't tell day from night or minutes from hours. And I couldn't dispel the biggest eye-opener of all: how political this Son of God had truly been, how *politically* incorrect. No one could deny that the carvings of his life were etched in spirituality and salvation, in the concept of eternal life. But never had I known the political backdrop of the tale. Never had I realized the biggest threat Jesus posed in his lifetime was a political one. He was a threat to leadership, a threat to authority, a threat to order. Hadn't the Pharisees gone after him because he threatened their status with the Jews? Even at the time of his birth, hadn't Herod ordered the killing of all males under two because this future king threatened his own ability to govern? Later on, in that Gospel of Luke that I loved so much, hadn't Herod's successor mocked and ridiculed Jesus when he failed to perform any "tricks" at the time of his arrest? Kings. Tetrarchs. Governors and Elders. Priests and Scribes. Those in power. Those in authority. They were the most threatened by this Jesus. They were the reason he was ultimately put to death. And it all came to light in the deep dark tones of this fourth gospel. It all came to light in this introspective and confessional Gospel of John.

Sadly, tragically, it ended just then—the spell, the trance. That simply. That uneventfully. No longer was I rapt by these incantations. No longer was I entranced by the tales of this New Testament. The shadowy confessionals of this fourth gospel reeled me back to reality with a forceful crash, frightening me, preoccupying me. Even the images of John differed vastly from those contained in the previous testimonies. The other three focused on water and land, on the symbols of earth and sky and nature. But the recurring imagery in John concentrated on light and darkness, on psychological warfare and sedition, even on stoning when, on numerous occasions, Jesus ran away to avoid being stoned by the Jews. The priests and elders chastised the people for listening to him and accused Jesus of being mad, even claiming he had a devil inside him. He was an insurrectionist all right, truly he was. Now I understood the nature of his arrest for the politically motivated act history intended.

What clarity I now possessed. What inner vision. The critic in me had come full circle. Jesus wasn't a common criminal. He was a political prisoner. He reminded me exactly of that: a prisoner of politics hung in ruthless display.

Never could I imagine the hopefulness that this understanding would offer me, the inner light it produced. At long last I was granted my hours of solitude. Even better—I had acquired real solace. Knowing the full extent of his struggles and the suffering he went through gave me strength. Understanding the pain he endured, and the isolation he must have felt, gave me the courage to overcome my own abandonment. Sure, I knew of his arrest and crucifixion, of the hurt he withstood. But even the brutality of the Passion had gotten altered in my mind, been sterilized somewhat. The manner of his death had lost its sense of horror, taking on that same watered-down, storybook quality of his pacifist image. Not with these new observations. Seeing Jesus as pursued and persecuted closed the circle. Seeing him as the pariah that his own people turned him into made his predicament all the more poignant and powerful.

What did all this mean? What did it mean for me, and more importantly, for this daughter to be born? *If* she was born. She certainly wasn't being sent here as a new Savior. It was obvious that Jesus would remain the only Savior the world ever knew and needed. And she certainly wasn't being sent here to undo anything he had done or to rewrite any of his deeds. His acts would always remain untouchable, immutable. What then? Why? What would she be able to do? What would she say? Would she perform miracles and heal? Would she teach and minister? I didn't know. I couldn't figure it out. Maybe she was being sent here to rescue Cubans from Fidel. To liberate us from the confines of Communism. Maybe since the Eagle seemed incapable of trampling the Alligator, and maybe since no other force on Earth had toppled Fidel in almost fifty years, the only person with the power to depose him would be this new daughter of God.

It hit me. Why I'd been admonished *not* to leave Cuba. Maybe this daughter's mission would also be political: to have Cubans shift their faith from Fidel to Freedom, from faith in Government to faith in the Gospels. Or maybe she was being sent to rescue Cubans from themselves, to separate the Cuban from the Canine. I was more troubled than ever, more confused than ever. I had embarked upon this journey to gather clues and get answers, but now I had more questions than answers, more theories than explanations. So much for the critic in me.

So much seemed unexplained, so much omitted. Why was it that, out of four Gospels, we knew nothing about his childhood? Nothing except the famous scene in which a twelve-year-old Jesus, already an architect of argument, was found discussing philosophical and theological matters with doctors and lawyers outside the temple. It was there that a worried Mary and Joseph asked him why he had tarried behind in Jerusalem, causing them such worry. But it was also there that Jesus answered them unapologetically. *"How is it that ye sought me? Wist ye not that I must be about my Father's business?"*

Hadn't the disciples learned anything else about his childhood? Where he had played? What he had thought and daydreamed about? Whether he had ever been disciplined? How he had gotten along with his other brothers? How Joseph and he had interacted? And what about Mary? Why was it that Mary barely appeared in any of the Gospels? The visitation by the Angel Gabriel was mentioned only in Matthew and Luke. Mark did not recount it, neither did John. Why did I imagine she had played a more central role in this all? That she had figured more prominently in her son's life? Yet she hadn't. Not really. How many times did Jesus disregard his mother coldly? Like the time he was told that she and his brethren were outside looking for him and he answered dispassionately, *"Who is my mother? Who is my brethren, if not those who do my Father's work?"* Or at the wedding of Cana, when Mary informed him there was no wine for the feast, and Jesus again answered her, *"Woman, what have I to do with thee? Mine hour is not yet come."* How badly I felt for Mary. No wonder Luke wrote, *"All these things Mary guarded within her heart."*

But it was in the Gospel of John where I saw just how much Mary had been marginalized. The images of this Gospel revolved around light and darkness and salvation and eternity, but the principal theme centered around Father and Son. Where the Father loved the Son and the Son loved the Father. Where if you hated the Son, you hated the Father.

Where everything the Son did was for the sake of the Father. And where Son and Father were so inseparable they were nearly as one; in fact, they *were* one. Even John's depiction of Jesus in this gospel was that of the incarnate divine word who revealed the Father to those who would receive Him. Nowhere, however, was there any mention of the mother or a revealing of her. Nowhere in this Gospel—or the other three—did I come across any consideration for the mother or of love for the mother or of the bond between mother and child. Even at the end of John, when Jesus was dying on the cross and Mary watched from nearby, where surely she suffered her own death while witnessing the death of her son, Jesus only said to her, *"Woman, behold thy son."*

How was this supposed to make a mother feel? If this visitation really had been true, and if a daughter really was destined to come into being, would she one day treat me in the same dismissive fashion? Would she one day disregard me because of her own spiritual calling? Would her sole focus in life be on her Heavenly Father and the work she was sent to do for Him? Would she forget all I had ever done for her or the sacrifices I had made? Or even that I had carried her light in my darkness? Truly, this bothered me. It gave me new cause for concern and worried me all the more. All these things did I now guard in my own heart. Who would I now use as a guide, if not Mary? How would I know what to do? How had Mary reared the son of God and how did one begin to raise God's daughter?

I'd had enough! This was pointless, fruitless. It was time to stop this spiritual sojourn. What did it even matter? There may have been a son, but there was no daughter. I had found absolutely nothing to answer my questions. No clues to any of this. And this latest insight only reinforced a strongly held belief: I didn't want to have children. I was a writer. A critic. A dweller in the land of argument. An insurrectionist against Revolution. I had no interest in being a mother and for good reason.

My journey was nearing its end. I felt it conclude as I closed up the Bible and that inner tube came floating back to shore. But it was not some distant coast I would soon be landing on, just old familiar terrain. As I drifted somewhere in that sphere between sound and silence, a familiar voice called out to me, a familiar knocking rapped on the door. I tried resisting. I tried fighting that current, but it was too strong for me, too powerful. It kept pulling me back until I came crashing into consciousness—the full throes of it! No longer was I stuck in a time warp. Minutes were separating from Hours, and Day was dividing from Night. Everything seemed familiar again except for this knocking on the door and the voice that accompanied it. The knocking was a pounding. The voice an urgent pleading.

"¡Clara!" it called out to me, the insistent voice of my Cuban mother. "I demand you open up this door, hija! Open it right now! Do you realize you've been in there for three whole days now? Please, hija! There's someone here to see you."

Three days? No! Had it really been that long? *Three whole days!* I couldn't believe it. Not when it had only felt like hours. Not when that candle by my bedside continued burning fluidly, eternally. Who was here to see me? Who and what was Mamá talking about?

"¡Clara, hija! ¡Open up, hija! There's someone here to see you and you need to come out at once! I'm not letting one more day go by without you eating! You hear me?"

I sprang up in bed. I jumped to the floor and headed over to the mirror. I was too scared to look at my own reflection, but I forced myself, glancing at the image of a frail and gaunt creature. I really didn't look that bad anymore. I seemed improved somehow. I even felt better. My face no longer appeared red or blotched. My eyes no longer sunken or lifeless. And it really must have been three whole days because I was starving, ravenous. I no longer felt nausea or motion sickness, but the ruthless pangs of hunger ripping through my abdomen!

"¡Clara, hija!" the voice called out again, the doorknob rattling and growling hungrily. "Open up, hija! Please don't make matters worse and open up!"

Oh, that Cuban mother of mine and her sneaky ways—*bless her*. I had always loved her with all my heart and always would. I had always shown her nothing but the highest respect and would continue doing so. But now I would manifest my affection all the more: love her all the more, appreciate her all the more, and heed her frantic beckoning at once! What was the matter with me? That was my mother calling me! But first, I must take care of something. Before heeding that rattling doorknob, I had to unseal this vault.

I went to remove the chair, the one wedged tightly underneath the door knob. Mysteriously, I no longer had to. The chair had dislodged itself and lay flat against the floor. How? How had this happened? Had someone or something come into my room? Had some otherworldly force visited me again? I looked up and down and all about the room and, in so doing, caught sight of my reflection again. I suddenly wanted to undress. I wanted to strip down and discard my drab and dirty clothes. My skin felt insufferably oily. My hair intolerably greasy. And a stench so unpleasant rose from my pores that I couldn't stand the scent of my own flesh. I removed my garments and let them drop to the floor. I was also starving and wanted something to eat. I had never eaten any, but I craved that Middle Eastern bread I had heard my father talk so much about: that soft, warm bread dipped in salt and oil and a hint of vinegar. My mouth instantly watered at the thought.

"¡Clara, hija,! Open up, hija! There's someone here to see you, someone you need to see! Not to mention you must be starving. Are you even alive anymore? Have you passed out again?"

"No, Mamá," I replied. "No, chica, I haven't. Just give me a moment, will you?"

What could I do? I had to go out there and face whoever was there to see me. I had no choice but to throw my drab and dirty garments back on, insufferable as they would feel against my flesh.

"Oh, hija! Thank God you've spoken! *¡Gracias a Dios!* It's so good to hear your voice, hija. Are you all right?"

The door to the vault finally opened. I flung it back all the way so she could judge for herself. *All right?* Was that what this woman had just asked me? Could she not behold I was all right? What was her problem? What was she so worried about? Didn't she know there was a reason for sequestering myself from the world for three days? A reason why I'd taken this necessary journey? Didn't she understand I had only been conducting my daughter's business?

With the door to my room wide open now, I felt greatly at peace again. Despite all I had learned and not learned and the frightening insights I had gained, I felt a semblance of solace. The long biblical journey of the last three days had alternately clothed and stripped me of calm and equanimity, but I felt my spirit immersed in solace once more.

But it wouldn't last long. I'd be stripped of all this comfort once more, much as someone is stripped of his garments before a taunting crowd. Before I ever stepped out of my room armed with the knowledge I now possessed, I knew who had come to see me. I could hear that siren's voice all the way from the living room as it intermingled with the much softer voices of Pilar and Angélica. I could hear the righteous indignation in her tone as it declared she would not be leaving until she spoke to me and saw me face to face.

Mihrta. My mother-in-law. The woman whose influence had reached far and wide into my marriage and who had made it her mission to destroy me. If anyone ever doubted the importance of the relationship between mother and son, there was no denying that significance when it came to my mother-in-law. Father and son meant absolutely nothing when it came to her. Thank God she would have nothing to do with my daughter. Thank God she was not related to her in any real way.

I might as well forget about showering. I doubted Mihrta felt like waiting. Besides, the sooner we got this over with the better. And what did showering matter? Such comfort was

solace

only temporary. Such solace was only secondary. What consolation was there in knowing that sure, you could wash and shower in the morning, but by midday you'd be drenched in sweat again? It mattered not the dirt that one carried on the outside, but that which one harbored within.

It had finally all caught up with me. I was so drained, so exhausted, I thought I would collapse right there on the floor. But I might as well forget about sleeping. And since washing was no real form of cleansing, I would go out there covered in sweat and grime and sand and clay. For not only had my mother-in-law come to pay me a visit, she'd come bearing momentous news. I could hear it down the hallway as she broke it to my sisters. I heard it loudly and clearly even as I stood distant shores away. Rigo had arrived safely in the United States and was doing just fine. So had Amalia and Henry and some fourth individual whom she knew not.

So the Maloja had made it. It had sailed triumphantly after all. But in just an instant of hearing that woman's voice and picturing her solid frame before me, it was I who found myself violently capsizing and sinking fast. That's what it felt like: that I was drowning, that I was dying. And in a way that's what I hoped for: that this world I had always known and callously been tossed about in would come to a quick and painless end, that it would all dissolve and I might know peace at long last. Yes, for just an instant it felt as if this impending moment might finally be the end of the world for me, and I was more than eager to embrace it, I was ready to die. But something kept pulling me back, a force greater than I who would not extinguish my life source. Not until I had answered each and everyone one of her questions to her full satisfaction.

What would I say? What would I possibly tell her? Every ounce of solace evaporated at the prospect of having to face this mother of all mothers and answer the swarm of questions surrounding Cojimar: why her son had left Cuba but I had not. Why I had prodded and coaxed my husband into fleeing his homeland, only to deprive a mother of her favorite son. She may have been overjoyed that he was graciously alive and intact on American soil, but it was hardly joyous words she had reserved for me.

It felt like the end of the world alright, but I did not need a last meal. I was no longer hungry. I no longer craved that Middle Eastern bread dipped in salt and oil. I felt sick to my stomach again, nauseous to the point of throwing up. I felt fatigued like never before and grimier than ever. I needed to scrape all the grunge of the last three days off every square inch of my body, even if it meant rubbing it all off with my bare hands. I needed to sanitize myself. I needed to purify my body against Rigo's scent and the way it clung to me so perniciously. At the mere mention of that name all the feelings of loss and pain came bearing down on me. Not like a cleansing wave of water, but a crushing wall of water. Sure, I was the one who had refused to leave, but Rigo was the one who had callously stranded me. Rigo was the one who had brought about the end of us—the end to everything.

I felt deathly ill again: physically, emotionally, spiritually. I felt shaken by a set of complications I had not contemplated. To hear such news, so soon, was to open up a wound much too fresh. Upon realizing that my husband had contacted his mother ahead of his own wife—especially now that I knew I had conceived and was undoubtedly with child—all those feelings of betrayal were instantly revived. It was definitely over between us. I truly couldn't stand him. And I may have only been three days pregnant, but already I was in the throes of all things maternity. During these last three days I had nurtured myself in a haven of freedom and fluidity and especially simplicity. But at the mere mention of that name, everything felt more complicated and I couldn't move again: all those feelings of abandonment were instantly resurrected.

... the story continues with ...

LUZ

book ii: complications

Now that Clara is ready to face the world again, how will she handle that unwanted visitor of hers in the form of her mother-in-law? And how will Clara react when she receives word of Rigo's whereabouts? Will she divulge what's truly going on? Why she really stayed behind? Or will Clara keep the secret all to herself? The next nine months will not prove easy. As Clara faces this trying predicament increasingly on her own, it will be a time of trial and tribulation, of conflict and complications. But what about the Creator and the Son of Man? Will the Creator admit He's up to something and there's more than meets the eye? Or will He continue to insist the Son of Man is completley off base? Finally, what about Cuba, that magical land where this miracle of sorts is taking place? Will it finally emerge from the turmoil and torment of these tragic days, or will it still be mired down in the swirling suffocation of this Special Period? While book i took us through the days leading up to that 'frenzied flight across the water,' book ii will take us through the challenges facing Clara's family during these troubled times. The story continues steadily and unflinchingly with—**LUZ, book ii: complications**—the second testament of Clara's story.

the author

Luis Gonzalez was born in Havana, Cuba, where he spent those all-important years of early childhood. But when his widowed mother of three fled Communist Cuba in the late 1960's, he found himself next in the Los Angeles enclave of Culver City, California. Though he quickly assimilated his new country and culture, and though he had no trouble mastering his new language, Cuba never left him. Cuba was always with him: inside him, driving him, calling him. He realized this more than ever when, in the 6th grade, he did his country report on Cuba and thus began a love affair with his homeland that continues to this day. It was only natural that Cuba should play a part in his writing, and even from grammar school age, Luis Gonzalez knew that writing was in his blood.

"I always loved to write, even as a young child. And I guess I've always been an indie author too because, when I was in the third grade, after only having been in this country a couple of years, I wrote two stories. One was called *The Magic Slippers*, the other was called *The Dolphins*. I took sheets of paper that I folded over and stapled and not only did I write the stories, but I illustrated them and made the cover and everything for them. I still have these two first books of mine and I look back on them now and wonder, wow, I really always was a writer. To this day those two items remain some of my most treasured possessions for they provide a glimpse into the passion that helped shape the person that I am, and if I'm anything, I'm passionate, and if I'm passionate about anything, it's writing."

It was also only natural that Luis Gonzalez would go on to study something in the language arts, and so he graduated from UCLA with a Bachelor's Degree in English Literature, and a concentration in Spanish composition and literature. As someone who is deeply moved and inspired by politics and religion and the arts, it was no wonder that he came up with the idea for his novel, LUZ, a story that grapples with all three realms. These days Luis Gonzalez calls San Francisco home where he lives with his wife and two of four daughters.

He's always writing in one way or another, for writing is more than just writing: a lot of writing takes place in your head before the words ever make it down to the paper. So even if he's enjoying or exploring the stunning Northern California landscape or he's debating religion and politics with family or friends, he's always writing, for out of those discussions little snippets always find their way to the surface of the creative page.

Proof

Made in the USA
Charleston, SC
23 July 2015